BY ALAN DEAN FOSTER

Published by The Random House Publishing Group

The Black Hole
Cachalot
Dark Star
The Metrognome and Other Stories
Midworld
Nor Crystal Tears
Sentenced to Prism
Star Wars®: Splinter of the Mind's Eye
Star Trek® Logs One–Ten
Voyage to the City of the Dead
. . . Who Needs Enemies?
With Friends Like These . . .
Mad Amos
The Howling Stones
Parallelities
Star Wars®: The Approaching Storm

STORIES:

Impossible Places
Exceptions to Reality

THE ICERIGGER TRILOGY:

Icerigger
Mission to Moulokin
The Deluge Drivers

THE ADVENTURES OF FLINX OF THE COMMONWEALTH:

For Love of Mother-Not
The Tar-Aiym Krang
Orphan Star
The End of the Matter
Bloodhype
Flinx in Flux
Mid-Flinx
Reunion
Flinx's Folly
Sliding Scales
Running from the Deity
Trouble Magnet
Patrimony

THE DAMNED:

Book One: A Call to Arms
Book Two: The False Mirror
Book Three: The Spoils of War

THE FOUNDING OF THE COMMONWEALTH:

Phylogenesis
Dirge
Diuturnity's Dawn

THE TAKEN TRILOGY:

Lost and Found
The Light-years Beneath My Feet
The Candle of Distant Earth

PATRIMONY

PATRIMONY

A PIP & FLINX ADVENTURE

ALAN DEAN FOSTER

BALLANTINE BOOKS • NEW YORK

Published in the United States by Del Rey Books, an imprint of The Random House Publishing Group, a division of Random House, Inc., New York.

DEL REY is a registered trademark and the Del Rey colophon is a trademark of Random House, Inc.

LIBRARY OF CONGRESS CATALOGING-IN-PUBLICATION DATA
Foster, Alan Dean.
Patrimony : a Pip & Flinx adventure / Alan Dean Foster.
p. cm.
ISBN 978-0-345-48507-6 (alk. paper)
1. Humanx Commonwealth (Imaginary organization)—Fiction.   2. Flinx (Fictitious character)—Fiction.   3. Pip (Fictitious character : Foster)—Fiction.
I. Title.
PS3556.0756P38 2007
813'.54—dc22
2007021494

Printed in the United States of America on acid-free paper

www.delreybooks.com

2   4   6   8   9   7   5   3   1

First Edition

Text design by Niqui Carter

For Pierre and Sylvie Clauzel,
Watching rockets climb over Africa,
With thanks for your help with more prosaic matters
On the same ground

PATRIMONY

CHAPTER

1

Make the right moves.

Easy for an Ulru-Ujurrian to say, Flinx reflected as the *Teacher* maintained its approach to the world that lay at the end of the decelerating KK-drive craft's present course. Easy for an Ulru-Ujurrian to do. But then, everything was easy for an Ulru-Ujurrian to say and do. Unimaginably powerful, preposterously playful, and possessed of talents as yet unmeasured—and quite possibly unmeasurable—they went about their daily activities without a care in the world—short of keeping busy by way of the unfathomable playtime that involved moving their planet closer to its sun.

Even that bit of outrageous astrophysics seemed simpler to Flinx than unraveling the mystery of his origins.

He had been given a clue. For the first time in many seemingly interminable years, a tangible clue. And even more than that, he had been provided with a destination. It lay before him now, a world he had never considered before, lying the same distance from his present position as his homeworld of Moth or, in a different direction, New Riviera and Clarity Held.

Clarity, Clarity. Under the proficient ministrations and attentive guardianship of his old friends Bran Tse-Mallory and Truzenzuzex, she would be recovering from the injuries she had sustained during the fight that had allowed him to successfully flee New Riviera, also known as Nur. While his love was healing physically, perhaps he could finally heal the open wound of his unknown origins. These chafed and burned within him as intensely as any cancer.

Gestalt.

A word bursting with meaning. Perhaps also a *world* full of meaning, as it was the name of the globe his ship was rapidly approaching. An undistinguished colony world, H Class VIII, with a single large moon whose orbit the *Teacher* was presently cutting. Home to a native species called the Tlel, as well as to a modest complement of human colonists. Rather eccentric human colonists, if the details contained within the galographic he had perused were to be believed. Not that he expected to interact very much with the general population. He was here to find something specific. Something for which he had been searching a long, long time, without any real hope of ever finding it. Now, for the first time in years, he had hope.

That is, he did if what he had been told was not a cynical dying man's final provocation—a last lie intended to exact a final measure of revenge on the youth responsible for his death.

I know who your father is, Theon al-bar Cocarol had wheezed on Visaria just prior to dying. Self-proclaimed sole unmindwiped survivor of the renegade, edicted eugenicist Meliorare Society, he had dubbed Flinx *Experiment Twelve-A* before gasping out *Gestalt!* and then inconveniently expiring. *Experiments are not supposed to have knowledge of their biological progenitors,* he had coldly insisted earlier.

To the Great Emptiness with that, Flinx had decided immediately. In his lifelong search for his origins he had pursued more than his share of dead ends. It would only be one more irony in a life filled to bursting with them if a lead supplied by a dying outlaw turned out to be the right one.

PATRIMONY

Equally important had been the expiring scientist's choice of words. *I know who your father is,* Cocarol had declaimed before gasping his last. Penultimate breath or not, Flinx had not confused the tense. Cocarol had clearly and unmistakably said "is." Not *was,* but *is.* So small a word, so full of promise. Was it possible, Flinx had been unable to keep himself from musing ever since that critical, piercing moment, that he might not only finally learn the identity of his father, but actually find him alive? It was too much to hope for.

So he did not hope. He had been disappointed too often before. But he allowed himself, had to allow himself, space in which to wish.

Intent on the fate of the galaxy and every one of its inhabitants civilized or otherwise, his mentors Bran Tse-Mallory and the Eint Truzenzuzex would almost certainly not have sympathized with his present detour. Much as she loved him, Clarity might not have sympathized, either. But she would have understood. Even with the fate of so much and so many at stake, there were private demons that had to be put to rest before Flinx could fully focus on external threats, no matter how vast in extent they might be. Save the inner universe first, he kept telling himself, and you're likely to be in better condition to make a stab at saving everything else.

Sprawled like a length of pink-and-green rope below the *Teacher*'s foreport, Pip lifted her head to glance across at him. Epitomizing the empathetic bond that existed between them, the minidrag's attitude reflected her friend and master's anguish.

"Am I selfish?" he asked the ship, after explicating his disquiet aloud.

"Of course you are." The *Teacher*'s ship-mind had been programmed for many things. Subtlety was not to be counted among them. "The fate of a galaxy rests in your hands. Or rather, in lieu of a cheap analogy, in your mind."

"Uh-huh. Assuming I exist in this hypothetical position to do anything at all about it, notwithstanding what Bran and Tru seem to think."

"In the absence of an alternative specifically encouraging, they seek surcease in the exploration of remote possibilities. Of which you are, like it or not, ostensibly the most promising."

Flinx nodded. Rising from the command chair, he strolled over to the manual console and absently ran his hand down the length of Pip's back. The flying snake quivered with pleasure.

"What do *you* think?" he asked softly. "*Am* I the last hope? Am I the key to something bigger, something more powerful, that visits me in dreams? Or whatever you want to call that perversely altered state of consciousness in which I sometimes unwillingly find myself."

"I do not know," the *Teacher* told him honestly. "I serve, without pretending to understand. I can take you wherever you wish to go, except to comprehension. That destination is not programmed into me."

Mechanical soul, Flinx thought. Not designed to pronounce judgment. In lieu of the advice of a superior intellect, he would have to judge himself. With a sigh, he raised one hand and gestured toward the port. Soon they would need to announce themselves to planetary control with an eye toward taking up orbit.

"What about this change of course? What do you think of my putting aside the hunt for the Tar-Aiym weapons platform in order to search for my father here, based on what the dying Meliorare told me?"

Understanding of certain matters might not have been programmed into the *Teacher*'s ship-mind, but contempt was. "An insupportable waste of time. I have run a number of calculations based on the facts and variables available to me. The results are less than promising. Consider: the human Cocarol may have simply been enjoying a final, embittered joke at your expense. Or he may not have known what he was talking about. If he did, circumstances may have changed since he was last conversant with the issue at hand. Since then, any knowledge he may have possessed concerning the identity or location of your male parent may have changed radically.

"Meanwhile, whatever lies behind the Great Emptiness continues this way. It is my opinion that your time would be better spent searching for the absent, ancient Tar-Aiym weapons platform that represents the only hope, thus far, of a device even theoretically powerful enough to counter the oncoming danger. A device with whom only you have had, and can initiate, mental contact." The silken yet tart mechanical voice paused briefly. "Have I at least succeeded in instigating within you a modicum of guilt?"

"The attempt is redundant," Flinx snapped. "No need to refresh that which never leaves me."

"That realization, at least, is encouraging," the ship replied. "Since logic and reason are having no effect, I search for that which *will* work."

In some respects chatting with the *Teacher* was easier than engaging in conversation with a human. For example, the ship never raised its voice, and if Flinx so wished, he could terminate the discussion with a simple command. On the other hand, unlike with another person, he could not turn away from it. The ship-mind was everywhere around him.

"As soon as I've settled this question, I'll resume the search. I promise." Pip looked up at him quizzically.

The ship responded, "What makes you so certain that you will settle it here? This is a question the answer to which you have sought on many worlds. As I have commented repeatedly, the dying human could have perished with a falsehood on his lips. It would not be overmuch to expect of one who had so long lived a lie himself."

"I know, I know." A pensive Flinx raised his gaze once more to the cloud-swathed new world looming steadily larger in the foreport. As he stared, the port continuously adapted to the changing light outside the ship. Another new world in a long list of those that instead of answers had thus far provided him with only more questions. "But after all these years, it's the most promising lie that I've been told."

Though Gestalt's human population numbered only in the millions, he was still surprised at the informality that infused the exchange of arrival formalities. According to the *Teacher,* the orbiting station-based automatic electronic protocol that challenged their approach did not even bother to inquire as to the nature of his business. This suggested that the planetary authority was either lazy, indifferent, or criminally negligent. As it developed, it was none of these. Orbital insertion protocol was a true reflection of the colonists' attitude and philosophy. It was not quite like anything Flinx had encountered before.

The lack of bureaucratic ceremony meant that he had to conceal only his true identity, and not the configuration of his vessel. The *Teacher* was able to avoid having to employ the complex external morphing he usually had to order it to undergo to disguise its appearance when visiting other worlds.

After equipping himself as best he could from ship stores according to the recommendations that were included in Gestalt's unpretentious but thorough galographics file, he headed down the corridor that led to the shuttle bay. Riding his left shoulder beneath his dark brown nanofiber cold-weather jacket, Pip had gone to sleep. A quick predeparture check indicated that everything was in place for him to take his usual leave from the vessel. The communit that would not only allow him to communicate with the *Teacher* but also allow it to keep track of him was secure in its pouch on his duty belt, which was itself concealed beneath the lower hem of the jacket.

Though not an iceworld like Tran-ky-ky, by all indications the surface of Gestalt was as chilly as a Meliorare's heart. It would, he reflected, be a change from all the temperate, tropical, and semi-desert worlds on which he had recently spent so much of his time.

"I'll be back soon," he declared aloud as the shuttle lock door curled softly shut behind him. A slight hiss signified pressure equalization.

"Famous last words," the *Teacher* murmured, addressing the observation as much to itself as to the lanky young human who was now slipping into harness inside the shuttle.

My father, Flinx thought to himself as he felt the subtle jolt that indicated the shuttle had dropped clear of the *Teacher*. My father *is*. So had insisted the dying Meliorare Cocarol. So many years spent searching. So much time lost wondering. Finding his father would not save civilization from the vast abyssal horror that was speeding toward the Milky Way from beyond the Great Emptiness—but it might help to fortify the hesitant, vacillating key that was himself.

In all his traveling he had never seen a planetary surface quite like that of Gestalt. Its waters were blue, its heavy cloud cover mottled white. Normal enough. But instead of ambiguous, perambulating scattering, the numerous continental landmasses ran north to south in roughly parallel, scimitar-shaped arcs, striping the entire globe with mountainous chevrons. Some of the larger bodies of land were loosely connected by wandering, thin strips of terrain, while others were completely isolated from one another by long stretches of open sea.

Each individual landmass consisted largely of rugged mountain ranges that had been squeezed up from the planetary crust by grumbling tectonic forces. There should be active volcanism, Flinx mused as he studied the surface that was rising swiftly toward him. Indeed, in the course of the descent he spotted several confessional plumes, their telltale trails stretching out straight and sharp as white feathers amid the rest of what was an otherwise typically anarchic atmosphere.

As the shuttle automatically leveled off on final approach, he marveled at the landscape that spread out in every direction. Valleys cutting through the incessant mountain chains flashed churning rivers. Bright flashes of alpine lakes lay strung like shards of shattered mirror among the green. And, startlingly, the blue. There was an inordinate amount of undeniably blue vegetation, he saw, in every imaginable shade and variation. In addition, the snow that capped the higher peaks and lay like cotton in shadowed vales and chasms was tinted a distinctive pink that occasionally deepened to rose. There must be something unique in the composition of the local precipitates, he reflected.

Finding one's way around such country would be next to impossible without modern technology. As the *Teacher*'s shuttle sped over valley after valley, dropping gradually lower and lower, he saw that one rocky, tree-fringed gorge looked much like another. Infrequently, a cluster of structures indicating organized habitation impinged briefly on his vision. Even at the shuttle's rapidly diminishing landing speed, these came and went too fast for him to tell if their origin was human or indigenous.

According to Gestalt's galographics, population centers of any kind were few and far between. Both the native Tlel and the humans who had settled among them favored their privacy. It was a trait inborn among the natives and elective among the humans.

The shuttle's voice, a modest echo of its starship parent, advised him to prepare for touchdown. It was a warning he always took seriously, even when preparing to land on a developed world. He had been prepared for touchdown ever since he had first settled into the seat. Sensing his heightened anticipation, Pip tensed slightly beneath the cold-climate jacket.

Only a few valleys on Gestalt were wide and flat enough to allow for the siting of a shuttleport. Tlearandra was located on the other side of the planet. Since it was also home to the offices of Gestalt's Commonwealth representative and the preponderance of potentially inquisitive secondary officials, Flinx had prudently chosen to land at Tlossene, the other principal metropolitan area.

Used to touching down at ports that were located well outside the boundaries of the major conurbations they served, he was startled when it appeared as if the shuttle was heading for the center of the city itself. Though eventually realizing this was an illusion born of descent velocity and angle of approach, he was still relieved when his craft made primary contact with an actual landing strip instead of the cluster of buildings whose rooftops it seemed to barely clear. The shuttleport was situated in a region of hard, dried river bottom that struck him as perilously close to inhabited areas. While it was true that Gestalt exported only small manufactures and conversely boasted only modest imports, thus negating any need for extensive port servicing facilities, the proximity of port to population struck him as irresponsible. He intended to inquire about the choice. Even though he could not think of one, doubtless there was a good reason why the port had been placed so close to the community.

It did not occur to him that maybe nobody cared.

Arrival formalities on the ground proved to be as thankfully unceremonious and perfunctory as they had been when the *Teacher* had first settled into orbit and been contacted by landing control. He had only to state his name (falsified), ship identification (falsified), and purpose of visit (conducting research on behalf of a company that for reasons related to commercial security preferred to remain unnamed—also falsified). It was thus under multiple fictitious pretenses and with considerable confidence that Flinx requested directions to the usual subterranean pedestrian accessway.

"This is Gestalt," an inordinately relaxed male voice informed him via the shuttle's internal communications system. "Nothing is paid for that receives insufficient use. That includes costly underground conveniences. We don't get many private craft here. There are no subterranean amenities for travelers such as yourself. Your landing craft's present orientation is positioned clear on my readout. Step out of your vessel and turn west. You'll see the main terminal. It's a short walk across the tarmac." A brief pause, then, "Weather's good today. If you're not properly equipped for the climate, you shouldn't be here. The valley in which Tlossene is located is almost three thousand meters up, you know. Or you do now, if by some odd chance you didn't prior to touchdown."

The controller's tone suggested someone chatting casually with a friend instead of that of a government official conducting formal business attendant on offworld arrival. The easy tenor, the absence of attitude, the lack of ceremony were truly refreshing compared with the flood of restrictive regulations and formal procedures Flinx so often was forced to follow when landing on other worlds.

But—step out and turn west?

"We only have two subsurface accessways," the controller explained in response to the new arrival's uncertainty, "both of which are currently in use by the pair of cargo shuttles you can see working off to the east."

Peering out the foreport in the indicated direction, Flinx could see the two much larger, bulkier craft parked on the indicated section of tarmac. Clunky robotic haulers and more agile automated loaders swarmed around several gaping service bays. No humans or Tlel were in view, and the industrious mechanicals paid no attention to the new arrival.

"Okay, I'll walk," he informed the controller. "What about Customs and Immigration?"

"Someone will meet you." A tinge of humor colored the rest of the reply. "It'll give SeBois something to do."

Flinx did not have to secure the shuttle—the ship would see to such mundane safety measures on its own initiative. As soon as the landing ramp was deployed, he made sure the skin-sensitive soft-sealing collar of his jacket was snug around his neck and over Pip, and exited through the lock.

The cold hit him immediately. Prepared for it, he was not surprised. If anything, the ambient temperature was less bracing than the shuttle's readout had led him to expect. No doubt the chill was mitigated by the intensity of Gestalt's sun at this altitude. His well-being was further enhanced by the planet's slightly denser-than-Terranorm atmosphere, which helped to compensate for the altitude. Inhaling deeply and deliberately, he could not tell any difference from sea-level breathing on any Earth-normal world. Beneath his jacket, Pip twitched slightly against him but was otherwise untroubled by the sharp drop in temperature. As long as she could find enough food to power her dynamic metabolism, she would be fine.

At the moment, food held no particular appeal for Flinx, since he had eaten prior to departing the *Teacher*. But he decided that if available, he wouldn't turn down a hot drink. While the emergency reserve that did double duty as a component of his jacket insulation could supply that, he preferred not to access its limited volume unless he had to. Besides, it was always nice to try something local.

Across the pavement and beyond the line of port buildings, the city of Tlossene crawled up a pair of opposing mountainsides that funneled into a sloping canyon in the distance. At the city's higher elevations, poured and fabricated structures gave way or filtered into blue and green alien forest. None of the structures was taller than half a dozen stories. Though a real city with a population in the hundreds of thousands, Tlossene was no grand metropolis. Many of the central buildings he could see clearly looked weathered but tasteful. Their external appearance fit what he knew of the history of Gestalt's settlement by humans. Scattered among them were distinctively dimpled domes and bulging egg-shaped constructions that hinted at a nonhuman sense of design. If these eye-catching edifices had not been built by the indigenous Tlel, they had at least been inspired by them.

In the far distance beyond the city soared peaks whose heights Flinx could only estimate. If he needed to know exact altitudes, he could always check with the communit on his belt that had been loaded with all the information on this world that was available to the *Teacher*. Reaching the bottom of the ramp, he headed away from the shuttle, strolling in the designated direction.

The pounding at the back of his head had nothing to do with the slight change in pressure from ship to surface. Such sometimes debilitating headaches were no stranger. As always, he would ignore the throbbing pain and attendant discomfort unless it became genuinely disabling. Only at such times did he reluctantly resort to medication or meditation. Sensing her master's discomfort, Pip shifted uneasily against his shoulder. There was nothing she could do but empathize.

If he were back on Arrawd, where the locals were in much more than one way of similar mind, his mind would be at peace. Or even if he were somewhere within that strange rain-forest-swathed world Midway—no, Midworld, he corrected himself. In all the Arm, those were the only two planetfalls he had made where he knew he could be reasonably certain of finding mental peace. Lips pressed tightly together against the pain, he strode grimly on. Learning the truth of the Meliorare Cocarol's last revelation would go a long way toward easing any discomfort he felt while on Gestalt.

He forgot about the all-too-recurrent pain in his head as he caught sight of something coming across the tarmac toward him. *Someone will meet you,* the amiable port controller had assured him. Flinx's gaze narrowed. Whatever was coming toward him—and it was coming fast—was no genial representative of local officialdom. It was neither human nor Tlel. As it, or rather they, sped in his direction, they were sending out silent feelings of fear, anxiety, and confusion.

They didn't even have legs.

The lack of visible limbs in no way hampered their progress. In fact, as they loomed larger in Flinx's vision, it was apparent that legs would only have hindered their chosen method of locomotion. There were at least a dozen of the bizarre creatures tumbling and rolling rapidly in his general direction. Tumbling and rolling frantically, if his perception of the primitive emotions they were generating was correct. About the size of a human head, each of the roughly spherical creatures was completely covered in mottled white and brown fur. Longer, denser bristles stood out to the sides like oversized whiskers. They propelled themselves across the tarmac with four arms that terminated in wide, flat, fleshy pads. Working in unison, these grabbed at the hard surface and pushed off powerfully. Somewhere beneath all that fur, he imagined, must be nostrils, a mouth or trunk, and possibly eyes and ears. For all that they appeared blind and dumb, they did not roll into one another.

Pursuing them was something much larger, far more ominous, and uncompromisingly threatening in appearance. As if to reinforce its menacing aspect, it was generating emotions that were as primitive as its obvious intentions. Hulking and bearish, it nonetheless traversed the pavement with a speed and grace that belied its bulk. Unlike its intended prey it did not roll, but instead lumbered forward on several dozen short, muscular legs that terminated in sharp-hoofed feet. White fur decorated with irregular splotches of pink combined to create an incongruously feminine façade. This initially disarming impression lasted only until one noticed the mouth. Almost as wide as the creature was broad, the protruding appendage skimmed along just above the ground, its horizontal maw gaping open. An enormous, trifurcated nostril set atop the blocky skull supplied the necessary air intake and outflow for the galloping carnivore, serving not only to fill its predatory lungs but also to allow the spatulate mouth to suction up anything in its path.

That explained the visible absence of teeth or bony ridges inside the flexible jaws, Flinx realized. The meat-eater didn't bite its victims, or crunch them, or bring them down with fang and claw. It simply, efficiently, and bloodlessly vacuumed them up. This particular alien carnivore, Flinx reflected, sucked.

The distance separating the desperate dozen of the round, rolling creatures and the whistling predator shrank as he looked on. That this frenetic display of local predation was taking place right out on the tarmac of one of the planet's main shuttleports would have been sufficiently surprising all by itself, even without the fact that the entire screeching, howling menagerie was bearing down on him at impressive speed. Perceiving the threat, Pip struggled to take to the air—only to find herself constrained by the soft-seal of her master's jacket.

Quadruple arms flailing wildly, a pair of the rolling furballs bounded past Flinx on his right. A trio shot past on his left. All five stank profoundly, emitting a pungent musk that was an olfactory reflection of their terror. It occurred to him that their route, rather than being arbitrary, might have been chosen with the intent of possibly placing a diversion into the path of their ravenous pursuer.

That, he realized a bit late as he reached for the pistol holstered at his service belt, would be him.

He had plenty of time to adjust the weapon's setting. The trouble was, the gun was properly secured in its holster. The holster was attached to his service belt. His service belt was fastened comfortably around his waist—beneath the jacket, whose front was snugly sealed against the local climate. Sharing some of the emotional tumult of the last roller as it swerved wildly past him, Flinx began to fumble a bit more hurriedly with the seal that kept the hem of his coat snug against his upper thighs. Oblivious to his concerns, the lumbering oncoming predator continued to head straight toward him. Flinx felt fairly sure that, unlike the rollers, it had no intention of going around. The broad, flattened, energetically suctioning mouth was more than capacious enough to vacuum him up as easily as it would have any of the fleeing, multiarmed furballs. Fumbling faster with the jacket's lower seal, he tried projecting feelings of uncertainty onto the onrushing meat-eater. When that had no effect, he strove to project fear. Too primitive or too preoccupied with the hunt to respond, the creature took no notice of his increasingly harried mental efforts.

Finally forcing her way free of the jacket, Pip took to the air. In the denser atmosphere, she had to work even less than usual to get aloft. Her iridescent body was a sudden burst of color against the blue sky. A blur of pleated blue-and-pink wings, she needed but a moment to orient herself before diving directly at the charging carnivore—only to hesitate in midair. The poison she spat was lethal when it struck the eyes of a target, and she was deadly accurate from a surprising distance. Only one thing kept her from dropping the whistling predator in its tracks.

She couldn't find its eyes.

Either like the fast-fleeing rollers it had none, an increasingly uneasy Flinx surmised, or else they were so deeply concealed beneath the coat of white-rose fur they could not be seen. As the beast drew entirely too near, suction from its mouth began to pluck at the legs of Flinx's thermotropic pants. Normally steady as sunshine, his fingers were uncharacteristically fickle as they fumbled ever more anxiously for the handgrip of his gun. The deep-toned whistling, he now noted, came not from the gaping cavity of the creature's distinctive, expansive mouth, but from the exceptionally large tripartite nostril set atop its skull. Mouth, nostril. Drawn by what must be an enormous lung, or set of lungs, air was sucked in through the vacuuming mouth and expelled through the bony structure atop the head. If he did not do something to halt or divert the monster, very shortly he would find himself in a position to study this fascinating example of adaptive alien biology from the inside.

As Pip darted and hovered overhead in a frantic but futile attempt to distract the lumbering carnivore, Flinx finally succeeded in pulling his pistol free of its holster and taking aim. Knowing nothing of the creature's anatomy and in any case not having any time to evaluate it, he pointed the beamer's muzzle at the center of the fur-matted skull. Hopefully, the brain that powered the animal was located in the general region between mouth and nose.

It was only when he had the pistol leveled and ready to fire that he noticed it was set on Heat, its lowest calibration, instead of Stun or Kill.

CHAPTER

2

Fingers working frantically, Flinx hurried to reset the weapon as he threw himself desperately to one side. At the same time, he could feel his feet beginning to slip out from under him as the full strength of the oncoming carnivore's predatory suctioning began to pull forcefully at his legs. Out of time and out of options, he raised the pistol.

A powerful odor of singed fur assailed his nostrils. The monster halted abruptly, its multiple legs bunching up beneath it like so many commuters trying to simultaneously pile into a transport featuring only a single open doorway. It stood where it had stopped, only a couple of meters from Flinx, swaying slightly on its plenteous foot-pads. Only when it keeled over onto its left side was he able to see the perfectly round fist-sized hole that had been punched clean through its skull from one side to the other. Exhaling, Flinx lowered the beamer.

He hadn't fired.

The man who had was coming toward him. Bolted to a secure right-shoulder mount, a rifle that was nearly as long as the diminutive figure was tall whirred smoothly and softly as it slid backward on its brace to drop down into resting position against the gunner's back. The shooter was clad in a single blue perflex suit designed to minimize weight while maximizing heat retention. The fabric over his right breast sported a couple of badly scuffed bronzed insignia. Though at first glance seemingly better suited to a diving competition than an outdoor stroll in Gestalt's rough climate, the one-piece outfit was at once more practical and less cumbersome than Flinx's makeshift cold-weather garb. Certainly if he lived on Gestalt, he reflected, he doubt-less would opt for something similarly comfortable.

Have to go shopping if I'm going to be here for a while, he told himself as he enviously eyed the approaching figure's suppleness of movement and lack of bulky attire. Edging away from the lifeless mass of dead carnivore, he started toward the individual who had fired the single lethal shot. He did so as much to put the still-warm corpse's stomach-turning smell behind him as to greet his rescuer. Behind him, the muted whine of port maintenance robots indicated the rapid ap-proach of sense-deprived mechanicals. Indifferent to the intensifying stench, they would systematically undertake the necessary cleanup.

Smiling, he extended a hand. Downward, since he was consider-ably taller than the man who had come to his aid. "Stimulating ar-rival procedures you have here."

The hand that gripped his fingers was small, dark, and strong as duralloy. White teeth gleamed in a dark face. It was impossible to tell if the official had any hair, since the integrated hood of the insulating perflex suit covered his head completely. His eyes were large and slightly almond-shaped. Though these were suggestive of Asian ances-try, the remainder of his features reflected the usual Terran homogeny. The only accent in his terranglo was local, the words emerging from his mouth slightly more clipped and formal than usual.

"No extra charge," he quipped. Turning, he looked on as a me-chanical loader picked up the carcass of the dead predator and uncer-emoniously dumped it into the cargo bay of a self-powered transport.

Pivoting in unison, the two mechanicals accelerated westward across the tarmac, heading for the nearest disposal bay.

"That's a kasollt that was coming for you. See them occasionally up in the foothills. They generally don't come into town. You're lucky to see one." His nostrils flared slightly, testing the air. "You wouldn't think a predator, trying its best to conceal itself, would stink like that. Or its prey, hoping to hide. But a lot of the local fauna has no sense of smell. That includes the Tlel. Strange bit of evolution, here. They make up for it by having specialized appendages on their heads that let them detect individual electrical fields. Like sharks on Earth." Turning back to Flinx, he eyed the youthful newcomer appraisingly.

Flinx's reply was measured. "I think I was lucky to see *you*."

The official's grin widened as he acknowledged the backhanded thank-you. "This port doesn't get many noncommercial arrivals. As soon as the kasollt was spotted chasing the olu herd out onto the field, some of us over in control thought it might be a good idea for one of us to come out and meet you personally." On his back, the intuitive rifle murmured softly by way of agreement. The man glanced at the shape that was moving around inside Flinx's jacket. "I see that you're not entirely alone. Just guessing based on the movement, I'd say your companion's an interesting creature."

"So I've been told." Through the fog of his breath, Flinx gestured toward the nearby complex of low-domed buildings. "Can we continue this inside? It's chilly out here."

"It's chilly everywhere here. This is Gestalt. Come on." Turning, his host led Flinx away from the shuttle. Behind them, the onboard AI observed their departure, retracted the landing ramp, and switched to Secure mode. Then it settled down in comfortable cybernetic hibernation to patiently await its owner's return.

"I'm Third-Level Port Administrator Payasinadoriyung." Before his guest could respond, he added, "Call me Paya." This helpful and downright necessary recommendation was followed by an expectant pause.

"Mastiff," Flinx told him, utilizing the alias he had already supplied to landing control. "Skua Mastiff."

Accepting this without comment, the official nodded in the direction of the well-equipped service belt that was concealed beneath the hem of Flinx's jacket. "You didn't defend yourself."

"I didn't think I'd need a gun here, on the tarmac. Consequently, the burst level on my weapon was set too low. I was trying to adjust it when you saved me the need."

Paya nodded understandingly. "Make sure it's properly set now." He jerked a thumb back over his right shoulder. "You've met the ka-sollt. Gestalt's home to multiple kinds of carnivore that all have one thing in common. They're all hungry, all the time. Even downtown, everyone here carries some kind of defense. Charged gloves, flashers, adjustable auralite, projectile weapon—next time I probably won't be around to moderate any informal encounters between you and the local fauna."

Flinx mulled the disconcerting advice. "I'll need an activated weapon even in Tlossene?"

"Anywhere you go walking within the city limits, yes." Paya's accompanying nod was emphatic. "The Tlel believe strongly in live and let live, even when the more aggressive examples of the local fauna do not. Essentially existing here as guests, the rest of us are obliged to go along with local values. So while it's not an everyday occurrence, there's always the chance of encountering something nasty roaming the streets. City maintenance does a pretty good job of keeping things clean and safe, but a knowing citizen is always on guard."

They were nearing the first building. Sheathed in the sprayed-on dark photogen that powered the structure, its curving outer wall flowed seamlessly upward like an inverted black wave to become the domed roof. The design was practical as well as reflective of Tlelian architectural influences.

Advancing through the triple entranceway, Flinx experienced a sequential and most welcome rise in ambient temperature. Slipping free of its carrying harness, Paya divested himself of his impressive weapon and secured it in a waiting open locker before directing Flinx to a small, slightly raised platform.

"A small formality." His tone was apologetic as he indicated that the visitor should stand within the platform's circumscribed center. "This will just take a moment. You won't feel anything. Try not to move, please."

Flinx nodded knowingly. "I'm familiar with the procedure."

Stepping up, he moved to the middle of the circular dais and turned to face the port official. He was careful to keep his hands at his sides and did his best not to blink as a soft light swept over him. This was accompanied by a deep humming of short duration. Less than a minute after it had commenced, the Arrivals documentation procedure was over. It had recorded his height, weight, approximate age, bone density, retinal pattern, brain-wave configuration, number and location of internal organs, presence and type of any prosthetics, the nature of the devices and instrumentation he was carrying on his person, and a good deal more, in addition to ascertaining the general state of his health. In even less time, it had done likewise for Pip.

Flinx could have found a way to slip into the city without submitting himself to the procedure. It was something he had accomplished successfully before, on other worlds. But his purpose here suggested that he might need to make use of official channels, or to speak with government representatives. Where and when possible, it was always better to operate and move about as an officially registered visitor. By the time anyone might by chance or curiosity happen to find themselves intrigued by certain unusual aspects of his presence and express a desire to put forth the effort to dig further into his background, he should be long gone outsystem.

Stepping down off the platform, he loosened the soft-seal at his neck. After the encounter with the kasollt and the walk to the terminal, the heat inside was almost stifling. Waiting nearby, the diligent Paya was studying the three-dimensional readout his communit was projecting into the air between them. Looking up, he smiled affably "Says here you're in extraordinarily good health."

Flinx indicated the device. "Bioanalyzers don't always show everything. As just one example, I suffer all the time from severe headaches."

The administrator sighed. "I'm a bureaucrat who deals regularly with the general public. I can sympathize." Raising an arm, he gestured down the corridor that led away from the Arrivals room. "We're done here. Have a nice time on Gestalt, and I wish you the best of fortune with your research. If you don't mind my asking, what are you researching?"

"History," Flinx told him.

Understandably misunderstanding, Paya nodded. "This world has an interesting history, though a slim one. Humans have been living here for a fairly long time, though the immigrant population has always been limited."

"By the Tlel?" Flinx inquired as they started down the hallway.

The official shook his head. "By choice. Gestalt is not a particularly hospitable world. This isn't Kansastan, or Barabas, and it doesn't offer new migrants the promise of a place like Dawn. Those who choose to settle here permanently are different from your typical colonist. It takes a certain singular mind-set not only to adapt to the planet, its limitations, and its climate, but also to live among the Tlel. Not everyone can handle it. Many of those who try manage for a few years, or five, or even a decade. Then they've had enough. The Tlel get to them, or the weather, or having to constantly keep an eye out for dangerous animals that on other colony worlds would be cleared from the vicinity of habitations."

"How about you?" Flinx teased genially. "Are you *singular*?"

The silent emotions the official emitted suggested calm amusement. There was no indication of suppressed suspicion. He had accepted this new visitor's definition of himself without hesitation.

"My wife and kids think so. My ancestors would think I'm crazy for choosing to live on a world like this. They all made their homes in warm, usually humid places. They'd find Gestalt too remote, too cold, and too dry. I happen to like it." He looked up at Flinx. "I also like the Tlel, in spite of the fact that they're completely oblivious to their own potent body odor. That's only natural, considering that they can't smell it. Or anything else. Most of us can manage the downsides or we couldn't handle living here. I hardly know you, but I have the impression that you'll get along just fine. Just a feeling." His tone switched from the familiar to the formal. "You have a place to reside?"

Flinx shook his head. For a moment, he was simultaneously afraid and flattered that the administrator was going to invite him to stay with his family. While that would have advantages, he preferred the freedom that privacy would give him. Still, he felt slightly let down at Paya's response.

"There are a number of decent places to stay in Tlossene. Almost all are set up to cater to the needs of visiting business travelers. As I said before, Gestalt doesn't draw the casual visitor. What's your preference? Luxury, economical, something in between?"

"In between," Flinx told him. He wanted to add *anonymous,* but that was generally not a description one appended to a request for a hotel recommendation. "If my research goes as I hope, I'll only be here for a couple of days."

The official eyed him closely. "I don't know where you've come from, and in any event it's none of my business, but it strikes me that anyone who'd go to the trouble of traveling between worlds to visit someplace just for a couple of days is either unconscionably rich, unutterably bored, or in a terrible hurry."

Flinx mustered a masking smile. "I'm neither rich nor bored, but I am in a bit of a hurry." *And it is terrible,* he added, but only to himself.

With a cheery wave and a last strobing smile, Paya escorted him to the opposite side of the terminal and saw him off.

The small automated transport that conveyed Flinx into town was covered by the usual transparent plexalloy dome, allowing him to study his new surroundings in comparative comfort. Rolling off an accessway, the vehicle paused to concede right-of-way to what looked like a cluster of two-legged rugs. Ambling across the busy route in single file, they appeared to lope in slow motion. Some were tall enough to have stood eye-to-eye with a fascinated Flinx— assuming he would have been able to locate any eyes beneath the blanket of long, flaccid quills that completely covered the creatures' conical bodies. Splayed feet sporting multiple digits provided support that was probably equally stable on snow or pavement.

A few of them turned in his direction as they crossed. He strained to make eye contact where no oculars could be seen, yet from the primitive animal emotions he was perceiving it was evident that they were aware of his presence. Or at least that of the transport craft in which he was riding. If they could not see it clearly, could they detect its faint electrical field? As he struggled to decide, he felt that he was overlooking something. It was a question he could have put to the helpful port official. Now it would have to wait until he could strike up a conversation with another equally knowledgeable local.

Proving the truth of Paya's word, the tolerant hired vehicle reflected the native concern for the welfare of Gestaltian wildlife by waiting until the last of the creatures had wended its way safely across the transport lane. Only then did it resume its course, taking him deeper into the city.

Tlossene was a city of eggs. Or rather, egg shapes. Without a flat or sharply angled roof in sight, the comparison was unavoidable. The use of bright colors somewhat diluted the initial impression. Apparently, there was no compunction against coloring the curving, interconnected buildings everything from robin's-egg blue to a startling mix of swirling fuchsia and teal.

While the majority of Tlossene's human inhabitants made use of the spaghetti-like network of sealed, climate-controlled tubular walkways that connected each building to its neighbors, enough citizens were out on the open pedestrian walkways to give Flinx a good overview of the population. These passing encounters also provided him with his first glimpse of Gestalt's indigenous species.

Short, resilient, and stocky of build, the Tlel were decidedly nonhumanoid. Patterns in their dense silicaceous fur ranging in color from beige all the way to blue-black distinguished one individual from another. In place of more familiar gelatinous, single-lensed individual eyes, each Tlel sported a glistening horizontal ocular that formed a semi-reflective crescent across the front of their skulls. What sort of images this unique vision organ conveyed to the Tlelian brain Flinx could only imagine, though they were obviously more than adequate.

In the absence of teeth, wide mouths were lined with interlocking layers of some hard keratinous substance. Tall oval ears curved sharply upward from the rear of the flattened, disc-like head. Beneath the area a human would have thought of as a chin, a cluster of a dozen centimeter-long black-and-white tendrils writhed and flexed, as if massaging the cold air. Cruising by in the transport, Flinx could not tell if these appendages were purely decorative or had some practical use. Perhaps they were the electrically sensitive organs to which the helpful port administrator had referred. Or maybe they were used in bringing food closer to the narrow jaws.

Air was taken in and exhaled through the mouth. Bearing in mind what Payasinadoriyung had told him about the natives having no sense of smell, Flinx was not surprised at the absence of anything resembling nostrils. Reaching all the way to the ground, a pair of thin, attenuated upper arms terminated in an anemone-like clutch of strong, grasping cilia instead of bony fingers or tentacles. He could not see whether the two legs ended in feet, pads, hooves, or something else because they were concealed in brightly colored leggings that spiraled up each native's lower limbs like striped candy.

In fact, every example of Tlel attire he saw was vivid and varied in color, design, and material. In addition to leggings and foot coverings, they wore loose-fitting vests, many of which were transparent in full or part. A few individuals sported specialized fabric coverings over their grasping tendrils. Perhaps, he thought, the bright shades and sharply defined patterns helped them identify one another when traveling through the pink-tinged snows that prevailed at higher elevations. Many also wore simple one-piece poncho-like garments that, like the vests, were largely transparent.

As with any new species, Flinx was looking forward to meeting some of them. Reaching down, he checked the translator that formed part of the otherwise purely decorative necklace he wore. Gestalt being part of the Commonwealth, its indigenous language was well researched. The *Teacher* had programmed the dominant tongue together with applicable dialects into the translation device as soon as he had identified that world as their next destination. He would not face the kind of communications problems here that he had on Arrawd, for example. In any event, he reminded himself, records indicated that a large number of Tlel now spoke at least some terranglo. A preponderance of any such linguistically talented locals was most likely to be found in a cosmopolitan urban center such as Tlossene.

A single brief snow flurry momentarily obscured the view ahead. Then it was gone, in a pink puff and a smothered sigh, a Gestaltian welcome no less idiosyncratic than that which had been proffered by the port official. Or by the ravenous kasollt, Flinx told himself as the transport pulled into the welcoming lobby of the hotel that had been recommended to him. As the vehicle slowed to a halt, a translucent flexwall flowed shut behind it, sealing out the wind and the cold.

The room he took, on the top floor, had a view through the curving transparent wall not only of shorter egg-shaped structures but of the mountains beyond the city as well. In the far distance even higher peaks could be discerned. Thanks to Gestalt's unpolluted atmosphere, their ragged outlines were perfectly sharp and clear. If only Clarity had been with him, he could have relaxed and truly enjoyed the view.

Spectacular as it was, he spared it only a glance. He was here in search of answers, not relaxation.

Still, knowing that his mind would be clearer, his thoughts sharper, he made himself wait until the following morning before starting in. He had waited his whole life to learn the truth of his origins. Apocalyptic revelations were always better contemplated on a good night's sleep.

Using his personal communit he could have accessed the planetary Shell from his room, or anywhere within the hotel, or even out on the street. He chose not to. Even with strong security wraps in situ, even with sweeper tics emplaced on the unit that would shadow his searching and shield it from any monitoring external source, he could still leave a trail. Making use of a simple, free public terminal while taking care to leave absolutely nothing in the way of personal markers behind would ensure that any curious probers would be able to trace his lines of inquiry no farther than that same terminal.

Further seeking to preserve maximum anonymity of purpose, he made it a point to explain to the hotel's human concierge that he was interested in seeing some of the local sights, whatever they might be. After spending half an hour asking enough questions to mark him as an interested but not particularly bright visitor and collecting sufficient information to convince any inquisitive parties of his unambiguously touristic intentions, he exited the hotel. Deliberately spurning automated transport, he elected to walk.

Outside, he felt no additional warmth through the boots he had chosen as the most suitable footwear for the chilly world of Gestalt.

In the current absence of snow, the layer of thermotropic paving passing beneath his feet remained temperature-neutral. Should snow or hail begin to fall, the sensitive material would respond by outputting stored heat to melt it.

He could have chosen a route covering the modest distance to the municipal hall that would have taken him through climate-controlled aboveground walkways. Instead, obliged as he was to spend weeks at a time sealed within the self-contained environment of the *Teacher,* he took the opportunity to revel in walking outside beneath the clear, clean, open sky. His view of cloud-swept blue was occasionally marred by the passage of a private or heavy cargo skimmer. Higher still, suborbital aircraft left occasional streaks in Gestalt's upper atmosphere. Far fewer of these were to be seen than on most inhabited worlds.

Despite being one of only two large cities on Gestalt, Tlossene still had more than a touch of the frontier about it. Some of this was no doubt due to the absence of any structure higher than half a dozen stories. Another reason lay in the penchant for Tlel-inspired architecture. Though he was not alone on the streets, the paucity of human pedestrians further reinforced the feeling of being on a world far outside the mainstream of Commonwealth commerce and communication. A perfect place, Flinx thought, for an organization such as the outlawed Meliorares to sequester secrets. A world where a visitor might look straight at something of significance and still manage not to see it. Like a certain long-sought-after paternal personage, for example.

While humans were scarce on the city's streets, the Tlel were not. Observing that there never seemed to be more than four of them together, Flinx wondered if there was some prohibition against them traveling in larger groups, or if four was simply considered some kind of optimal number for an outing. Perhaps in the presence of more than four of their kind it became difficult for them to distinguish individual electrical fields. Several times he saw them in conversation with local humans. At least a couple of the latter appeared to converse fluently without the aid of mechanical translation devices such as the one he wore around his neck. Once, he also saw a tall, lone Quillp ambling along, its elongated skull retracted downward toward its body as far as its flexible neck would allow. Other than fellow humans, it was the only non-Tlel he encountered in the course of leaving the hotel behind.

Of thranx he saw none. While humankind's closest allies would have found Gestalt's dense atmosphere appealing, its cold climate would scare off all but the most determined—or possibly masochistic—of that tropic-loving species. No thranx would visit this world willingly, he knew. To be posted or sent here, a thranx would have to have offended more than propriety.

As he neared Tlossene's municipal hall, he encountered representatives of yet another of the Commonwealth's sentient races. More naturally suited to the local climate than either Quillp or human, a pair of ever-active, bundled-up Tolians disappeared through its main entrance. Gestalt was one world, he reflected, where being born with a fur coat was an advantage rather than burden. He prepared to follow them.

Approaching the entrance, he observed several Tlel making minor repairs to the building's decorated exterior. Utilizing a patchpaster of unmistakably humanx origin, they were busy at work halfway up the side of the five-story structure. He paused outside to watch, captivated by the fact that they employed neither lift packs, scaffolding, safety harnesses, nor anything other than their ciliumtipped arms. Apparently useless for climbing, their legs and blocky, legging-concealed feet dangled freely over the street. The strength in those long, thin arms was clearly considerably greater than he had initially estimated.

As he looked on, they swung easily from one location to the next, carrying the patchpaster with them while continuously adjusting its spray. On further reflection, the seemingly unbalanced alien anatomy made sense. Broad splayed feet were for walking on snow and mud. Long, sinewy arms were for going over higher, rougher impediments, perhaps by swinging through vegetation. If he had the time and the inclination once he had fulfilled his purpose here, he decided, it would be interesting to spend a few days out in the backcountry closely observing the Tlel in their natural habitat. But not too closely. The malodorous body odor that emanated from them was more than merely conspicuous.

Taking into consideration different senses and what they revealed about others, he found himself wondering what *his* personal electrical field "smelled" like to a being capable of detecting it. As someone who possessed a unique sense of his own in the form of the ability to perceive the emotions of others, he felt a sudden kinship with the Tlel who were at once blessed by the possession of such an inimitable facility while being cursed by the absence of a much more common one. When humans among them spoke of how things smelled, of odors and aromas and scents and stinks, how could the olfactory-deprived Tlel possibly respond other than with bewilderment?

Unlike some corresponding facilities of municipal importance on more developed worlds such as recently visited Visaria, there were no guards at the entrance. Security was not entirely absent, however: only more unobtrusive. He knew this because a Tlel armed with both a humanx-manufactured sidearm and a traditional slim, conical knife approached as he entered and addressed him in the guttural wheeze of the dominant dialect. As Flinx fiddled with his translator, he reflected on the strangeness of meeting the gaze of a creature that had no eyes in the familiar sense: only a lens-like arc of photosensitive organosilicate material. The disc-shaped head was tilted back on the short neck, staring up at him. He had a brief, unconscionable urge to wonder if it would spin if he slapped it sideways.

The wide mouth beneath the eyeband parted, and the grumbling challenge was repeated. While the gripping cilia at the ends of both arms splayed outward to help balance the stocky body, the tendrils beneath the chin area flexed in a fashion that could only be called impatient.

"Just a minute—I'm getting it. Takes a moment for the presets to adapt to actual auditory input. There!" Speaking into the translator's pickup, Flinx heard his own words transcribed into the aural gargle of pharyngeal and epiglottal consonants and hard vowels that passed for Tlelian speech.

It transpired that the sentinel's concern was not with the human visitor but with his much smaller, slimmer, and largely concealed companion. Noting how thoroughly the motionless Pip was buried beneath his jacket, Flinx found himself wondering how the Tlel had divined the flying snake's presence. Peering past the sentry, he could not see any kind of obvious detection gear. That did not mean it was not present, he reminded himself; perhaps it was camouflaged as a reading device, a bit of décor, or the floor itself.

He hastened to explain that Pip was his close companion, that she was under his complete control, and that she posed no threat to anyone. This confessional was at least half true. He did not outright lie and say that she was harmless. His swift explanation and genuine openness apparently sufficient to satisfy the sentinel and any unseen colleagues, the Tlel turned away, rumbling by way of parting something perfunctory that Flinx's translator did not catch.

As expected, the public terminals available for accessing the Gestalt Shell were located on the ground floor. Out of more than two dozen, only one was in use. That was not surprising. Though a sufficiency of such free terminals was mandated on every civilized world, most citizens preferred to use their personal communits to communicate, range their local Shell, and gather information.

Always wary of standing out or drawing attention to himself, he settled into an empty booth at the far end of those that were not in use. A standard citizen's request activated the booth's visual and verbal privacy screen. Now no one could look in on him or hear any verbal commands he might choose to voice. Anyway, unlike occasions during which he had been obligated to perform illegal searches or scans, what he was going to do now was perfectly legitimate. Or so it would have seemed to anyone standing alongside him within the booth.

They did not see him slip the mazr into an open port. It would not only mask his inquiries from anyone who might use the terminal after him but also thoroughly homogenize, shunt, self-encrypt, and rephrase his requests so that they resembled perfectly conventional searches for everyday, sanctioned information. Without the use of the mazr a deep-thrust query on "Meliorare Society," for example, might trigger an automatic follow-up alert somewhere. That was unlikely, especially on a laid-back world like Gestalt. But Flinx had not succeeded in staying always a step or two ahead of those pursuing him by taking informational as well as personal security for granted. The hard lessons he had learned when he had illegally penetrated a main hub of the Terran Shell several years earlier had led him to take more proactive precautions prior to making such intrusions.

Taking a seat in the booth's single chair and slipping the tiara-like, featherweight, pale green induction band over his hair, he let it automatically adjust until the fit was snug against his forehead and over his ears. Detecting the presence of an operator, the terminal swiftly read his E-pattern and activated the neural connection. Above the concealed projector located within the shelf in front of him, weft space began to take shape. When the glow had strengthened sufficiently, he readied himself to input.

Much to his surprise, he found that he was trembling slightly. Worried by the conflicting emotions she was receiving, a concerned Pip poked her head out from beneath his jacket. Though no overt threat was discernible, she remained edgy and alert. Reaching up and across with his left hand, he stroked the back of her head and upper body. It could be argued that the habitual response was intended more to relax him than her.

Taking a deep breath, he double-checked to make sure the mazr was running before voicing the initial queryought as clearly as he could. "Does the edicted Meliorare Society have any history on the planet Gestalt, also known by its indigenous name of Silvoun?"

As expected, the response of the planetary Shell was as near instantaneous as it was brief.

"No."

Concise and conclusive, he told himself. Well, he had expected nothing less. Now that he was in, with a query that theoretically contained the potential to alert certain security nodes but had not done so, he found that some of the tension eased out of him. The mazr was doing its job.

"What do you know of a Commonwealth citizen named Theon al-bar Cocarol?"

As it had with his initial inquiry, the Shell came up empty. It was the same when he repeated the query using the now-deceased Meliorare's alias, Shyvil Theodakris. Though he was already less hopeful than when he had sat down, he was not yet disillusioned. His preliminary queries had been blunt and undemanding. To ensure that the Shell had access to the full range of Commonwealth knowledge, he pulled up a general sybfile on the Society itself. That, at least, should be readily accessible to anyone with an uncontroversial interest in the straightforward history of Commonwealth science.

The Shell hub responded immediately and exhaustively, presenting him with the complete official history of the Meliorares: how they and their activities had been discovered and quickly placed under edict, the nature of their banned eugenics experiments, how they had been hunted down one by one, tried, convicted, and sentenced, and an analysis of the small but sordid chapter they represented in the history of Commonwealth biological research.

It was the sanctioned history that the Shell gave him. He allowed himself a small smile as he perused the proffered information. Not everything had worked out exactly as the official records stated. For one thing, a certain Meliorare experiment named Philip Lynx was still at large, harassed and besieged both within and without, but as yet wholly himself and most decidedly unmindwiped. He shifted in the chair, mentally preparing himself. It was time to probe deeper, and differently.

He started tunneling.

Some of what he did was legal, some not. Having previously penetrated the Terran Shell itself, he had no difficulty avoiding the internal floating security of the considerably less well-defended Shell on Gestalt. Its secure sections opened for him, if not like a book, at least in a pattern of three-dimensional sybfiles—a flower of information. Despite the cool air within the administration building, perspiration began to bead on his forehead as he dug and drilled and pushed ever deeper into the depths of the local hub.

He found little that was palpably illicit—this was not Visaria, after all—and a good deal that certain citizens had reason to wish to keep hidden, but nothing whatsoever related in any way, shape, weft, or form to the dead Meliorare Cocarol or to the disturbing proscribed society to which he had belonged. The deeper Flinx wormed, the more discouraged he became. Risking discovery, he entered his own true name, his nickname, and even what he had learned of the personal history of his mother. All to no avail, all for naught. There was nothing. Not a hint in words, not a glimmer in weft space, not a suggestion of anything connected to the Society, to his ancestry, or to him.

When probing directly yielded nil, he tunneled sideways. He searched in reverse, trying to find the tiniest possible chyp of information that would allow him to work in a different direction, along another node. He promulgated requests that were grounded in fantasy and fancy as much as in fact. Everything he tried came up the same. Empty.

Physical hunger, as primitive and unsophisticated an intrusion as it was demanding, caused him to glance at his wrist chrono. He was startled to see that he had been in the booth nearly all day. His throat was dry. It had not occurred to him to bring along anything to drink or to take a sip from his jacket's emergency supply. Contemplating options, he realized reluctantly that even if he wished to stay and continue the investigation, Pip's active metabolism demanded that she be fed. Why not take a break?

He wasn't getting anywhere, anyhow.

Cramped muscles unlocking, he broke the connection, slipped the neuronic headband off over his head, and replaced it in its holder. A simple tug and twist removed the mazr from the console; he quickly slipped it into a pouch on his belt. The device would leave behind no trace of its masking presence. Seriously disheartened, he exited the booth and then the building. Neither the Tlel nor the few humans who were still working inside gave him so much as a curious glance.

It was dark outside and, in the absence of Gestalt's bright sunshine, noticeably colder. The material of his jacket and pants immediately responded to keep him warm. Pip burrowed even deeper beneath his protective attire, a warm muscular cable relaxed against his inner shirt and chest.

There were only two Shell hubs on Gestalt: one in Tlossene and the other on the far side of the planet in the second city of Tlearandra. There was nothing to be gained by flying halfway around the globe to pose it the same queries. The hubs' content, operation, and resources would be identical. Law as well as custom demanded it, since one unit would have to be available to refresh the other in the event either suffered a catastrophic failure. Should he go there, only the scenery would change. Nor was Gestalt big or important enough to warrant the existence of a private, access-restricted hub. For example, there was no military presence significant enough to justify such an expense. The chill that was beginning to creep over him had nothing to do with the nocturnal climate. It arose from disappointment, and from within.

Maybe the *Teacher* was right. *A waste of time,* it had called his impulsive detour to Gestalt's system. That, and *selfish.*

He had tried the planetary Shell and found it wanting. Probed long and deep and learned nothing for his efforts. It was past time to resume the search for something more real, more tangible, in the form of the brown dwarf-sized Tar-Aiym weapons platform that Bran Tse-Mallory and Truzenzuzex had pleaded with him to locate. It was apparent he would learn naught here, unearth nothing on this cold, minor world, about either himself or his paternal ancestry.

He did not cry, but he wanted to.

On Visaria a dying Meliorare's words had provided the best hope of finding out something about the nature and identity of his father. If despite his most intense searching they had led him nowhere but here, where would he look next? In the absence of any other clue or information, how would he pick up the DNA thread? Should he even bother to try? Perhaps it was simply one of those things he was destined never to know. He would gladly have traded it for one of the many dispiriting, somber, sobering things he did know.

The lights had come on in the city. In the clear, oxygen-rich air Tlossene's many-domed and gracefully curving structures took on the appearance of a fairy-tale town, albeit one in which contemporary high-tech had utterly replaced fantasy. Photoemitting walls illuminated the streets. Even at this comparatively early hour these were largely devoid of human pedestrians, though Tlel were present in number. Their guttural chuckling and gabbling filled the night with a steady burble of contented alien chatter. It was all that disturbed the otherwise perfectly still air. He kept his translator switched off. At the moment, he did not especially want to know what they were saying. At the moment, he did not want to know what anyone was saying.

Maybe, as the *Teacher* had suggested, the devious Meliorare Co-carol *had* expired with little more than a teasing lie on his lips, sending the youth responsible for his death off on a desperate wild-goose chase. Flinx refused to countenance the possibility. Not yet, anyway. He would try again, somehow. There were other ways of finding things out. Methods that were not as fast or efficient as directly querying a planetary Shell, perhaps, but still serviceable.

For starters, he would ask around.

CHAPTER

3

He began the following morning, starting by accessing freely available Shell sybfiles via his communit. These readily offered up the names of a number of organizations and businesses fronted by individuals who had lived on Gestalt all their lives. They represented a broad cross section of settlers. He quickly winnowed the list down to those involved with immigration, obscure social activities, and any that might offer services to citizens who had reason to be exceptionally protective of their personal privacy. He was looking for any person or commercial concern that might have contact with other individuals who had more than the usual reasons to keep the details of their identity discreet. In particular, he was looking for one such individual who more than a quarter century earlier had sold or donated sperm to the Meliorare Society and might subsequently have fled to the minor colony world of Gestalt.

Though still extensive, the final list represented the best he could do based on a preliminary search. He had to start somewhere. Simply checking every male inhabitant of the appropriate chronological age was certain to prove an interminable as well as unrewarding task.

Furthermore, the Meliorares had manipulated his DNA to produce results to their taste, to fulfill a specific design. His paternal donor might as easily be short and dark-haired as tall and redheaded, and of any age over the necessary minimum of forty. Flinx felt that he was likely to have more luck looking for distinctive, revealing social traits than for specific physical characteristics that might be nothing more than coincidence.

Nevertheless, whenever any male who fell within the appropriate age parameters cropped up on his initial list, he felt compelled to run at least one cursory check of that individual's history. Men who chose to live alone also came in for particular scrutiny, as did those companies that maintained even the most peripheral involvement with gengineering or other types of biological research. While it struck him as unlikely that his father would be so foolish or disdainful of his past as to become openly involved with such enterprises, rigor and possibility demanded that they still be investigated.

His ability to tunnel the Shell helped immensely. Hundreds of years ago, the search process would have taken forever, or rendered insufficiently specific replies. Most of the searches he ran, though not all, were perfectly legal. Those privacy shields he encountered he brushed aside. Gestalt's Shell and germane technology were not primitive, but neither were they particularly sophisticated. As days passed and he worked his way through sybfile after sybfile, he reflected on how much, and yet how little, his life had changed.

Look at all the progress I've made since Mother Mastiff took me under her wing, he thought as he sat and worked at the public terminal in the administration building. Why, I've advanced all the way from stealing things to stealing information. And so far not very encouraging information, at that.

Once, on the third day of searching, he thought he was seriously on to something. Paid in advance, a local investigator—even a world as minor as Gestalt had need for such services, it appeared—circumspectly provided him with a list of artisans who had dropped out of and no longer belonged to any formal planetary aesthetic associations. Some of the documented iconoclasts doubtless objected to association policy, some to the need to belong, and some had abandoned the organizations out of sheer irascibility.

Scrutinizing this registry of creative malcontents, Flinx found a number whose personal information was privacy-guarded. Brushing aside these protections, he came across one composer who not only was the appropriate age but also physically resembled him in several respects. Furthermore, and most intriguingly, Sadako Basrayan was not a native Gestaltian but had emigrated from Earth itself some twenty years earlier.

Flinx could hardly restrain himself. Even the *Teacher,* contacted through his communit, allowed as how its owner might just possibly have stumbled onto a lead that held a shade more promise than fantasy. Ostensibly to discuss the musical accompaniment to an opera he was writing, Flinx managed to arrange a meeting with the reclusive Mr. Basrayan. Once assured by his guest that the colorful minidrag accompanying him was only reflecting her master's excitement when she rose from his shoulder to buzz the living room, the relieved composer readily if unknowingly complied with Flinx's needs. Basrayan did this not by suggesting music that caused his younger visitor's imagination to take flight, but by sporting a great deal of hair. Though it was black and not red, Flinx was not discouraged. He only needed one such strand, which he surreptitiously co-opted halfway through the visit from a chair the composer had been occupying.

Running any DNA sequence was a simple enough process. Not wishing to take the time to return the sample to the *Teacher,* an excited Flinx utilized a self-service analytical facility in Tlossene. The service would extract the musical Mr. Basrayan's genetic code and compare it with a sample of Flinx's own.

The following day he accepted the service's hard copy with hands that did not shake. But his face was flushed. Initial excitement and high hopes soon gave way to crushing dejection as he eagerly scanned the readout. The codes did not match. They were not even close. Tossing the costly analysis into the nearest public waste disposal, he strode grimly out of the facility and back onto the street.

Weeks later, he was on the verge of giving up when he found himself engaged in terse correspondence with one Rosso Eustabe.

As with many of the contacts he had made, Flinx met this latest in what so far had been an endless parade of unhelpful personages in the front lobby of his hotel. There, he and various locals with whom he had worked long and hard to cultivate contact would indulge in drinks and snacks at his expense. Introductions and casual conversation would be followed by the passing of information from a visitor to the tall young man who had extended the invitations—information that had so far provided Flinx with nothing more than a multiplicity of insights into the nature of some of Gestalt's least sociable denizens. He had encountered and interviewed enough grumpy, grouchy, disaffected, irritable, semi-sane, cantankerous iconoclasts to last him a lifetime. The fact that he could on occasion himself be accounted among their number was a detail he unconsciously overlooked.

Eustabe did not exactly lurch into the lobby, but it was clear that his motile abilities had been more than slightly compromised by a lifetime of hard work, and perhaps also ingestion on a regular basis of organic compounds less than beneficial to one's health. Rising from the adaptive chair that had become intimately acquainted with his backside in the course of the previous several weeks, Flinx methodically extended a hand toward this latest in the seeming endless line of nonconformist informers. His guest accepted the welcome with the one of his hands that was still flesh. The other, together with the arm to which it was attached, was wholly synthetic. Unlike the majority of people who had incurred the need for extensive prosthetics, Eustabe had not bothered to obtain one that duplicated the appearance of his real arm. The plasticine and carbonfiber webwork and synflesh overlay that comprised the fingers, hand, and arm of his artificial limb was an unrelieved, unadorned gray. Or perhaps its owner had not wanted to spring for the additional credits necessary to purchase a perfect duplicate, Flinx reflected.

In addition to the arm, the other man's stride suggested that all or part of his right leg was equally mock. So were both ears, and there were signs of inexpensive skin regeneration work on his neck and forehead. His face was beaten, weathered, experienced, making him look older than he probably was. Except for some filaments of light brown that had somehow succeeded in not being overwhelmed, the gray stubble that adorned his chin and the rest of his face was the same color, if not the same composition, as his prosthetic left arm. Sometime, somewhere, Flinx's latest informant had suffered and survived a horrific accident. The man's emotions betrayed no evidence of any personal historical catastrophe, however; nor could Flinx peer inside him to identify any possible complementary internal replacements. At his young host's invitation, Eustabe flumped down in the chair opposite.

"I'm Skua Mastiff," Flinx told his guest.

"Rosso Eustabe."

Flinx found it difficult to put together an assessment of the man's feelings. One moment the newcomer seemed completely relaxed; the next his nerves knotted sharply, as if something was after him. Probably something was, Flinx decided, though whether real or imaginary he could not have said.

"Word out is that you're doing sociological research for an off-world data company." Eustabe's real fingers kept scratching, scratching, at the arm of his chair, as if trying to dig a hole in which his hand could hide. Responding, the reactive material of which the arm was manufactured kept flexing in a futile attempt to accommodate the continuously fluctuating nervous pressure.

"That's right." Flinx tendered the automatic smile of a traveling professional. It appeared quite genuine. As well it should, its owner having had plenty of opportunity to practice it in the course of preceding interviews. "I've been assigned to gather statistics on Gestalt. As I informed you through our correspondence, we're particularly interested in those eclectic Commonwealth citizens who for reasons of their own choose to withdraw from society at large yet continue to show an interest in changes among their own kind. Artists, for example, who frequently depict in their work different states of humanity. Or cosmetic biosurges who sometimes find themselves working outside the bounds of what is commonly thought of as good taste. Also those who shun widespread contact with their own kind for reasons that are not readily apparent."

"I remember." Eustabe was nodding, his expression uncommonly like that of a wise family member who knows where all the bones are buried. "I think I might have one for you."

As he had done during so many previous interviews, Flinx methodically detached his communit from his service belt, activated it, and instructed it to record. "Go ahead."

Eustabe scratched at his steely chin stubble with the fingers of his real hand, seeking tactile feedback. "There's the matter of payment . . ."

"The terms of which you agreed to when you responded to my request for information." Trying not to appear overly indifferent, Flinx forced a repeat of his earlier smile. "And also as agreed," he continued perfunctorily, "if your information leads to a usable contact, a further bonus will be paid—by my company."

Eustabe nodded thoughtfully. "I'm a private contract transporter. I've got a long-range heavy-lift skimmer and I make a living delivering supplies to backcountry residents. Quite a few of those here on Gestalt."

"So I've learned," Flinx responded noncommittally.

The oldster shifted in his chair. Though he could not be certain, Flinx thought he heard the man's right leg whine when it moved. An integrated servo in need of maintenance, he decided. Eustabe probably needed money.

"Okay then. There's this one fella, about me age, goes by the name of Anayabi. That's all, just 'Anayabi.' Uses only the one name."

Feeling suddenly tired, Flinx sighed. "I'm afraid that's not enough to qualify an individual for my company's study. Or to meet the criteria for a bonus payment." Relaxing on his neck and shoulder, Pip glanced up sleepily. No one was looking in their direction. By now the hotel staff, mechanical as well as human, was used to (if still not entirely comfortable with) the minidrag's presence.

"I'm just telling you." Eustabe's tone turned slightly defensive. "As you might have noticed, meself, I ain't quite all there natural-like, if you know what I mean." When Flinx's silence indicated that he did, indeed, know to what his guest was referring, the other man continued.

"Most times, most folk, they don't react openly to the prosthetics. Or if they do, they try not to show it. Polite being, they are. But this guy, this Anayabi moke, after a couple of deliveries I make to him, he up and right-out starts chattering about it."

Flinx perked up slightly. "About *it*?"

"You know." Eustabe leaned toward his host. "The nonmeat parts of meself. Me arm"—he raised the cybernetic limb in question— "and the other parts. Starts asking me all kinds of questions about them. How did I come to need the synthetics, how did they feel. How did I respond to their presence emotionally as well as physically, that sort of stuff."

Interesting, but—not much more, Flinx felt. And hardly conclusive of anything. The kinds of questions any curious albeit admittedly tactless person might ask. Or more specifically but in no wise especially revealing of anything other than his profession—a physician, perhaps. Having nothing else planned for the next hour, anyway, he decided he might as well let Eustabe ramble.

"Go on."

"It wasn't just the questions. I've dealt with plenty of the like before, many times occasioned." Leaning forward, Eustabe lowered his voice slightly, as if he was about to impart something significant as well as unexpected.

"What was odd about this fella was that he didn't just ask questions with his voice. He asked them, too, with his *eyes*. The first couple of times, I didn't pay attention much. Then it started growing creep on me. I mean, he was making me feel like a specimen in a lab, or something."

Deep inside Flinx, something tightened ever so slightly. "Please, continue."

Eustabe sat back in the chair, which morphed to accommodate him. "By the time I made my fifth delivery out his way, I'd had enough. So I straight-up called him on it. All the questions and the staring. Wasn't worth the tip. I told him outright to back off. Well, he right up and apologized. Insisted he didn't mean to offend in any way, that it wasn't at all in his temperament. That it was just his nature to ask questions about things that interested him, and one of the things that interested him mostest was how human beings can change themselves to make themselves better."

Flinx swallowed hard. Sensing the surge in her master's emotions, Pip awoke and lifted her head to locate the source of the disturbance. Whatever it was, she decided, it was clearly not the harmless human seated nearby. "Better people?" Flinx asked tentatively of his guest.

"No-so," Eustabe replied. "Better human beings. Those were his exact words." Letting out a derisive snort, he reached for the bowl of snacks the hotel had set out on his chair's end table. Detecting the heat emanating from his open palm, the snacks obediently leaped upward to fill it. As he munched something then moaned pleasurably, he squinted at the tall young man seated across from him. "He sufficiently interested in human changes to qualify him for your survey?"

Change. Make better. Keywords underlying everything the members of the Meliorare Society stood for. The members—and possibly also those who, while not formal members of the organization, had freely assisted them in their work. Assisted them by contributing their own knowledge, expertise, experience—and in more than several cases, genes.

This hermetic Anayabi could be nothing more than a retired physician or decertified gengineer, or perhaps a curious biologist with a hobbyist's interest in general eugenics. "What does this Anayabi look like?" Flinx could not keep himself from asking. "Skin color, eye color, body type, approximate age . . . hair color?"

Eustabe's face screwed up slightly. "That all relevant to your survey?"

Though he was much younger than his guest, Flinx had in his comparatively short lifetime seen a good deal more. This experience informed his brisk response. "Does it matter to you if it is?"

The older man sat motionless for a moment. Then he nodded understandingly. Any additional words or queries would have been superfluous. "Couple centimeters taller than me. Average build, pretty solid for someone his age. Living away out where he does, I imagine he gets some serious exercise. Or uses a good toner. Skin color about like yours." Flinx's heart skipped a beat. An unjustifiable reaction, perhaps, but an irrepressible one. "Didn't notice the color of his eyes. Black hair, cut real short. He and I are about the same length of sentient existence, I'd guess."

Eustabe's description made the subject sound as if he was also the appropriate age. "Any accent?" Flinx remembered to maintain the illusion that this was a proper scientific interview by feigning interest in the operation of his communit, which continued to record the interview.

"Unadulterated Gestalt, insofar as I could tell. If not native, then someone who's lived here a long while. Long enough to sprinkle his chat with Tlel terms. That's as clear a mark of a long-termer as you can find."

Would his father give himself away as a possible collaborator of the Meliorares by showing such explicit interest in the adaptability and improvement of another human being? On the other hand, who on Gestalt would have reason to suspect that such questions might have their origin in such an illegitimate history? This Anayabi's questioning and studying of someone like Eustabe might be perceived locally as nothing more than the tactlessness Eustabe himself had initially felt it to be. Harmless, if tasteless, chatter between one of hundreds of recluse settlers and a deliveryman. To ascribe to it anything of greater significance one would have to look at it from an entirely different perspective.

The perspective, he knew, of one all too familiar with the Meliorares and their work.

Though she was unable to locate the source of it, Pip fluttered her pleated wings as she shared her master's increasing excitement. This Eustabe was presenting him with a long shot, Flinx knew. An extreme long shot. Almost as great a long shot, albeit on a much reduced scale of physical values, as relocating the perambulating Tar-Aiym weapons platform. His lips pressed against each other. If he could take off across a sizable section of the Arm in search of the latter, he could damn well spend another day or two checking out the former. More than one long shot in his past had proven worth the pursuing. Clarity Held, for example.

"Young Mr. Mastiff, sir?"

"What?" Dragging himself back from contemplation of several unrelated curvilinear forms, Flinx remembered that he was supposed to be conducting a formal interview for an unidentified employer. "Yes, this Anayabi, uh, fella of yours certainly sounds like he might fit the profile of the kind of folks we want to include in our survey. Do you happen to have any additional information on him?"

Eustabe shook his head. "I just made my scheduled deliveries, that's all. I never had a hundredth the interest in him-wise that he did in me. You can try researching him through the Shell, but it's my experience that folks who like that much physical privacy take care to shield their personals as well. If you go looking, I don't think you'll much find." He smiled broadly. "If he can fit into your survey, then I expect your bonus will fit into my account."

Setting a secure, private link between their respective communits, both men worked in silence. While Flinx transferred the specified bonus credit to Eustabe's personal account, his guest provided Flinx with what little additional information his personal sybfile contained on the hermetic Anayabi. The mostly speculative peripherals did not interest Flinx half so much as the coordinates of the settler's residence.

A quick check showed that the locale in question lay at the extreme limit of a standard skimmer's range. Its very remoteness was a good sign, though pre-arrival research had indicated how seriously many of Gestalt's iconoclastic artists, writers, and self-proclaimed philosophers valued and protected their privacy and isolation. So, too, Flinx knew, would anyone who had once had professional intercourse with the Meliorares. Anyone with any common sense, that is.

He had to force himself not to utilize his own communit to link to the Shell, but to wait until he could once more access a public terminal to research the cryptic Gestaltian resident named Anayabi. He was at once disappointed and pleased to discover that Eustabe had been correct. There was nothing in the public records beyond the most basic listing to be found on anyone by that name. Only a single, terse, uninformative identification string through which Mr. Anayabi could be reached via the Shell. Nor did inputting the coordinates Eustabe had supplied produce any information beyond a location on a topological abstract. There was no description of the inhabitant of said location or his occupation; no mention of any family or category of abode. Like so many of his fellow settlers, the secretive Anayabi had elected to disclose nothing about himself beyond what was necessary to identify and record him as resident on the planet.

Was this notable lack of information simply typical of Gestaltian reclusiveness, Flinx pondered restively, or just possibly indicative of a man with something to hide?

As it turned out, it would take him at least one additional day to find out.

The headache that woke him before sunrise the following morning defeated his every effort to moderate the pain. The medications he always carried with him, the precisely programmed neural stimulator he wrapped around his head—nothing worked. He spent the morning, then the afternoon, then the evening lying in bed, alternately medicated to a stupor and uncomfortably asleep, as wasted as the day itself.

As always during such excruciating episodes, a fretful Pip watched over him. Though she had witnessed her master in the throes of cerebral agony many times before, she suffered through such repetitive episodes with as much concern as she had when he had first experienced them as a child. By the time both the pain in his brain and the side effects incurred from his efforts to mute it had diminished sufficiently for him to function normally again, night had fallen, along with any hope of accomplishing anything of significance in the small remnant of what had been a thoroughly dissipated day.

Even though he awoke the next morning feeling physically drained but otherwise all right, he held off proceeding until he was reasonably sure his head was not about to launch from his neck. Such punishing events would not drive him from Gestalt, and they would not deter him from his goal. Though it was hardly a reassurance, he knew he could die from a cerebral hemorrhage just as easily on Earth or Moth or New Riviera as he could on Gestalt. History and experience had taught him that no medical treatment extant could alleviate his condition.

However crippling his headaches became, he was not leaving Gestalt until he had exhausted every possibility attendant on the dying Cocarol's words. Though he would resume by investigating the lead Rosso Eustabe had given him, it by no means represented the only prospect. Anayabi was not the only eccentric living in isolation on this world. Further digging might well turn up others.

The skimmer that arrived at the hotel in response to his requisition was not new, but it looked perfectly serviceable. He could have called forth his own transport, bringing it into town from its docking bay in the shuttle, but such a display of obvious independent wealth might have occasioned unnecessary and unwanted comment. No youthful, midrange fieldworker for an offworld company would be likely to have access to such an extravagance. Instead, it would be expected that he would have to hire the necessary vehicle locally. So that was what he had done.

Preliminary research had also suggested that it would be good form, as well as socially proper, for him to engage a native escort. He did not need a guide, of course. Once the coordinates Eustabe had supplied had been entered into its AI, the skimmer would navigate its own route to the described destination. While Flinx would have preferred making the journey on his own with only Pip for company, his extensive travels had demonstrated on more than one occasion not only how important it was to adhere to local customs, but how frequently they tended to prove unexpectedly useful as well.

The rented skimmer was not as fast as his own, nor as straightforward in its construction and controls, but it was built with an eye toward the terrain and climate where it was deployed. The familiar transparent plexalloy shield was heavier than usual and double-strength, both to protect against the weather and to further insulate passengers from it. A purely utilitarian vehicle, the unstylish craft was intended to convey people and cargo from coordinate A to coordinate B efficiently and without lugging any false pretensions along with it. Squat and unlovely, it would have drawn no admiring gazes on any developed world. Faster, flashier models were also available from the rental company, all of which Flinx spurned. As always, the less attention he drew to himself, the better he liked it.

Though indigenous escorts were available for hire in Tlossene itself, the agency that had rented him the skimmer suggested he contribute to the human-Tlel economy by engaging one from any of several outlying towns. With nothing to recommend a particular village over another, he logically chose the one that lay along the route his skimmer was going to follow anyway.

With the rented craft stocked with the limited supplies he would need for the journey, he performed a perfunctory routine check of its functions, made sure its internal vorec was properly keyed to his voice, set a bowl of treats on the floor for an eager Pip, and, with the minidrag munching away, directed the skimmer to lift off from the roof of the rental facility (one of the few nondomed structures in Tlossene) and head northwest to the town of Sluuvaneh. Ten minutes into the flight, assured that the craft was performing efficiently, he allowed himself to relax and spoon his way through one of the self-contained, self-heating meals stocked in the vehicle's stores.

The country through which he was soon traveling was as beautiful and pristine as it was alien. Once beyond the last suburb of Tlossene, the semi-urbanized landscape quickly gave way to what a human would have described as unbroken boreal forest—albeit one that was twisted, angular, and all too blue. Gentle hillsides gave way to more rugged slopes cut by streams that were alternately rushing and raging. Gestalt's denser atmosphere did nothing to inhibit the wild white water below. Given the planet's modest and widely dispersed population, both human and native, he was not surprised by the absence of roadways. Transport by skimmer and aircraft negated the need for investment in such impractical and expensive infrastructure.

Ranging from a familiar subdued green to a startling deep azure in hue, some of the tree-like growths whose tops his vehicle skimmed were well over a hundred meters in height. Few branched in Terran fashion. Instead they tended to conserve such efforts until their respective crowns were reached, whereupon each growth exploded outward like the tip of a used firecracker. Below these heights, thickets of lowlier growths fought for soil, space, and access to sunlight. When cruising over more open terrain, Flinx sought in vain for a glimpse of a single flower.

He did, however, espy some local fauna. Several times, flocks of slender-winged flying creatures with long, straight beaks altered course to avoid crashing into the skimmer or being overtaken by it. In keeping with the somberness of their surroundings, they tended to range in color from gray to black. On the other hand the herd of wackensia, as the skimmer's limited-knowledge AI identified them, were boldly striped in turquoise and mauve. They fled from the skimmer's shadow on multiple legs, their flexible cropping mouths flapping with their rippling gait, reminding him of shorter, less aggressive variants on the carnivorous kasollt that had confronted him at the shuttleport.

As he traveled farther from Tlossene, he gained altitude. Peaks that had been distant from the city drew gradually nearer. The distinctive heliotropic tinge to the snows that covered their crests was unlike anything he had encountered elsewhere. Some unique mineralization, he mused, that ascended with evaporation or transpiration only to precipitate out again as pink snow. With more pressing matters on his mind than local atmospheric chemistry, he did not bother to query the skimmer's AI for a more detailed explanation. Shifting his attention back to his current qwikmeal, he dug his spoon into the steaming bowl of mixed vegetables and meat of an uncertain origin.

It would not do to confront on an empty stomach the man who might or might not be his father.

CHAPTER

4

The town of Sluuvaneh was no primitive assemblage of smoking huts and hand-tilled fields. While the size of the majority of small, domed, pastel-hued buildings clearly marked them as individual residences, there were also a number of distinctive larger structures whose functions Flinx could not immediately identify from the air. One boasted an impressive field of antennae of varying shape and size. Local communications center, he speculated. Others suggested the presence of low-level or boutique manufacturing facilities. At least two landing sites for visiting vehicles were clearly marked out. Both featured large structures—domed, of course—intended to provide protection from the elements for local vehicles as well as offer temporary shelter for visiting craft. Buildings and touchdown pads were immaculate, free of debris, and as contemporary as any counterpart on more populous Commonwealth worlds.

His approach had been monitored by local traffic control ever since his rented skimmer had crossed Sluuvaneh municipal limits. Automated instructions directed him to set down at the northernmost of the two welcoming ovals. Communicating with his skimmer's AI, local navigation as efficient and current as anything in Tlossene took control of his craft. Guiding it smoothly into one of the beckoning hangars, it parked the arrival neatly between a pair of slightly smaller craft. One of these looked brand new while the other sat beaten and battered on its charging pad, badly in need of an update and refurbishing.

Not being a government representative, a deliverer of goods, or in any other way significant, Flinx's arrival was not met. For all anyone in Sluuvaneh cared, he was welcome to sit in his skimmer until his supplies ran out. As near as he could perceive, there were not even any emotions aimed in his direction. Gathering up Pip, he checked to make sure his translator was activated as he exited the rented transport.

As it developed, even the translator was not necessary. Many of the town's Tlel inhabitants spoke terranglo, he soon learned. Sometimes broken, sometimes more a variety of local pidgin than grammatically correct, but consistently comprehensible. After chatting with a couple of workers at the landing area, he turned off the translator altogether. It appeared that engaging a native escort to accompany him for the few days' travel it would take to reach the man who might, just might, be his natural father was going to be even easier and more straightforward than he had imagined. If only his intermittent headaches didn't put him in a hospital before that meeting could take place. Though he had yet to master the problem, he had lived long enough to realize that the impatience that led to stress was more dangerous to him than a boatload of zealously upwardly mobile AAnn. Stress, he reminded himself, that invariably fertilized the slightest tingle and throb at the back of his head.

Given its location and the smaller stature of its inhabitants, the streets of Sluuvaneh were both wider and better maintained than he had anticipated. The town was an idiosyncratic amalgamation of traditional native design and advanced Commonwealth technology. As with a great many of its sibling communities scattered around the planet, it might be isolated physically, but its inhabitants were in constant contact with the planetary Shell and related support facilities. Just one example took the form of the conventional automated navigation facility that had taken control of Flinx's skimmer as soon as it entered the relevant traffic zone and guided it to a perfect, gentle touchdown.

The robotic personal transport vehicle that conveyed him to the town center was similar to many he had ridden on other worlds, with the exception that half the seats had been removed. They had been replaced by Tlelian floor pads to better accommodate traveling natives. As there were no human or Tlel residents requiring transport from the landing site at the particular moment when he stepped up onto the transport platform, he ended up having the vehicle all to himself as it pulled away from the loading area.

Almost immediately, Flinx's vehicle was humming along down a street that separated neatly aligned rows of domed, brightly colored Tlel homes and businesses. Confirming their presence in the community, a few humans were out walking, but unlike the case of the much larger and more cosmopolitan Tlossene, he saw no evidence to suggest the presence of any other Commonwealth species. Sluuvaneh, apparently, was too unimportant to attract even Tolians.

It took several minutes of cruising through town for it to register on him that no street or byway was perfectly straight or sharply angled. From domed houses to curvilinear avenues, something in Tlel custom, it appeared, mitigated against straight lines. He found himself wondering if he would find himself held in better regard if he slouched. Pip's appearance, at least, ought to engender nothing but admiration. Lethal or not, she was all curves.

Information obtained in Tlossene led him to the Tlel equivalent of the local chamber of commerce. It was something of a shock to see Tlel, clad in their often transparent or translucent outer attire and colorful leggings, operating the same kind of equipment one would find on Moth or Earth. While some species had to have human- or thranx-designed instrumentation re-engineered to fit their individual anatomical requirements, the clusters of prehensile cilia located at the ends of long Tlel arms had no difficulty operating controls intended to be manipulated by thicker, clumsier human fingers or chitinous thranx digits.

As he strode deeper into the building, he was conscious of needing a shower. On the other hand, since the Tlel had no sense of smell, his human body odor was unlikely to offend anyone other than himself. If not his scent, then did his body's electrical field precede him? How far from his epidermis did it extend, and at what distance could it be perceived by a Tlel? How did they distinguish between the fields of a living creature and, say, that of a battery-powered communit? Did the presence of electronics confuse them in the same way that releasing a liter of perfume into a room would overwhelm the olfactory senses of any humans within? Could one sense be considered superior to the other as a means of sampling and evaluating one's immediate environment?

No need to burden himself with such questions, he told himself firmly, when there were other matters that foremost demanded his attention.

There were no barriers, no internal walls within the building. Where humans would favor individual work cubicles, the Tlel clearly preferred unobstructed lines of sight. Swallowing and steeling himself against the overpowering stench, he ignored the paired reek of the duo of busy Tlel he approached. As soon as they acknowledged his presence, he proceeded to state his purpose. He spoke in terranglo, slowly and clearly, ready to resort to his translator if his words were not understood.

"My name is Philip Ly—Skua Mastiff. I'm a visiting researcher from offworld who is heading into the northlands. I have a skimmer and supplies and I need an escort." He gazed at the two horizontal eyebands that were, he presumed, staring in his direction. The sensation was more akin to eyeing a pair of dark-tinted mirrors than a set of eyes. That their owners were aware of his presence and listening to him could not be denied, however. Their emotions confirmed this.

It was soon clear that he would not need his translator. One of the two workers advanced toward him. As well as the high, narrow ears that protruded from the rear of the disc-like skull, half the black-and-white hairs atop its head were inclined sharply in Flinx's direction. These upper specialized growths were what were giving their owner a "picture" of the human's electrical field. The longer, more flexible appendages beneath the jaw must be employed in feeding, Flinx decided. Opening its wide, flattened mouth, the native exposed the opposing layers of hardened, shiny, horn-like masticating material within. The words that emerged were decipherable, if more than a little mangled by the Tlel's vocal apparatus.

"Which uv yu is the dominant?"

"Which . . . ?" Glancing down, Flinx saw that Pip had stuck her head out from beneath his jacket and was subjecting the expansive work area to serious inspection. "I am," he replied, adding a probably useless smile. "That is, I am unless she objects." Pip eyed her master quizzically and, conveniently, said nothing.

"Yu are heading tu the north." As he spoke, the first speaker's associate was busily manipulating the controls of a portable console. Taking notes, Flinx wondered—or checking to see if he was wanted by the authorities? The highly developed sense of paranoia that had kept him in good stead since he was a child functioned whether he wanted it to or not. "What is yur purposepurpose?" The Tlel's tone was flat and almost stern. Flinx stiffened slightly.

"As I said, I'm a researcher, working for an offworld firm. My work involves traveling around and interviewing individuals who fit a certain social and psychological pattern."

"*Clalak,*" the official coughed. "Would yu like tu interview me?"

"Uh, I'm only here to interview human residents."

"Is something wrongwrong with my kind, that yu du not want tu interview me?" Swaying slightly on its pair of blocky feet, the Tlel leaned purposefully toward him. "Does it have something maybe tu du with this incomprehensible perceptive ability yur kind call 'smell'?"

"It's got nothing to do with that," Flinx replied hastily. Unsettled, he struggled to explain further. "It's just that—"

He broke off. While he could not understand the odd sequential noises the two officials were presently uttering, their emotional state was open to him without the need for translation. In contrast with the standoffishness their words conveyed, he thought he could detect a lightness of being combined with a certain distinct ease and air of . . . air of . . .

They were laughing at him.

He could not indicate that he knew that, of course. So he simply stood silently and waited for the speaker to resume his end of the conversation.

"Forgive bad manners," the official told him. "We want yu tu understand that there is not muchmuch fur those in ur position tu du here in outside-city way station community like Sluuvaneh. Therefur we must find ur entertainment where we can. It is a thing Tlel share with yur kind. Be confident no offending is intended."

"None taken," Flinx assured him—or her. He still was not confident of his ability to distinguish between the sexes, not even on an emotional level.

After having added little to the ongoing verbal exchange, the second official stepped forward. His eyeband continued to focus on the device he held gripped securely in more than two dozen flexible cilia.

"Yu swearswear by the law-givings uv the Tlel as well as yur own government, that which is called the Commonwealth, that yu are come tu Tlossene and thence tu Sluuvaneh fur no illegal purpose, and that yur intentions are honorable and in keeping with allall local traditions, customs, and courtesies."

"I du," Flinx replied with a straight face.

The specialized fur atop the second official's head rippled like burned grain in a breeze. Flinx knew there were devices that could detect when a person was lying by analyzing minute fluctuations in an individual's electrical field when he was made to answer specific questions. Could the Tlel do so naturally? If so, they might by their very nature be one of the more honest species in the Commonwealth.

For whatever reason, the interrogating speaker fiddled with his (Flinx had by now decided both of his interrogators were male) device until it projected a three-dimensional image accompanied by simple Tlelian script. Rotating the result, he made certain it was clearly visible to the visitor. As Flinx eyed the projection, it rotated slowly above the instrument, giving him a 360-degree view of the subject. The image was that of a differently attired Tlel.

"This is escort Bleshmaa, whu is experienced but not aged, with knowledge uv where yu desire tu go. Standard rates apply, with applicable commission tu the town general account."

Flinx had never before chosen an alien companion from looking at its image. Given his limited knowledge of Tlelian convention, it seemed as good a method as any. After all, he was relying on these two officials for help and advice. If they vouched for this Bleshmaa, that should be good enough for him. In lieu of any obvious alternatives, it would have to be.

"Very well. I accept the recommendation and thank you for your help. Where and when can I meet this gentleman?"

More airy emoting accompanied a reprise of the previous amused gargling. "Bleshmaa is notnot gentleman."

There were indeed, he noted a few minutes later as the escort he had agreed to engage left her workstation and ambled over to join them, subtle differences between male and female Tlel. In contrast

with humans, sexual dimorphism was not as blatant but, once understood, was easy to recognize.

Clad in the by now familiar transparent vest and elaborately decorated leggings, Bleshmaa had a neck shorter than those of the Tlel
whom Flinx knew to be male. An unobtrusive difference, but one that
he learned was common and consistent among the locals. Though just
as flat as those of her male counterparts, his escort's skull was not as
wide. Personal adornment was restricted to the same kind of cosmetic
fur-tinting that was practiced equally by both sexes. The lower portion
of the body tended to broaden out as it approached the upper legs.

"I am Bleshmaa." Like a loading bucket on the end of a small
crane, one cilium-tipped limb rose toward him. A handful of worms
encircled his proffered fingers to complete the approximation of a
primate handshake. The gesture was not unexpected. Humans, he
knew, had been living alongside the Tlel for a long time. The cilia
contracted gently. It was like shaking hands with a warm-blooded
squid. When it was over, the digits did not so much withdraw as slide
off his fingers.

"Nice to meet you." He hesitated, then added helpfully, "You can
call me Flinx. It's an old nickname."

"Claladag," she responded. "Like a title."

"No, not a title," he corrected her. "Something less . . ." He
shrugged. The definition was not important. "Yes, like a title." Looking down at himself, he indicated the iridescent green triangular-
shaped head that was regarding the new arrival attentively from its
resting place within his partly open jacket. "This is Pip."

Bleshmaa's eyeband regarded the minidrag. "Fur its size, very
strongstrong *flii,*" she commented.

Flii was the Tlelian term for an entity's individual electrical
field, he recalled from his intensive pre-arrival research. Another
word cemented in his slowly but steadily expanding vocabulary. "I
need to go north to interview another of my kind," he told her. "How
soon can you be ready?"

"I am not partnered. Can leave now." She turned to the patient, watching officials. "They will see tu it that the necessary forms are appropriately flooded using my values. I will report total billable time upon returning."

Flinx would have thanked the pair of helpful bureaucrats again had they not turned and walked away, returning to their work. He found himself alone with his escort.

"Yu have coordinates?" she asked him. He nodded. Pivoting, she started for the exit. "Then time spent talking here is useless evaporation. Also costing yu money."

Appreciating her concern while trailing in her wake, he could not have agreed more.

Not only did Norin Halvorsen not look like what he was, he did not even look like his name. He was short and bald except for scattered, fitful swirls of dark brown hair that clung to the side of his head, with a paunch that was just large enough to demand attention. This was complemented by a puffy face, a bulbous and perpetually sunburned nose, eyes that might have twinkled were they not set in a permanent squint, and a mouth that unaccountably appeared frozen in a perpetual grin. He looked more like a badly out-of-shape elf than a scavenger of other people's miseries, which was a polite way of defining what he did for a living.

Halvorsen tracked down those who owed money, services, or bits and pieces of themselves to sometimes honest, sometimes less-than-reputable concerns. He did this with absolute disregard for the designated unfortunate's personal situation. To Halvorsen, the term *mitigating circumstances* was an oxymoron. Those unlucky enough to come to his attention might lose a vehicle, a business, a home—or a significant body part. He was not above employing physical violence to carry out his work, up to and including threatening bodily harm to otherwise innocent spouses and children. To Halvorsen, a guiltless child was just another correlated asset, albeit an irritatingly noisy one. Moreover, children's bones were easier to break than those of the adults he was employed to chase down, and they rarely fought back.

In short—and he very nearly was—Norin Halvorsen the person was as disagreeable as his profession: a noisome if fitting match. He was a foul and forlorn person to be around, unless he had just been paid. The rest of the time he had little use for humanity and even less for other sentients. He was proud of the fact that for each and every known nonhuman species he had invented a personal, unique, and highly offensive slur.

Unlike many others who practiced the same odious occupation, Halvorsen prided himself on his professionalism. Not a day went by that he failed to scan every available form of media, legal and otherwise, for prospective business. He also paid close attention to local and planetary gossip, no matter how lowly its nature or disreputable the source. The infrequent overlooked diamond, he was wont to reflect philosophically, was occasionally to be found buried in piles of excrement. He had no compunction about rooting through the latter in search of the former.

Take the surreptitious appeal his highly specialized search software had recently finished decoding, for example. Concealed within a line of the mundane greater Commonwealth news that was diffused daily via space-minus transmission, it consisted of a sizable reward that was being offered by some eccentric outfit calling itself "the Order of Null." This was to be paid for the verifiable demise of an apparently unremarkable citizen name of Philip Lynx, who sometimes went by the terse nickname of Flinx. Halvorsen had never heard of the individual in question or the faction that wanted him dead. His ignorance in these twinned respects, the fact that he knew nothing about either, troubled him not a whit.

What he did know was figures. The one promised by the Order of Null was substantial, electronically escrowed, and waiting for whoever could deliver certifiable proof of the unknown Mr. Lynx's death. As to the nature of the individual who had been thus perversely singled out—his character and morality, family and dreams, personal probity or individual worth—this in no wise whatsoever impinged on Norin Halvorsen's conscience. The gentleman in question might be a saint, a sinner, or representative of the 99 percent of imperfect humankind whose makeup fell somewhere in between. It made not the slightest difference.

The great majority of such automated reports offered their diligent reader nothing more than interesting reading and occasional unexpected entertainment. Only rarely did they augur anything substantial. This new one focusing on the citizen Lynx certainly did. Halvorsen sat up a little straighter as he studied the floating image his desk unit had automatically generated in the air before him. This just might be, perhaps, one of those rare instances.

Because his expensive, well-maintained, continuously updated custom programming had, quite unexpectedly, made a match.

A recent arrival to Gestalt, the individual his instrumentation had sculpted out of the air above the desk went by the name of Skua Mastiff. Other than that, he fit the details and imaging supplied in the illicit appeal flawlessly. The straightforward visual reconstruction was a perfect equivalent. Height, build, hair and eye color, skin tone—other than adopting an alias, this Flinx person had made no attempt to disguise himself. The presence of a rare winged Alaspinian pet, also visible in the sybfile Halvorsen's instrumentation had illegitimately pilfered from Port Immigration via illegally accessing certain supposedly secure portions of the Gestalt planetary Shell, provided the clincher when it came to making the identification unconditional.

Such apparent indifference to personal appearance on the part of an individual others of his kind badly wanted dead suggested a number of possibilities, every one of which raised a warning flag within Halvorsen the professional. For example, this Flinx might not be aware that a sizable reward had been offered in return for his termination. Or—he might know of it, and feel he was safe on a world like Gestalt. Or he might know of it, and feel so sure of his ability to defend himself that physical disguise was a safeguard he could safely forgo. As he picked up his communit, into which the information from his desk had automatically been transferred, Halvorsen was equally confident in his ability to claim the pledged payment. In the course of his ignoble career he had run to ground and successfully dealt with wanted families, groups, and teams. One individual, no matter how self-assured or well-trained, no matter how lethal the implied capabilities of his exotic pet, inspired little trepidation.

Idly, he wondered who this Flinx was, what he might have done, or whom he might have offended to inspire such a splendidly hefty incentive for his demise. Halvorsen did not waste more than a minute or two on such speculation. The only raison d'être he required to justify his intermittently murderous dealings was the number of zeros that followed the initial number on an offer of remuneration.

Following lunch, he instructed his exclusive and highly sophisticated instrumentation to embark on a planetwide scan for the newly arrived visitor. Even taking into account this Flinx-Lynx person's lack of any serious attempt to disguise himself, the search was concluded absurdly soon. Moreover, his objective had been in Tlossene itself as recently as the previous day. I might have passed him on the street, Halvorsen reflected as he rose from his chair. The hotel where the visitor had stayed was only a short hop away by public transport. If they had any information on the intentions or habits of a guest who had so recently checked out, this was going to be a quick job indeed. Quick and clean—that was how Halvorsen liked them, his professional life being so very different from his private one.

Of course the hotel management could not possibly think of releasing nonauthorized personal information on one of their recent guests. The human clerk Halvorsen spoke with did, however, let slip in the course of the conversation with the pudgy and squat albeit polite figure confronting him the number of the room where the guest in question had stayed. It was a harmless morsel of information. Though regretful at not obtaining what he sought, a smiling Halvorsen voiced his thanks. Simultaneously, he amused himself by mentally flaying the handsome and barely contemptuous young clerk until not an inch of skin remained on his red, raw, screaming body. Keeping his fury to himself as always, he left the reception area and settled himself in one of the several thick, highly responsive chairs that dotted the outer lobby.

Pretending to view a local tridee cast, he utilized his customized communit to remotely riff the files in the hotel's subox. Preset to make a match should it find the appropriate one, it did so within seconds, generating a sybfile that a grunting Halvorsen swiftly devoured. Every detail of the guest's stay, from the food he had ordered into his room to any communications that had been passed on to him via the hotel's subox to how often he had used his room's facilities to sanitize his clothing, lay open to Halvorsen's perusal.

Of particular interest were multiple contacts with several rental agencies. Inventing and feigning a relationship to the now departed guest "Skua Mastiff," Halvorsen contacted each of these enterprises in turn, claiming to be holding something of importance that his good friend Mr. Mastiff had left behind at his hotel. Both less protective of their client's privacy and more concerned with their respective reputations for helpfulness, each agency responded with appropriate concern. Only one, however, acknowledged having had commercial intercourse with the young visitor in question.

Visiting that agency in person, Halvorsen killed time until his ever-questing instruments had quietly and furtively extracted the information he needed from the agency's subox. Whether owned by an individual, a company, or various branches of government, every skimmer in use on Gestalt had a location tracker integrated into its instrumentation. Found commonly in skimmers used on Earth or Hivehom or any other highly developed Commonwealth world, trackers were of proportionately more importance on wilder, less populated worlds such as Gestalt. They allowed the location of each vehicle to which they were affixed to be pinpointed from multiple sources by satellite relay at any time of day irrespective of inclement weather or awkward terrain, and continually updated the craft's position.

According to its integrated tracker, Halvorsen noted as he once more studied the readout on his communit after leaving the agency, the skimmer the visitor had rented was presently occupying a stationary position in the northern town of Sluuvaneh.

This was going to be almost too easy, he reflected contentedly. The Tlel community in question was located less than a day's travel from Tlossene. Considerably smaller than either of Gestalt's twin capital cities, it would offer a tall redheaded offworlder little room in which to hide even if he realized there was reason for him to make himself inconspicuous. While Halvorsen made it a point not to dally when engaged in business, neither did there appear to be any untoward urgency in pursuing this particular quarry. The unpredictability of the weather on Gestalt also had to be taken into account. For that and other reasons, whenever it could be avoided he preferred not to fly at night.

There was no rush. He had plenty of time. Judging by his actions subsequent to his arrival on Gestalt, this Flinx individual plainly had no idea anyone local might have more than a passing interest in him. Halvorsen could take it easy, check out his equipment, enjoy a proper supper, and start out first thing tomorrow morning. By evening of the next day at the latest, he would have in his possession incontrovertible, verifiable proof of a corpse to pass along via space-minus beam to the group called the Order of Null. He could expect the pertinent hefty credit transfer to follow directly.

Business was always best, he hummed to himself serenely as he made his way back to his waiting vehicle, when it was possible to conduct it calmly and with a minimum of fuss.

A few dark clouds had shouldered their way to prominence among the less threatening white cumuli that gathered every morning around the jagged peaks of the high northern mountains, but otherwise the following day dawned clear, crisp, and chilled. Perfect for a quick direct flight to Sluuvaneh, the making of a few surreptitious inquiries, and a swift execution. Halvorsen was at ease as his skimmer lifted from the rooftop landing pad of his building. Set on autopilot, it accelerated rapidly northwest in the direction of its programmed destination while its owner relaxed and studied the pornographic images the craft's central projector inveigled for him out of the climate-controlled interior. In between glancing up at the perverted inventions, none of which was new and only some of which he any longer found stimulating, he passed the time checking and cleaning and checking again the gleaming, highly specialized black handgun that reposed in the carrying case spread open across his lap.

It was a menacing little appliance. Unlike many contemporary hand weapons, it had no Stun setting, no life-preserving paralysis parameters. It was designed to do one thing and one thing only, and that was to terminate the life-force of motile organics. The nature of the disruptive charge that it unleashed was such that it was not necessary to strike a vital area or organ in order to accomplish its task. Hit on a hand, a foot, the tip of a finger, that individual would expire just as speedily and absolutely as if struck in the heart. Though Halvorsen was a sure hand and excellent shot with a wide variety of weapons, the gleaming, beautiful black slayer was a personal favorite. The lazy man's means of assassination, he mused to himself. Not only did it kill instantly, but because it was nonexplosive there was never any untidiness to clean up afterward.

Though the public landing pad at Sluuvaneh held a dozen skimmers of varying size and origin, thanks to the information supplied by the rental company Halvorsen had no trouble homing in on the location of the one belonging to his quarry. At this rate, he reflected as he slipped the black slayer into its concealed vest holster, he would be finished with the job and back home in Tlossene in time for dinner. Disembarking from his vehicle, he sauntered casually across the heated tarmac in the direction of one of two nearby service hangars. The information available on his handheld communit was identical to that simultaneously being displayed on his craft's command console.

Perhaps his quarry's skimmer needed repairs, or a recharge, or simply a systems update. He smiled to himself. He was about to save the offworlder the cost and inconvenience of any repairs.

There was one skimmer parked in the front of the hangar where the signal was coming from. Halvorsen hesitated when he saw the craft, frowning slightly. It was a commercial rental, all right, but bigger than the model whose identification he had appropriated and belonging to a different company. How had his information become so scrambled? Tensing as he approached the battered, well-used vehicle, he observed that the signal was not coming directly from it, but from a point slightly behind it. He accelerated his pace.

An increasingly anxious stroll around the far side of the parked vehicle revealed not the expected second skimmer but an extensive service and repair area. Replacement parts, containers, vacuum-sealed shipping crates, tools, analyzers, and adjusters in a bewilderment of sizes, shapes, and standards filled work consoles and were piled on the floor space between them. As near as he could see only a single human was present, working patiently alongside several equally engrossed Tlel. With his sense of smell recoiling from the combined stink of native and lubricant and holding the communit unobtrusively at his side, he approached the woman.

"Morning, ma'am."

Despite the Tlel-tolerant ambient temperature inside the service hangar, she was sweating profusely. Wiping perspiration from her forehead, she turned to look at him. A glance down at his communit's readout showed that the signal from the skimmer the offworlder had rented was stronger than ever. So strong, in fact, that he should have been standing inside that very craft right then and there, instead of out on an open hangar floor preparing to question a dowdy middle-aged technician.

"Good morning, sir. May I help you?"

Halvorsen's frustration was increasing exponentially. Leaning slightly to his right, he peered past her. Looking up from his work, one of the Tlel technicians stared in their direction. To avoid meeting that glistening alien eyeband, Halvorsen turned away. His rudeness was deliberate.

"I was supposed to meet a friend of mine here today." He recalled applicable aliases. "Skua Mastiff's his name." Pivoting slowly, he studied the interior of the hangar. There was no place to hide anything larger than a car. Manifestly, it held only one skimmer. "I was supposed to meet him here, but this isn't his transport I see parked."

While replying, the woman fiddled with a piece of apparatus he didn't recognize. Probably all she ever got to fiddle with, he thought snidely. "Oh certain, *clodat*. He was here."

Was. Interesting, Halvorsen suddenly found himself reflecting, coldly, how a simple change of tense could turn an ordinary three-letter word into a pernicious four-letter one.

The woman continued. "Left early this morning." As she spoke, she continued to adjust the circuitry sprayer she was holding. Turning slightly to her left, she gestured toward a small, glassy, rectangular shape sitting atop a worktable surrounded by a dozen or so other sealed modules in varying states of disarticulation. "That's the tracker off his rental. Said he wasn't sure it was working properly. I told him it was against the law to go out into backcountry without one, and he said he knew that, but that he had an important appointment he couldn't miss and that he didn't need to go more than a few kilometers from town." She shrugged, apparently not noticing the angry flush that was rapidly adding color to her visitor's cheeks.

"It was his call, friend. I'm not the one who'll have to pay the fine if he gets caught skimming around without a locator. That's be-tween him, the law, and the company that rented him the transport in the first place." She nodded once more in the direction of the re-cently extracted device. "Told him I'd have it checked out and ready for reinstallation when he gets back tonight."

If he gets back tonight, a fuming Halvorsen seethed silently. The visitor might have told this pasty-faced woman the truth—or he might choose not to return for a few days, or a couple of weeks. When he finally deigned to do so, it might be via a circuitous route that would make him difficult to intercept before he bade final farewell to this happy, smelly world.

Halvorsen briefly considered returning to Tlossene and doing nothing more proactive than waiting for his quarry to finish his gal-livanting around and show up at the shuttleport. Such a course of action presented complications of its own. His diligence might draw the attention of curious authorities, or he might simply miss his transiting quarry while in the process of doing something as simple as eating, sleeping, or attending to demanding necessary bodily functions.

One possibility the exasperated hunter discarded from the outset was any thought of trying to sneak aboard the visitor's private shut-tle, there to lie in wait for its wandering owner to return. Such craft were invariably equipped with defenses designed to deal harshly with snoopers and interlopers. Furthermore, the shuttleport itself was often busy. Even if he did manage the timing so that he could confront his quarry, there was always the risk of encountering poten-tial witnesses.

No, to ensure the safety and success of the modest enterprise on which he was presently embarked, he needed to find his target and deal with it as far away from Tlossene, as distant from the innocent eyes of curious bystanders, as possible.

Unsurprisingly, when questioned the phlegmatic technician had no idea as to her recently departed customer's destination. The tall young offworlder had not volunteered the information, and she had not regarded it as any of her business to inquire. Which lack of information left the irate Halvorsen no choice but to commence the arduous and disagreeable task of asking questions around town. Much as it repulsed him, this meant not only interacting with the local Tlel but being polite to them, as well. Having no other choice, he held his nose both literally and figuratively as he strode from place to place in search of information that might give him a clue which way his absent, perambulating "friend" might have gone.

He spent a furious, wasted day in search of clues before finally finding one the next morning in the person of a native functionary working at the central administration center. *Clue* was the operative description, since "he said he going north" was as specific as this even more than usually malodorous individual could be. Though damningly ambiguous, it was the only information on his quarry's plans that Halvorsen was able to unearth. The administrative functionary, of course, had no reason to suspect that a fellow human's motivation in inquiring as to the route taken by one of his own kind was anything other than benign.

A delay. That was all it was, Halvorsen fumed as he made his way back to his own craft. This taking off without a tracking locator was very inconsiderate of his quarry. Fortunately, Halvorsen's skimmer was equipped with sophisticated tracking equipment that did not rely for success on following the clear signal of another vehicle's safety instrumentation. Catching up to his target would require a couple of days longer than he had anticipated, a bit more expenditure, a little more wear and tear on both himself and his equipment, before he finally ran the man down. Though the provisional aggravation quotient continued to rise, he knew it was only a matter of time until he would be able to claim the stipulated reward. It was often so. One sometimes had to spend more time and money than originally envisioned in order to make more of the latter. The only thing he could not amortize was his own irritation.

PATRIMONY

So upset was he at the unexpected turn of events and in such a rush to resume the pursuit that before he left town he neglected to check with the repair technician to see if there was actually anything wrong with the locator his quarry had left behind to be "checked out." Had he lingered long enough to learn that it was in fact in perfect working order, the surprising revelation just might have proven sufficiently unexpected to give even Norin Halvorsen pause.

CHAPTER

5

One way that escort and employer passed the time as the skimmer cruised steadily northwestward was to work on improving their knowledge of each other's language. In this the willing and voluble Bleshmaa had the clear advantage, since she already spoke very good terranglo while Flinx's knowledge of Tlelian barely qualified as minimal. Ten meters below the skimmer, the crests of the highest alien treetops unfolded like cauliflower florets in a recurring eruption of green and shocking blue.

"Nono," she told him, employing the characteristic Tlelian doubling of a word to indicate emphasis. *"Clelet cleleen jlatat.* Notnot *jliteet."*

Flinx tried again. As befitted a moderately expensive rental, the skimmer's seats were warm and comfortable. Plush but not pushy. Outside, the lush but chilly surface of Gestalt sped past at a constant speed maintained by the skimmer's automatics. Pip dozed nearby, only occasionally glancing up whenever her master or his new friend grew more than usually excited.

Bleshmaa, it developed, was not presently conjoined. Both she and her deceased mate, who had been killed in a backcountry encounter with something large, hairy, and tooth-laden called a sleang, had supplemented their income by escorting not only human visitors and settlers but also other Tlel into some of the more primitive, less visited expanses of Gestalt's wild northland.

"Clelet cleleen jlatat." Flinx repeated the phrase clearly despite the fear that by doing so correctly he risked swallowing his own tongue. The feeding cilia beneath Bleshmaa's flattened, horizontal chin rippled in a brief wave of approval.

"Muchmuch better. If yu continue tu progress, tomorrow we will try some more advanced action words."

The farther north they traveled, the more variable and unpredictable the climate became. The good weather continued to hold, however. Nothing beyond the occasional light hailstorm or brief shower interrupted the spectacular view outside. Flinx was most impressed with the ferocious rivers. Descending from the high mountains that marched down from the northern pole, these roared southward in what seemed to be a multiplicity of never-ending cascades of churning, frothing water anxious to reach the equator. The glint and flash of white water was particularly striking where it cut through tall stands of fibrous growths that were azure or cobalt in hue. Against dense alien forest, the rushing rivers resembled shifting cracks in a vast pane of blue glass.

When not initiating her employer into the mysteries of Tlelian enunciation, Bleshmaa busied herself with typical native amusements. Some were simple enough to improvise without external input. Others required downloads accessible via her own basic but perfectly adequate communit. Due to Gestalt's long association with the Commonwealth, advanced technology had made more than casual inroads into Tlel society, transforming it in ways her ancestors could not have dreamed. Like most of her kind she was as comfortable with the progressive advances and with the skimmer's full complement of sophisticated instrumentation as was her current human employer.

The fourth day of steady flight found him three-quarters of the way to his goal: the coordinates that had been supplied by the helpful Rosso Eustabe. Accessing information from the skimmer's instrumentation via his own communit, he continued to hunt for additional information on the enigmatic Mr. Anayabi. As with his original probe conducted from Tlossene's administrative center, search after surreptitious search turned up nothing new. In lieu of hope of actually learning anything, he had given to substituting persistence, a quality that had served him well in the past.

His attention was drawn sharply away from his research by the voice of the skimmer's AI. For a change, the message did not involve the weather. The announcement was as terse as it was utterly unanticipated.

"I must please ask you to secure yourselves in your seats, as we are currently under attack."

Taken aback, a startled Flinx asked the AI to repeat the alert. It promptly did so, in the same even tone of voice. As alarms went, Flinx thought the rental craft's excessively polite.

Throwing himself into the forward passenger chair, he instinctively pushed back into the crash padding and allowed the safety harness to activate around him. While it did so and as an agitated Pip settled onto his shoulder, he looked around wildly, searching for the source of the declared threat. A quick scan of the deep blue sky through the craft's transparent plexalloy dome revealed no imminent danger; no diving aircraft, no incoming kinetics, no paralleling vehicles of any kind. Bemused, he started to press the AI to project whatever it had detected into the air above one of the forward consoles.

Then he felt it.

The hlusumakai came diving out of the brilliant white sun, heading straight for the skimmer. A bare moment after Flinx's cantankerous special Talent sensed the creature's murderous intent, he saw it. Swift, septuple-winged, golden-hued, and furry, the aerial predator had eyes as big as the skimmer's aft port, a trailing cranial crest of feathery crimson tassels, and a mouth large enough to swallow Flinx whole. One outstanding feature dominated the remarkable beast's appearance. Like a great golden sail, a translucent membranous arc formed an enormous spine-supported, fan-shaped semi-circle from one side of the creature's head to the other.

As the hlusumakai swept past, pulling up at the last minute to avoid a head-on collision with the skimmer, Bleshmaa flinched in her seat. Letting out an untranslatable cry and moaning in obvious pain, her long arms doubled up to allow their cilia to grasp her flattened head, she remained upright on a floor pad only due to the support of her automated safety harness. At the same time, several readouts on the skimmer's instrument console went temporarily crazy. In contrast, all Flinx felt was a slight tingling.

"I will now proceed to take evasive and defensive action."

The voice of the AI was as calm as if it were delineating standard arrival procedures at Tlossene shuttleport. Sharply descending several meters, it dropped dangerously close to the cerulean crowns of several of the highest forest growths before resuming flight on a more or less level path. Leaving her perch on Flinx's shoulder, an angry Pip fluttered and beat at the transparent canopy like a frustrated, oversized butterfly, seeking the open air beyond and a chance to strike back. Meanwhile a concerned Flinx, disregarding the skimmer's request to remain in his seat, had thumbed the manual release on his harness to go to the aid of the obviously beleaguered, suffering Bleshmaa.

"My head!" Her alien whimpers reminded him of a distressed kitten. The Tlel did not cry, not in the human sense. But the emotions were undeniably akin. "Hlusumakai attacks with very strongstrong *flii.*" She managed to recover her equilibrium enough to gesture outside with one long arm. "If I not protected by partial diffusion mechanism integrated as safety measure into all Tlel transportation, I might be dead now."

"Dead?" Flinx had seen no poison spewed, witnessed no strike of fang or claw, observed no emission of a natural explosive or disabling gas. Come to think of it, other than a possible attempt to intimidate through sheer size he had not seen the hlusumakai initiate any kind of hostile action whatsoever. Then he remembered the short-lived but unmistakable reaction of several of the skimmer's instruments. They had gone momentarily crazy when the creature had been at its closest to the skimmer.

The Tlel had the ability to sense the electrical fields emitted by other living beings. The carnivorous kasollt that had tried to vacuum him up subsequent to his arrival at the shuttleport had possessed the same natural faculty. What if a native predator had evolved the ability not only to sense such fields, but also to overpower them with some kind of projection? In the same way that a human would be blinded by contact with Pip's caustic venom, could a Tlel's highly evolved electrosensory facility literally be short-circuited by a high-powered blast from another denizen of Gestalt?

In Flinx's widespread travels he had encountered creatures that could blind by focusing and concentrating light, and others that could stun by emitting deafening blasts of sound. Why not a disrupter of natural electrical fields as well? Much in the fashion of a solar flare or lightning discharge, a sufficiently powerful natural emitter might for a split second even generate a strong enough pulse to momentarily interfere with the electrical systems of a modern vehicle. Just as the skimmer's instruments had been momentarily affected.

He recalled his fleeting view of the diving hlusumakai's flaring cranial membrane. A sexual attractant—or some kind of organic transmitter? The burst emitted by the beast had only given him a slight tingle—because unlike Bleshmaa, he possessed no highly developed capacity for detecting electrical current in others, no wide-open sensory apparatus for the attacker to disrupt. Similarly, a sound-generating creature would have little effect on someone who was totally deaf. Just as the olfactory-deprived Tlel would be immune to the odiferous persuasions of skunks.

PATRIMONY

A glance upward through the transparent canopy showed the imposing dark mass of the hlusumakai pacing the skimmer overhead. Perhaps it was puzzled, Flinx reasoned, as to why its peculiar intended victim continued onward above the treetops instead of plunging to the ground like proper prey, stunned into immobility. As he stared, the predator's shape changed. Folding its multiple wings, it plunged like an arrow and began to grow larger. Pip continued to bang against the skimmer's unyielding canopy, desperate to gain open sky in which to fight.

"Here it comes again!" he shouted more forcefully than he intended. Whimpering and rocking slightly against her safety harness, Bleshmaa folded both arms across the front of her head, completely blocking her arc of vision.

Gazing deliberately at the fast-diving hlusumakai, Flinx readied himself to try to project onto it. He would conjure a sense of danger and attempt to frighten it off. As it happened, his questionable effort was not needed.

No Gestaltian enterprise worth its liability insurance would allow a rental skimmer out into the wilds of the northlands without suitable protection and appropriate defenses against the manifold dangers that lurked there. Its partial diffusion screen had served to keep Bleshmaa from being numbed into insensibility. Now it responded to the hlusumakai's second attack with a more proactive apparatus. This took the reassuring form of an integrated pumper built to unleash explosive shells. Having identified the target from its initial pass, the skimmer's targeting apparatus locked on. Deploying from a port in the craft's ventral side, the protruding weapon swiveled, locked on, and fired once.

Not wishing to have to pause in his journey in order to clean the skimmer's canopy, Flinx was relieved when the hlusumakai blew up well off to the craft's starboard side instead of directly overhead. Or worse, forward. Blood, shattered bone, and torn flesh rained down on the forest below, unexpected manna of Gestaltian biblical proportions for the hungry scavengers undoubtedly roaming among the cobalt growths.

"Evasive and defensive action concluded." The skimmer's AI voice was identical to the one it had used when it had first declared the emergency. Unlike the *Teacher,* it was not sophisticated enough to have a command of emotional modulation.

Careful not to exert too much pressure on her strong but slender arms, Flinx helped a trembling Bleshmaa out of her safety harness. Though her wide, flattened feet provided a stable base for her tapering body, she still swayed slightly for a moment or two after he released his grasp on her and stepped back.

"Very painfulpainful," she declared when she finally spoke again. Tilting back her disc-like head, she focused her cryptic eyeband on him. "Yu humans are so very different from us. Sometimes it is a lucky thing tu be blind. But yu are ignorant uv the beauty uv the *fliiandra.* Yu will never—*see* it. Nono," she corrected herself. "That is not the right wording fur what I am trying tu say. I think in yur language there *is* no right wording."

He nodded, because it seemed the proper thing to do. "Yes, I'm afraid that the beauty and mysteries of the *fliiandra* will always remain an enigma to me." A hand gestured outward, past where Pip was humming back to rejoin him. "On the other hand, I am immune to the danger posed by the hlusumakai and any others like it."

"Passengers will please resume safety seats," the AI suddenly declaimed.

Both Flinx and his escort looked around apprehensively. This time he could detect no homicidal animal emotions rushing toward them. Bleshmaa sensed no oncoming disruption of her *flii.*

"I don't see anything," he finally declared aloud. *Nor perceive anything,* he added, but only to himself. "Another hlusumakai?"

"The problem is not organic in nature," the skimmer explained. "We are approaching an area of very turbulent low atmospheric pressure. If you prefer, I can set down and wait for it to pass."

Flinx considered. "How long do you estimate, at our present speed, it would take to go around it?"

"It is a fairly large, active area moving rapidly south-southeast and transecting our present course. Perhaps a day or two."

"How long to fly straight through it?"

"Approximately one hour."

Flinx had battled and survived serious weather on a host of worlds boasting wildly disparate climates. Where rough conditions presented an obstacle, he had always found it better to get through them as quickly as possible. He would not waste days sitting on the ground waiting for a storm to pass, or even one going around it, and he so informed the skimmer's AI. Besides, how bad could it be?

Very soon he found himself presented with yet one more reason why Gestalt did not rank high on the list of those humans and thranx who were desirous of emigrating to another habitable world. In fact, he soon found himself completely engulfed by that particular reason.

It was a thunderstorm to match the mountains through which the skimmer was currently flying, though perhaps *flying* was not, at that moment, the most truthfully descriptive word. *Rattling* would have been more accurate, or even the hoary term *bucking* that related not to mechanicals but to the violent gyrations of a certain domesticated Terran ungulate. Despite its robust engine and advanced stabilization technology, the skimmer jumped and slid wildly through the violent air currents. Powerful downdrafts threatened to send it crashing into trees whose weirdly outstretched upper branches began to resemble beckoning hands. The besieged, wind-tossed craft actually did "top" a couple of native growths, sending splintered branches and spore-laden spongy packets flying. The rental agency, a grim-faced Flinx reflected as he vibrated helplessly in his seat's safety harness, would not be pleased with the appearance of the vehicle's underside when he returned it.

Rain machine-gunned the transparent canopy. It alternated with heavy hail and occasional blasts of snow as Gestalt's atmosphere threw everything in its meteorological arsenal at the stubborn skimmer. Not so idly and given the current circumstances, Flinx found himself wondering if removing the craft's locator and leaving it behind in Sluuvaneh might have been a less-than-optimal way of disregarding procedure in order to protect his privacy. On the other hand, if anyone at the rental agency happened to currently be tracking the weather in the northlands, they would not be worrying about their vehicle. According to its locator, their skimmer was at present safely and comfortably at rest in a well-protected service hangar in Sluuvaneh.

As he gritted his teeth and held on, both physically and mentally, he reminded himself that this was not New Riviera. Then again climate, terrain, and isolation combined to create exactly the sort of discouraging place that would appeal to the hermetically inclined. Someone like, he could not keep himself from yearning hopefully, his father.

Raising his voice in order to make himself heard over the banging and rattling against the plexalloy of the current hailstorm, he shouted at his escort. "Is the weather like this often up here? Should we put down and wait it out?" He was starting to think that where local Gestaltian meteorology was concerned, maybe allowing a little extra travel time was the better part of traveling valor.

Despite the unabated violence of the current storm, however, Bleshmaa did not seem at all concerned. "Weather in north can be viciousvicious, as yu see, but usually not longlong." She was looking, he noted, not at him but at the forward console readouts. "I agree with skimmer-mind. We will be through this very soon. Not tu be worried. Besides, ground here is covered with snowdriftings. If forced landing necessary, would be very soft."

Another Tlelian attempt at humor, he thought. Or maybe not.

His escort was as good as her doubled words, however. Five minutes after he had seriously considered directing the skimmer to find a landing site where they could wait out the tempest, it subsided as swiftly as it had overtaken them. Impenetrable rain-swept darkness gave way to an uncertain drizzle. Then the clouds parted, to reveal blue forest carpeting the steepest slopes they had encountered thus far. Towering pink-tinted cumuli clustered protectively around the highest peaks like giant cherubs guarding a goddess. Turning slightly farther to the west, the skimmer began following the course of yet another ferociously churning wild river.

"I am going tu open canopy slightly." Disdaining the artificial supports that had kept her upright during the worst of the storm, Bleshmaa slipped out of her safety harness. A curious Pip hovered behind her, fascinated by the two sets of grasping cilia whose supple curling movements were not so very different from those of her own coils. The flying snake was a presence the native had already learned to tolerate.

Disengaging from his own fastenings, Flinx reached up and outward in a long stretch that emphasized his lean frame. "Letting in some fresh air?"

"Yu will see." In the absence of a physical smile on the native's wide, flattened face, he found that he was able to perceive an emotional one. "I think yu will enjoy."

A portion of the port-side canopy slid down into the skimmer's lightweight composite frame. By design, the craft slowed its speed to reduce drag and allow for onboard observation without instruments. Scrubbed clean by the storm, alpine atmosphere heavy with oxygen flooded the single compartment. Having experienced firsthand one more reason why offworlders might not want to live on Gestalt, Flinx now found himself enveloped by a reason why they might.

It was the most wonderful air he had ever inhaled.

Filtered and flushed through the immense undisturbed alien forest below, richer in oxygen than the atmosphere of Earth or Moth or even Nur, the air that filled the skimmer was infused with the full, unadulterated fragrance of the blue forest: redolent of scents half remembered and swirled with others he was unable to isolate and identify. The simple act of breathing threatened sensory overload. Similarly stimulated, an equally exhilarated Pip proceeded to turn a series of backflips and pinwheels that suggested her respiratory intoxication exceeded even his own.

"I . . ." He had to pause long enough to take in another wonderful, invigorating lungful of air. ". . . see what you mean."

Standing near the opening but not sticking her head outside the canopy, Bleshmaa, too, was drawing in breath after breath. "It is wonderfully clean and clear, is it not? No contaminants ever drift this far north. A visitor does not need a sensor capable uv detecting airborne poisons, because there are none. The atmosphere uv the northlands is safesafe."

"Of course it is," Flinx responded, "but it's so much more than that! The aroma, the sheer combination of fragrances is simply—"

He broke off. She was staring at him. He could sense the confusion in her mind even if he could not see it in her wholly nonhuman face.

Fragrances? Aromas? What are those? her feelings seemed to suggest. It hit him hard. The extravagant perfumes the blue growths were releasing, the full-bodied bouquets—she could not detect any of them. Nor could any member of her olfactory-deprived species. They *could* measure such emissions scientifically. Instruments would tell them something was being added to the atmosphere in the same way others could detect the paths of subatomic particles by recording their paths. But like all Tlel, Bleshmaa had no sense of smell. The phantasmagorical, pungent perfumes of the blue boreal forests of Gestalt must remain forever an unknown quality to those who had evolved among them.

By the same token, he went on in ignorance of anything organic in the skimmer's vicinity that might be generating electrical impulses. While he could smell the spectacular forest, she could "smell" him and Pip and doubtless the skimmer as well by sensing and measuring the strength and type of current that ran through their brains and bodies. He found himself wondering. If some djinn or sorcerer of legend could somehow offer him the ability that among sentient species was unique to the Tlel, would he trade one sense for the other?

Of course, he knew nothing of what an individual's electrical field "smelled" like. Was it like a scent, or more like a clashing of bright colors? Or perhaps more like the emotions his own singular ability allowed him to perceive? In the absence of the requisite biological equipment, how to imagine such a thing?

Not only could the Tlel not whiff their marvelous surroundings, they could not whiff one another. That ability was left to visitors and settlers who arrived with the properly evolved detection mechanisms pre-installed. He did not have to inhale deeply to smell his escort. Her body odor, to which she and her kind were completely oblivious, fell somewhere between a stench and a reek. Even were he tactless enough to point this out and complain about it, it would not matter.

She would not know what he was talking about.

CHAPTER

6

The storm that had bounced the skimmer around like a wood chip in a wind tunnel was not the last they encountered as they continued northward, but it turned out to be the most severe. By comparison, the occasional subsequent snow flurries and intermittent assaults by windblown hail seemed almost benign. Allowing for the skimmer's need to follow a route through deep canyons to avoid having to crest ten-thousand-meter-high mountain peaks, another day or two of comparatively easy travel should find him and his escort at his chosen destination.

Then would come the initial encounter and introduction. Hopefully, it would be followed by a cordial interview and, if fate and fortune were with him, the means to obtain the minuscule volume of organic material that would allow him to determine with certainty if he bore any genetic relationship to the person he had spent a bit of time and money to meet. And if, in the end, nothing along the line he hoped for eventuated from that?

He would return to Tlossene, and he would try again.

For now, it was enough to relax and enjoy the uninspired but nourishing qwikmeals the rented skimmer's cooker served up, to chat with his ebullient escort about her people and their culture, and to continue his hesitant forays into the throat-spraining complexities of the Tlelian language. Much as voyagers on the ocean grow familiar with the motion of a boat and thereby gain their sea legs, he had become accustomed to the occasional jolts and bounces the northland weather imposed on the skimmer.

The small missile that flew past, however, was another matter entirely.

It had happened so fast that the craft's AI had not even had time to make a warning announcement. One moment they were cruising along as usual: Flinx in his forward seat, Bleshmaa busying herself in back, Pip coiled on the console in front of him. The next, the skimmer took a lurch to port more violent than any induced by wind or storm. Out of harness, he was nearly thrown from his chair.

"I must please ask you to secure yourselves in your seats," the synthesized voice hastily declared, "as we are—"

"I know, I know!" Ignoring the preprogrammed regulation warning, Flinx stumbled to the rear of the skimmer. From a standing position and despite her sturdy Tlelian posture, Bleshmaa had been thrown to the floor. He helped her up, for the second time in as many days careful not to put too much overbearing human weight on her upper arms.

"Someone is trying tu kill us." Her disbelief was palpable. It was as much question as statement. He shared her bewilderment. Taking evasive action, the skimmer slammed back to starboard, nearly throwing them to the floor together this time.

He did not venture to disagree with her analysis. But who, and why? Here on Gestalt, of all places! He had no enemies here.

He quickly corrected himself. That conclusion was self-evidently mistaken.

In any event, on the all-too-numerous occasions in the past when he had been confronted by other sentients whose intentions toward him had tended to the homicidal, they had invariably declared themselves as well as their objective. As the skimmer rocked and weaved, dodging the occasional explosive projectile flung in its direction, no angry voice spat from its speakers, no accusatory projection coalesced in its interior. Whoever was pursuing them was apparently content to commit murder anonymously.

Except that with Flinx as the intended target, no would-be murderer could remain completely anonymous.

Despite the skimmer's violent bucking as it fought to avoid obliteration, he reached out with his Talent. The source of the enmity that was pursuing him opened immediately to his probe. Its most notable characteristic was a cool detachment. The individual who was trying to kill him was not particularly angry. Yes, his emotions were heightened by the exhilaration of the chase, but insofar as Flinx could tell the man's feelings were devoid of personal rancor. It was a state of being Flinx recognized immediately because he had encountered it previously. The feelings of professional assassins such as the Qwarm differed noticeably from those whose actions were inspired by raw emotion. The man (as usual, it was easy for Flinx to identify the gender of the individual whose emotions he was perceiving) who was pursuing him was not entirely all-business. There was a feeling of excitement, a sense of glee at what he was doing, that was starkly at odds with what Flinx had once sensed in the mind of a Qwarm. His pursuer was not a member of the Assassins' Guild, then. They truly were all-business, as cold and unfeeling when cutting throats as a designer cutting fabric.

The skimmer sought salvation in low clouds. The attempt did nothing to throw off the pursuit, or even to slow it down. Clouds, fog, snow—in these days of heightened instrumentation that rendered climate of any kind invisible, weather made bad camouflage. That the man hunting him was properly equipped for his murderous work was evident by the alacrity with which his own craft followed Flinx's through the cloud bank where his and Bleshmaa's shuttle had sought refuge.

The forest would have offered more cover, but darting through the densely packed growths would have forced the skimmer to slow, thus rendering it an even easier target for the craft on its trail. It and its occupants were not entirely helpless, however.

Though the rental was equipped to protect those it transported from the depredations of inimical fauna, no maudlin regulations prevented it from defending itself when attacked by sentient beings. The same shell-pumper that had messily dispatched the attacking hlusumakai now fired back at the pursuing craft. In forcing it to take evasive action of its own, their pursuer fired less often, choosing its shots with greater care.

That one would eventually hit home was likely, Flinx knew, given that his skimmer's ability to keep flying and dodging was severely circumscribed. A commercial rental, not a stingship, it was being asked to perform maneuvers for which it had never been designed. The assassin on their tail knew that just as well as Flinx himself, he reflected. It would be interesting to know why the man wanted Flinx dead. Under tight control, however, the killer's emotions offered no clue as to his motivation.

There was a loud *bang,* as if a large container full of trash had been dropped onto the plexalloy canopy. The skimmer endured an abrupt drop of several meters and broke off several treetops before recovering altitude. He did not have to ask the AI for an explanation. One was supplied anyway. The calm, emotionless tone of the skimmer's voice was maddening.

"We have been hit. My defensive weapon has been disabled and is not repairable. I will continue evasive maneuvering." A pause, then, as air roared around them, "I have made several efforts to contact the craft that is assaulting us, in an attempt to obtain an explanation for the hostile and dangerous behavior it is displaying. Neither it nor any plausible organic occupants have responded."

If he had been with his own skimmer from the *Teacher,* Flinx knew its far more advanced weaponry would already have dispatched the pursuing vehicle. His craft mounted concealed armament that was not only illegal but also well in excess of that available to most non-military transport. Seeking as low a profile as possible while on Gestalt, he had opted instead for the local rental. Now he was paying for it. In more ways, possibly, than one.

Still, even though the rental skimmer's own weapon had been put out of action, they were not entirely defenseless. He still had his pistol—as well as access to another, far less visible weapon. In order to make maximum use of its potential, certain forced adjustments would first have to be made to the skimmer's present tactics. Orthodox instructions would have to be manually countermanded. Fighting to keep his feet as the deck rocked and bucked beneath him, he turned his full attention to the craft's console.

In the pursuing skimmer, Halvorsen was hard-put to rein in his frustration. Judging by the make of skimmer that his quarry had rented, it ought to by now be a smoking ruin somewhere on the ground below him. Instead, its unexpected ability to avoid obliteration was continuing to delay his return to Tlossene. Must be a newer model, he told himself. He sighed. Its strained efforts to evade his assault were only postponing the inevitable. Especially now that its single defensive weapon was out of action.

Secure in battle harness while his own craft's automatics managed the pursuit—indeed, managed it far better and more efficiently than any organic pilot could have done—he contented himself with firing at the target whenever it fell within range of his own skimmer's weapons. In this almost leisurely manner he sought to murder the occupants of the craft that was desperately trying to shake him. It could not do so, he knew. There was no chance its internal AI could outthink his far more sophisticated craft's instrumentation. His skimmer had been specially modified to win this kind of chase. A rental whose principal function was the shuttling of people and light cargo back and forth between towns would eventually run out of evasive options. One by one, his own skimmer's adaptive intelligence would record them. As soon as one previously utilized maneuver was repeated, as it inevitably would be, his craft would be ready to respond with a corresponding fatal blow.

Diffidently, he checked the chronometer. Another ten minutes, he told himself, and no matter how new, his quarry's AI would surely have run out of evasive options. Twenty at most. If a lucky shot didn't precede a predictive one. Either way, he was confident he would be on the ground scraping up proof of his labors before the hour was up. That was why he did not employ his vehicle's most powerful weapons. Utterly obliterating the frantically dodging craft in front of him would be counterproductive. He needed to be able to recover at least a little intact DNA to attest to his accomplishment in order to collect the promised payment.

Struggling to keep erect, Flinx did his best to secure Pip inside his jacket. He didn't want her flying free inside the wildly gyrating skimmer. For one thing, despite her exceptional aerial skills, an unexpected jolt of sufficient violence could send her crashing into dome or deck.

Also, he had something else in mind.

"Open rear canopy!" he bellowed, directing the command to the skimmer's AI.

Well behind him, a frightened and shaky Bleshmaa flashed her horizontal ocular in his direction. "Open? What fur du such a thing, Skua Mastiff?"

"Call me Flinx," he yelled back. If he was going to die, he resolved, he did not want to do so with a lie lying on someone else's lips. Even a nonhuman's. Even one who had no lips. "I'm not through fighting back!"

Though it briefly demurred, the skimmer's AI finally opened a small section of the rear canopy. Screaming cold wind promptly rushed in to fill the skimmer's interior. As he stumbled toward the rear of the passenger compartment, Flinx drew his pistol. Inside his jacket, an agitated Pip bumped and twisted against his chest. Unable to unfold and spread her wings, she kept her movements restrained. He knew his companion. Sensing the threat to her master, she would immediately detect the opening in the canopy and zoom out to attack their pursuer. Fast as she was, however, she would quickly be left behind by both speeding craft. Having nearly lost her on several previous occasions on other worlds, he had no intention of losing her here.

Turning to watch the human, an uncomprehending Bleshmaa fought to keep her balance while clearly wondering what her apparently daft offworld employer had in mind.

"Cannot confront skimmer-mounted weapons with handgun! Target is tuu far away! Pleaseplease, come back and close canopy!"

"I'm a pretty good shot," Flinx shouted back at her. "We have to try something."

She was right, of course. At this range and under current conditions, with both craft swerving and bobbing madly, the best pistol shot in the Commonwealth could not hit the skimmer that was shadowing them. Besides which, before it would allow itself to come within range of a hand weapon, its own much heavier armament would blow their own craft to bits.

If it was fired, he thought determinedly. No doubt whoever was controlling the weapons could not imagine a scenario under which the larger craft would close the gap between them without making use of such an advantage. Flinx, however, could.

"Reduce speed!" he yelled in the direction of the skimmer's console.

Mad he surely was, Bleshmaa must have decided. "Order countermanded!" she gargled hastily in quite serviceable terranglo.

"Reduce speed!" Flinx repeated, as forcefully as he could. "I am the renter of record here!" The AI should recognize his voice, not Bleshmaa's, and should respond accordingly.

Cilia crawled over his lower left arm. "This is matter uv dying, not commerce protocol!"

"That's why you need to trust me." He shrugged her off. "If you have a better idea, I'm listening." Squinting into the cold air and over the slightly bulged stern of the skimmer, he struggled to level his pistol. Precise aiming would have to wait. At present and though he knew it was right behind them, he could not even see the pursuing craft.

"Complying," the AI responded. "Reducing speed. At this time I feel it is appropriate to point out that certain damage is covered by the insurance option that you elected to take at the time of renting. Damage not covered under the present circumstances includes . . ."

Flinx ignored the AI's recitation of what expenses were covered and which he would be responsible for in the event of the skimmer's destruction. The craft was only following preprogrammed procedure, he knew. As a distraction, it was negligible. It did not prevent him from continuing to hold his weapon aligned with the rear of the vehicle. It did not prevent him from half closing his eyes and concentrating.

It did not prevent him from projecting.

Beneath his jacket, Pip's coils relaxed as she detected her master's efforts. With only two other sentients in the immediate vicinity, Flinx had no difficulty focusing on the one who was behind the imminent threat. In the swirling, almost freezing atmosphere at the stern of the skimmer it was hard to hold the pistol steady. The weather did not, however, affect the feelings he cast forth as sure and accurate and true as any explosive projectile.

Secure in his harness, safe from the violent jolts and swings his craft was abiding, a confident and patient Halvorsen suddenly sat bolt upright and blinked. As his skimmer suddenly and unexpectedly closed on its target, he knew he should be firing one or more of its integrated weapons. Instead his hands hovered, palms facing downward, fingers trembling slightly, several centimeters above the pertinent controls. Nor despite straining his brain could he find the right words to activate them using verbal instructions. Had he been wearing an induction headband, it was doubtful that at that moment he could have summoned the will to put forth even a mental command.

Despite the rapidly increasing proximity of the target, he did not fire. Not because something had suddenly gone wrong with his skimmer's weapons systems, nor because his quarry was out of range, but because he had, inexplicably, undergone a sudden change of heart. For someone oft accused of not possessing one, the abrupt shift in sentiment was striking.

His fingers quivered as he sought to depress one of several contact points that would send death in various high-tech forms streaking toward the other craft. Why do such a thing? he found himself thinking. Isn't there enough misery in the universe? We all of us are going to die soon enough. Even Norin Halvorsen was going to die. Probably in some wretched, depressing hole somewhere, sick and alone, with no one to murmur a kind word or two over his decaying bones. Taking up space better reserved for neutral neutrons, wasting oxygen, contributing nothing to a society of fellow sentients—that was what his life had come to. That was the pitiful summation of his miserable existence. What he had believed passed for enjoyment was nothing more than the instinctive utilization of various primitive stimulations designed to numb his nerve endings. In striving to survive, he had done little more than anesthetize his soul.

He started to sob. A small, submerged part of him was screaming, shouting its outrage, trying to revive the cool calculating killer that reveled in professional accomplishment, expensive liquor, and cheap women. Normally dominant, this segment of his character had at present been reduced to a small squeak buried beneath a tsunami of despair. Had Halvorsen been able to identify the source of this anguish and gloom he might have had a chance to fight back, to resist it. He could not. He could only suffer beneath the weight of a crushing despondency the likes of which had not affected him since the earliest days of his unspeakably dismal childhood.

If he was not going to fire, the professional, calculating part of his mind that still functioned insisted, then he needed to back off. Or at least to change course or commence evasive maneuvers of his own. But he failed to issue the necessary orders to implement those actions as well. All he found himself able to do was sit in his harness and sob a steady stream of melancholy whose source remained a mystery to him.

That source was looming rapidly larger as the pursuing skimmer drew steadily closer to its decelerating target. Standing straight and tall and exposed to the elements in the rear of that craft was a singular slim figure. Staring unblinkingly into the approaching cockpit of the second skimmer, it was holding something tightly in both hands.

A gun. A hand weapon of a style that was known to Halvorsen but had been modified with a flourish that was new to him. It was not a large gun, but it did not have to be.

Move! a part of him shouted frantically. Shoot back, dive, climb, do *something*—or the skinny son-of-a-bitch is gonna etch you a new hairline. Lower down. Wonderingly, Halvorsen found himself wrestling with his own unresponsive body, trying to find the missing will to make his impassive limbs function. Desperation and fear proved strong enough to finally force one hand downward, toward the skimmer's console and the weapons controls embedded there.

At the same time, Flinx fired.

His shot struck Halvorsen's skimmer just as it started to climb. Penetrating the plexalloy canopy, the beam missed its weeping target. It did, however, pass through a portion of the craft's control console. A number of critical connections were instantly severed, melted, or fused. Rising from the console, smoke began to fill the interior of the pursuing skimmer. As a consequence of this damage, it took evasive action by banking away from its quarry far more sharply than its pilot would have preferred. But not before getting off a single blast of its own.

Subsequent shots went completely wild. Unleashed more with frustration than skill, every one of them went wide. Air was seared, tree-like growths were incinerated, but none came anywhere near the rented skimmer—except for the first one. As he ducked reflexively, Flinx's carefully wrought emotional outpouring was jolted by the attack. One consequence of this was that he projected even more strongly on his pursuer than he had intended.

Rattled to the core of his being by the potent emotional projection, Halvorsen tore himself out of his harness with a cry of utter despair. Fully intending to end it all by cracking the skimmer's canopy and flinging himself outside, he was saved only by the smoke that was now filling the interior. Coughing and choking, he was unable to see his damaged instruments or voice the necessary command. Instead, he stumbled several times before collapsing to the deck. Alternately weeping and coughing, he lay helpless, his right thumb jammed in his mouth, his legs drawn up against his chest in full fetal position.

Only the planning that was the hallmark of an astute professional saved him. Badly damaged, his craft sought instructions on how to proceed. When none were forthcoming, and perceiving that its master was at present unwilling or unable to respond accordingly, the skimmer's advanced AI reverted to the installed programming that was designed to deal with just such an emergency. Reversing course, with speed and maneuverability reduced, it headed home.

That greatly-to-be-desired option was not available to Flinx's craft. At close range, Halvorsen's final, agonized shot had severely damaged not only the craft's instrumentation, but also its power and propulsive systems. Fighting with the manual controls, barking desperate commands in a harried mixture of Tlelian and terranglo, and despite her best efforts, Bleshmaa was unable to halt its sudden, sharp descent.

The plunge threw Flinx off his feet. Yanking open his jacket, he let Pip out. Freed, she immediately took to the air inside the compartment. She did not try to escape out the opening that still gaped in the rear of the canopy. The hostile mind that had been threatening them was now distant and moving rapidly away. The real and present danger was not one that could be dealt with by her singular abilities.

Rolling over, Flinx struggled to his feet and staggered forward to rejoin the frantic Bleshmaa. Devoid of the elaborate backups that were built into the *Teacher*'s skimmer, the simple rental craft was finding it impossible to cope with the damage Halvorsen's weaponry had inflicted on its vital components. Never far below, the flaring crowns of the great Gestaltian forest loomed steadily larger through the transparent canopy.

"Pull up, pull up!" As Flinx threw himself back into his seat's harness, there was no response to his verbal directive. The skimmer's AI was dead, leaving them entirely on manual control. He looked over at Bleshmaa. "We're going down—find a flat place to land!"

Even as he voiced the appeal he could see that he might as well wish for the smooth tarmac of a shuttleport and for its own master AI to take control of their damaged craft and automatically bring it in to a safe, gentle touchdown. The surface below was as thickly forested as any field of ripe grain. Where bare ground showed through, mounds of naked rock thrust sharp stone fingers skyward. Directly ahead, a soaring cliff marked the far side of the valley through which they were rapidly descending. Crumbled scree at its base promised a landing even rougher than that offered by the thick forest below.

As he became convinced they were going to slam into the granite rock face, Bleshmaa's cilia executed a frenetic dance on a pair of control contacts. The mortally wounded skimmer shuddered, fell— and turned to the left. Left, left, ever so slowly, until he was certain it was going to impact the snow-streaked black rock ahead.

Then more valley appeared, cut by white froth. He barely had time to register the abrupt change in terrain when Pip let out a violent hiss somewhere aft of his right shoulder, there came the terrible high-pitched shriek of splintering composite, and the light went away from his eyes.

Only for a moment. It was soon replaced by diffuse sunshine, the crackling and moaning of disintegrating structure, and an entirely new sound: that of rushing, churning water. Cold it was, and pouring excitedly into the interior of the downed skimmer where portions of the plexalloy canopy had been snapped away. Already it was over his ankles and climbing energetically up his legs. Nor was it the only thing in motion. The skimmer was still moving: erratically, intermittently, but continuously forward. Loud crunching and grinding noises came from below. He could feel the recurring impacts beneath his feet as the splintering craft was systematically torn to pieces by the rocks over which it was being dragged.

Bleshmaa had managed to set them down on the only relatively flat surface for kilometers around—smack in the center of one of north Gestalt's innumerable raging rivers. The grating sounds he was hearing came from the skimmer sliding and banging over the unyielding, uneven riverbed.

The craft slewed suddenly sideways. A fresh incoming torrent struck him in the face. Swallowing some, he choked on the icy flow, shook it off, released himself from his seat's harness, and began battling his way toward the nearest breach in the canopy. Having no idea how deep the river was, he knew he had to get out before the skimmer filled completely with water. Hovering above him now, immune to such land-bound perils, an anxious Pip hissed encouragement.

The edges of the fissure in the plexalloy were not sharp, and he was able to grasp both sides with his bare hands. Outside and beyond, a riverbank lined with twisted blue growths any one of which would have stood out starkly in a park on Nur or Earth or Kansastan was gliding past at an uncomfortably swift pace. Gripping the broken canopy tightly, he prepared to pull himself out and swim to shore. A sudden realization stopped him.

Where was Bleshmaa?

Cursing silently, he paused in the opening to look back. Because of the rising, rushing water it was difficult to see anything inside the damaged, rapidly submerging skimmer. He shouted, trying to make himself heard above the river's roar. When no response was forthcoming, he growled silently one more time, then plunged back inside.

She was halfway out of her harness. It was all that held her upright. It was not necessary to be familiar with Tlelian biology to realize that she was unconscious. In the absence of any eyes to see closed, her limp limbs and utter nonresponsiveness, both verbal and emotional, were proof enough. Wrestling the alien body out of the seat as icy river swirled and surged around them, he slung the flaccid form over his left shoulder. It was surprisingly heavy.

By now the skimmer had sunk far enough so that water merely poured through the multiple gaps in the shattered canopy instead of rushing in furiously. While it was easier now to make his way outside and onto the intact portion of the sinking craft, the constant damp cold was beginning to overwhelm the ability of his special clothing to counteract it. After all he had been through in his short but hectic life, after defeating menaces both sentient and unthinking, it was sobering to think that he might die from something as primordially austere as hypothermia.

For the moment, swimming to shore was out of the question. The skimmer was banging and bouncing its way down a succession of Class V rapids that were disturbingly broad in extent. Setting his escort's body down alongside him, Flinx studied the near shore. Better to pick a spot, however daunting it appeared, and swim for it than wait for the skimmer to sink completely or break up beneath them, leaving him no choice when to make the attempt. Though a good swimmer, he knew that white water and cold would combine to rapidly sap his remaining strength. Once committed he would have to swim hard and fast, as it would be impossible to return to the skimmer. Glancing up, he could only envy Pip. Riding the air currents above the river, she effortlessly kept pace with the helpless, sinking transport.

Whether because it was too low on the emotional scale to be noticed, or because he was cold, tired, and preoccupied, Flinx failed to notice the diving jaslak. As a consequence, he also missed its unique style of attack, whereby it did a complete revolution in the air in order to maximize the impact of the lump of solid bone contained in its tail. Though it missed Flinx's head and struck his shoulder, it still hit him hard enough to knock him down and dizzy. Feeling himself sliding off the skimmer's broken, sloping canopy, he fought to hang on and keep from slipping into the river.

Both eyes focused on the injured potential prey, a second jaslak came diving headlong out of the sky. Trailing its bone-heavy tail behind a pair of broad furry wings, it dove straight at the struggling Flinx. Usually one blow from the club-like tail sufficed to knock a quarry off a rock or out of a tree, but this strange animal floating downstream was larger than the flock's usual prey. It was clear that it would take several blows, precisely directed, to render it insensible. Only then could all the members of the flock safely descend, to land on the body and pick clean the damp flesh with their protruding, incisor-laden jaws.

Taking careful aim, the second jaslak spun—and howled in mid-flip as a thin but potent stream of toxin struck not one but both eyes. In acute pain, it brought its wings to its face as it fell toward the river, plummeting harmlessly past a still-dazed Flinx as he pulled himself back up onto the skimmer alongside the motionless Bleshmaa. Still in its service belt holster, his pistol would make short work of his aerial attackers—once he was out of the water and his head had cleared enough for him to activate the weapon and take aim.

As their comrade splashed into the river and was swallowed by the roaring, boiling foam, other jaslaks folded their wings to their sides and plunged to the attack. It was likely they had never before encountered another flying creature as swift and nimble as the Alaspinian minidrag. Agile as an oversized hummingbird, Pip danced circles around her stymied assailants. Two crashed thuddingly into each other, sending both tumbling into the water, snapping and yowling as they fell. Struck by a second spurt of the flying snake's venom, another dropped screaming to smash against a protruding boulder.

Loath to let such a fine meal escape but unable to get past the murderous flying creature circling protectively above it, the rest of the flock gradually fell away, letting wind fill their wings to lift them higher as they sought easier prey elsewhere upstream.

It was not necessary for Flinx to say *thanks* aloud. His constant companion could read his emotions even if he could not quite decipher hers. It was also possible that she recognized the significance of the smile that now transformed his expression. Turning away from the patrolling minidrag, he looked down at the Tlel he had dragged clear of the skimmer's rapidly filling interior. Ignorant of the location of Tlel lungs—or even if the natives of Gestalt possessed analogous organs of respiration—he could not tell if she was still breathing. Beneath the sodden, transparent upper garment, however, her torso was still warm. The feeding appendages beneath her jawline quivered like semi-invalid eels. He hesitated at gripping her cilia lest in their chilled condition he inadvertently damage one of the delicate digits.

His attention diverted by a rising roar, he looked up- and downriver. The sound arose from an as yet unseen source. It took him a moment to identify it. Alas, it was not the rumble of an approaching rescue craft. Instead, the source of the thunder was entirely natural.

Unable to gain a more elevated perspective, he could not tell the height of the waterfall the helpless skimmer was fast approaching. From the increasingly deafening rumble he estimated it to be at least twice the height of the worst rapid they had so far run. That being the best-case scenario, he knew it was time to abandon the skimmer and strike for the nearest shore no matter how difficult the route or inhospitable the potential landfall.

At first he started to slip his right arm around Bleshmaa's neck, much as he might have done in preparing to tow a human. After taking into consideration the extreme slenderness and unknown carrying capacity of that particular Tlel body part, however, he decided instead to try a chest carry. Fortunately, his arm was long enough to reach around the entire upper portion of the escort's conical shape and beneath both long arms.

In the river these trailed beside her like seaweed. By now he was too numb, mentally as well as physically, for the cold water to affect him. He was less worried about becoming chilled than he was about growing drowsy. Increasing lethargy would be a sure sign that hypothermia was beginning to set in.

Though he swam hard for the heavily vegetated shore, the force of the current increased as the river drew closer to the falls. For every meter he gained shoreward, he felt he was slipping twice that far downstream. The roar of the still-unseen cataract was loud enough now to reverberate in his ears. Trying not to think of how high it might be or what unyielding rocks lay jumbled at its base, he concentrated on kicking and paddling.

Azure undergrowth, dark and promising, grew steadily larger in his vision. His grip on the trailing, dragging body of Bleshmaa was so tight that his fingers had cramped into a hook. Judging by the unrelenting thunder of it, the threatening cataract was very near now. But so was the shore.

The physical feeling of something giving way as he banged into and off a submerged rock was matched by a sudden lightness. Momentarily bewildered, he saw that he still had his unbreakable grip on the female Tlel. Something else had been lost to the implacable current, then. With a start, he realized what it was. His service belt was gone, ripped off by the formidable flow. Belt, pistol, communit, first-aid apparatus and medicinals, emergency food rations—everything gone, gone, all gone, swept away in the dark, fast-moving water like a dead serpent. Without the aid of the belt's gear he had little hope of survival, let alone rescue.

Going after it would mean abandoning Bleshmaa to the current and to the approaching cascade. Furiously treading water, he debated for perhaps ten seconds. By then it was too late. The belt had surely been swept beyond immediate recovery now. Maybe he could retrieve it later, somewhere downstream. It *might* be rolled and pushed to shore. More likely, he realized despondently, it would wrap itself around an underwater rock or snag, never to greet the anxious eyes of its owner again.

He resumed digging water. If he didn't make it to shore very soon, the matter of his belt's destiny would be rendered moot. He and Bleshmaa would expire within the river, or go over the looming falls to be broken on the rocks below. Only Pip would know of the time and manner of their passing, and be left to mourn.

His flailing right hand contacted something hard and unyielding. No attacking predator this time, but a protruding branch, so dark blue it was almost purple. He grabbed for it gratefully.

It pulled away from him.

His one exhausted thought was that he had no time for any more surprises. A second branch or root bobbed in the water slightly farther downstream. As he drifted toward it, he reached out anew. For a second time, the promise of safety drew away from him. Some kind of instinctive, reactive defense mechanism on the part of the parent plant, he found himself thinking, unable to keep from analyzing his surroundings even with death stalking him by, literally, degrees. Maybe the river was full of aquatic herbivores that liked to gnaw on water-loving tree limbs. Maybe, the inopportune line of thought logically continued, the river was full of creatures that liked to gnaw on other things.

The realization caused him to expend his remaining energy in a sudden burst of effort. Exerting all his strength, he kicked hard, simultaneously paddling frantically with his free hand. The effort thrust him forward through the water just enough to push his chest out on land. The fragment of beach was cold, it was hard, and it most certainly was not dry, but it was solid beneath him. Half pulling, half kicking, he willed himself out of the river, dragging the dead alien weight of his escort behind him. Water sloughed away from his body, leaving behind only the chill that was its shadow.

Rolling over, he sat up, breathing hard. Settling on a bush nearby, Pip watched her master intently. Faint burbling noises came from Bleshmaa. He hoped she hadn't swallowed a lot of water, because he did not have the faintest idea how to go about performing emergency resuscitation on a Tlel. After sitting for a while as his thermotropic clothes slowly shifted away the tiny beads of water adhering to them, he crawled over to sit closer to his unconscious escort. If not exactly warm and dry, neither was he in imminent danger of freezing to death. Silently, he thanked the unseen, unknown manufacturers of the high-quality attire he wore. In ancient times, he knew, anyone who had undergone a similar icy submersion would have perished as the primitive fabric of their water-soaked garments turned to a frozen cocoon around them.

Damp and cold, his translator necklace still hung around his neck. That was fortunate, because his weary brain was having enough trouble forming coherent thoughts in his native terranglo. For the moment, at least, venturing anything in the throat-twisting Tlelian language was beyond him.

"We're clear of the river," he murmured to her. Only when he spoke did it strike him that there was absolutely no other sound to be heard in the immediate vicinity of the beach beyond the erratic snarl of the nearby waterfall. "How do you feel?"

"Not—gud." The words emerged feebly, like a failed effort. "Something brokebroke—inside."

He would have disregarded propriety even if he had known the physiological intricacies of the Tlel. Taking his time, he examined her from flat head to broad feet. At first nothing seemed amiss, or missing. Pulling aside the battered poncho-like outer garment, he lifted up the right half of the transparent vest beneath. That was when he saw that her entire left side had been caved in. In the absence of blood he had not noticed it earlier.

"Excuse me" was all he could think to mumble as he began, ever so gently, to feel of the flesh beneath the short, glass-like fur. Her skin quivered under his touch. He could not tell for certain, but the partial collapse of the upper body cavity seemed quite extensive. Maybe even, he told himself, too extensive. He sat back, gazing down at her.

"Sit me up," she wheezed weakly.

"I don't know if that's such a good—"

"Upup." When she started trying to push herself into a sitting position, bracing her weight with arms that threatened to give way at any second, he leaned forward to help her.

She sat that way, staring. First at the forest, then at the sky. She asked questions. Some of them he was able to answer; others he could not. A number of them had to do with which way the river into which they had crashed was running. After a while, she raised one arm and pointed. All the manipulative cilia were lined up and pressed together to form a single thick digit.

"That way. Nearest civilization lies . . . that way. Yu go fur help. I cannot walk. Will stay here and wait yu return."

She did not know about the lost service belt, he realized. How could he tell her that without it and the equipment it held, his chances of reaching anything remotely resembling civilization, much less in time to return and save her, were minuscule? Not that he intended to leave her, anyway. She was being more than disingenuous if she thought that in her present injured condition she could survive the forest for more than a few days. He started to remind her of the obvious.

She did not respond. When he put a hand on her upper right arm and squeezed, she still did not react. His next breath was long and drawn out. Surviving the forest was not something she would have to worry about. She would not, in fact, have to worry about anything any longer. She could wait for his return without trepidation.

She had no eyes to close, but he noted that her formerly moist and bright eyeband had both dimmed and dried out.

A weight settled on his shoulder. Seeking warmth, Pip had left her bush. Pulling his collar out away from his skin, he waited while she slithered down under his inner shirt. Her flesh was cold at first, but warmed quickly.

He recalled the nature of the rugged, forbidding country they had overflown before they had been attacked. High mountains, sheer precipices, raging rivers, ice and snow, alien forest inhabited by hungry predators, and who knew what else. He had nothing left in the way of equipment except his translator, which would not help him in dealing with famished carnivores. He had that, and Pip, he reminded himself. Pondering his situation, he decided that any reasonable person would concur that he had no chance of getting out of this alive.

Certainly not if he continued to squat by the riverside feeling sorry for himself, he mused. Mother Mastiff would have been appalled. He could almost hear her berating him for such fatalism. Berating him, and boxing his ears. He promptly proceeded to do something else he thought he could not do. He smiled.

It was a start.

Climbing to his feet, he considered his surroundings. Cold, inhospitable, growing dark, starting to snow lightly. Pink snow. He needed warmth, hospitality, light, shelter from the harsh weather. He would not find it here, muttering to himself and bemoaning his misfortune. "Therefore," he declared aloud, "I had better get moving."

He started hiking in a southwesterly direction, as Bleshmaa had recommended. Very quickly she faded into and became one with the pink snow and blue growths behind him. Soon the forest swallowed her up, and she then was gone altogether.

CHAPTER

7

If the great northern Gestaltian forest had seemed quiet by day, the nocturnal silence bordered on smothering. Before daylight vanished completely, Flinx managed to raise a feeble palisade of fallen branches and clumps of an odd, thorny bush the color of lapis that gave off a disconcerting scent of burned meat when he pulled it out of the ground by its roots. Settling himself back against the tree he had chosen to serve as the rear wall of his temporary shelter, he ruminated that he would already be dead of hypothermia if not for the thermosensitive clothing that not only kept him warm but by now had almost dried itself out. How long the heavily stressed specialty garb would continue to do so under such difficult conditions he did not know.

While in the utter absence of light he could see very little, his singular Talent allowed him to perceive a great deal. Though largely devoid of sound, the forest that surrounded him and Pip was raucous with the ragged, rampant, primitive emotional broadcasts of creatures anxious to eat and those desperate to avoid being eaten. Less intrusive than the more powerful, fully formed emotions of sentient beings, these primal transmissions nevertheless generated a soft buzz in his brain that was impossible to ignore. The occasional brighter flash of shock or surprise was easily recognizable even though the species involved were alien to him. They invariably indicated something about to be killed or devoured.

Thanks to his unique ability, he could sense presences all around him where any others of his kind would have been left literally in the dark. The same was not true for the Tlel, however, or for many of the creatures that inhabited the forest. In the absence of light their individual electrical fields, or *flii,* would stand out clearly to any creature possessing the ability to sense them. Including his own, he realized. From time spent as a childhood thief he knew how to move silently to avoid being heard, and later years had taught him how to utilize whatever camouflage was available to conceal himself from sight, but how did one veil one's personal electrical field? Certainly not with branches, or piles of snow, or thick clothing. Albeit to a lesser extent, Pip must also be generating *flii,* he knew. Any Tlel engaged in a search for the downed skimmer should be able to locate them by identifying their distinctive alien emanations.

So, too, he realized, would prowling predators.

Snuggling back against the tree and its oddly spongy exterior, he wondered if one's individual *flii* grew stronger or weaker in proportion to exhaustion. If the former, then he ought to be broadcasting a signal all the way back to Tlossene. He was left pondering the possibility even as sleep overtook him.

He awoke warmer and more refreshed than he would have believed possible. Fatigue had certainly played a part in his sound sleep, but there was more to it than that. He was almost comfortable, as if some thoughtful passerby had draped him in a spare blanket or two. Blinking sleepily, he brushed at whatever was batting against his face. At first he thought it might be falling leaves. Then he remembered that the tree-like growths of Gestalt did not have leaves.

It was Pip, beating frantically against his forehead, nose, and cheeks, trying to rouse him from the comfortable but dangerous stupor into which he had fallen. Perceiving her concern, he smiled encouragingly as he projected a feeling of reassurance.

"Easy, long lady. Not only am I not dead, I'm feeling a little better, actually." Scales gleaming metallically in the morning sun that was sifting down between the tall boles, she backed off. He moved to stand up.

He could not. No warm blankets enveloped him—but something else had.

It was the tree. He had spent an hour or so the previous evening wedging himself between the odd, rippling folds of its exterior, seeking as much shelter and warmth as such minimal sanctuary might provide. A Terran tree would have ignored his efforts. One on Midworld might have seeped acid to dissolve the interloper, or used flexible vines to throw him aside. Here on Gestalt, it seemed that at least one species of tall growth was able to respond accommodatingly.

During the night, folds of its blue-gray exterior had expanded up and around him. Like the irritant in an oyster, he was in real danger of becoming completely encased by the tree's outermost layer. He might not be transformed into a pearl, but a burl was no better destiny.

It took a good half an hour of squirming and twisting to free himself. Had Pip not awakened him he might have eventually awoken only to find himself irrevocably locked within the tree, able to see, breathe, and scream but unable to free himself. Though the tree had reacted to his presence without malice, its actions would have resulted in a slow, horrible death nonetheless.

Brushing fragments of pithy, malleable fiber from his jacket and pants, he took stock of his surroundings. Sunlight bouncing off patches of snow forced him to squint. He had nothing with which to improvise a set of goggles to mute the glare. He struggled to remember. In what direction had the dying Bleshmaa pointed? Unable to recall exactly, he settled on following the river. As he started out, he tried very hard not to think of hot food, hot drink, or, for that matter, anything that emitted heat.

Before the day was done, he had learned to avoid one especially graceful, willowy tree. As if slapdashed by an artist in a hurry, it flaunted streaks of bright yellow on its trunk. Instead of a crown of expanding branches, bush-like clusters popped out of its entire length. From these exploded feathery dots with barbed points. Pulling one after another from his clothing after passing too close, he suspected that they were not poisonous. Parasitical, but not poisonous. The projectiles contained the tree's seeds, which it sought to plant in anything soft, organic, and motile. Had the growth detected him because of the heat he was generating, Flinx wondered, or by sensing his *flii*? It was a known fact that plants as well as certain animals were sensitive to electrical emanations.

In any case, the stickery seeds were harmless enough—so long as none struck him in the face.

Following the river and without any definitive destination in mind, he tried his best to keep descending. If nothing else, the lower he went, the warmer it would become. Eventually and with luck, a continuous descent might even lead him to a village, if not back to distant Sluuvaneh. Thinking of that community reminded him of poor Bleshmaa. He wondered how the Tlel mourned their departed.

Water was no problem, but if he did not find something to eat within a day or two, the inhabitants of that town would be given the opportunity to perform a unique double funeral.

Stumbling down a slope strewn with rocks, glassy bushes, and turquoise-hued saplings that snapped like plastic under his grasp, it struck him yet again that as a privacy-preserving ploy, leaving behind his rented skimmer's location tracker had been a less-than-stellar idea. Eventually someone at the rental company would get nervous and initiate a search for their missing craft. Other than knowing that he planned on traveling north from Sluuvaneh, however, they would have no idea where to look for him. Even if it had not been broken into fragments following its plunge over the waterfall that had nearly claimed him as well, Flinx realized how difficult the ruined vehicle would be to spot from the air. In any event, he could not sit around waiting to find out.

He did, however, have his privacy.

His one real chance lay with his own ship, the *Teacher*. If it did not hear from him after a designated interval, it was programmed to assume he was in difficulty. His shuttle would lift from its parking pad at Tlossene's shuttleport and start looking for him. Its internal AI was designed to perform a relentless search until it homed in on his personal communit.

Which, even if still functioning, was either trapped with the other equipment on his service belt somewhere at the bottom of the river into which the skimmer had crashed, or floating indifferently downstream. That was another reason why he continued to follow the course of that same river. If his shuttle managed to locate the submerged unit, it would respond by beginning a search that would take the form of an ever-widening spiral with the device as its nexus.

None of which was likely to happen before he perished from hunger, exposure, attack, or accident. The *Teacher* would not even activate a shuttle search for another several days. But with nothing else on the horizon to offer encouragement or cheer, such hopes were the best he could come up with.

At least he was not alone. Periodically, Pip would descend from her inspections of the surrounding treetops to wriggle back beneath his jacket. She would ride there until his body heat had warmed her anew. Thus refreshed, she would slither out, spread her blue-and-pink wings, and again take to the sky. Watching her dip and soar among the blue-green alien boles, he reflected on a bit of serendipity: the same blue, pink, and green skin color that made her stand out in the forests of her native world of Alaspin served to camouflage her presence on Gestalt.

Her coloring did nothing to mask her *flii*, however. Twice while airborne she was attacked by predators. One was sinewy to the point of invisibility, with long, slender transparent wings that rendered it even more difficult to see. She just did avoid its attack by braking sharply upon catching sight of it and soaring straight up. It was an aerial maneuver the predator could not match. After trying and failing to corner the elusive minidrag against a tree trunk, it finally gave up and glided away.

The second attack on Flinx's winged companion was less direct and more insidious.

From time to time she would pause to rest in the branches of a tree. Since with few exceptions the majority of forest growths put out branches only from their summits, this frequently placed her out of his line of sight until she once again spread her wings and took to the sky. It was a rare bole indeed that featured branches between crown and ground in the fashion of a Terran tree. One such sturdy exception held out the opportunity for her to take a break within sight of her ground-bound companion. Choosing a limb that was halfway up the trunk she touched down lightly, folded her wings against her sides, and gripped the woody surface with her ventral scales.

The tree promptly tried to grab her.

While not as subtle in its actions or as fast-reacting as the ferocious carnivorous plants Flinx had encountered on Midworld, the brown-spotted blue tree that did its best to trap and ingest the minidrag would not have been out of place in their company. Flexible strips of pseudo-bark retracted like coiled springs, folding shut around Pip with the audible *cracks* of a dozen whips being snapped simultaneously. She avoided them by simply spreading her wings and rising straight up. Evolved to seize unwary visitors by their feet, the dynamic growth was stymied by the fact that Pip had none. As she hovered safe and unharmed above the booby-trapped branch, Flinx saw the deadly coils slowly relax and lie flat once more. They were not large enough or strong enough to pose a danger to him should the occasion arise when he might have to climb such a tree, but anything Pip-sized or smaller and devoid of wings would have found itself immediately restrained. Scrutinizing the growth, he looked for a mouth, but could not find one.

Half-transparent aerial carnivores one couldn't see clearly, predatory trees, no food, no certain path, constant cold—at least, he told himself, things couldn't get any worse.

Then it started to snow.

As on previous occasions, he found himself wondering exactly which trace minerals were responsible for the splash of pale pink that tinted the snowflakes. They descended around him in languid spirals, as if the sky were bleeding. As drifts began to accumulate, it became harder to make progress. He was grateful for the presence of the river that had swallowed his skimmer. Its chortle and clatter offered company, albeit of the inorganic kind, and gave him a route to follow, even if one that led only downward.

Stumbling through the cold and snow, he was burning calories the way a gambler burns house credit. Both he and Pip had to find food soon, or all the fresh snowmelt in the world would not keep them going.

Accompanying a brief break in the weather came an opportunity to try local nourishment. This presented itself in the form of a squat, thick-boled growth that was the color of burnt turquoise. Empty dumbbell-shaped shells lay scattered around the plant's bulging base. Examining several of the baby-blue husks he saw that their interiors had been scraped clean, though by what kind of animal he could not tell. The odd shapes were some kind of nut, he theorized. The multitude of cracked and emptied shells hinted strongly at the edibility of their contents. How would his human digestive system deal with it? How would the alien nutmeat respond to his gastric fluids? He was so hungry he was on the verge of not caring.

Some sharp-eyed, slow-footed inspecting of the ground produced a double handful of unopened pods. Setting one on a flat rock, he smacked it solidly with another chunk of loose granite. The action exposed the pod's interior. Like its parent growth, the nutmeat itself was a speckled blue. The color did not dissuade him. Right then, he would gladly have bitten into a bright green steak. He reached down to pry out the shell's contents—and got a shock.

Literally.

Pip was in front of him instantly. Sitting up, he waved her aside. "I'm okay," he told her. "Surprised, but okay." The fingers that had tried to extract the nut tingled as if his entire hand had gone to sleep.

A cautious search of where he had been standing before the shock had knocked him down led him to the shell. It was empty now. A unique method of seed dispersal, he told himself. If each nut was like a storage battery, waiting for some unsuspecting herbivore to bite down on it before flinging it aside, it did not explain the abundance of empty shells that ringed the tree. It made sense that at least one herbivore had evolved a method for dealing with the growth's heavily defended reproductive system. Perhaps, he told himself, whatever fed on the fallen nuts was immune to their stored energy. Or possibly it possessed a means for safely discharging the potentially lethal shock. A better one, he told himself, than he did.

Nutritious though they might be, he decided to give the tempting nuts a pass. A more powerful jolt from a larger one might do more than just knock him backward and down. The thought of trying to eat a handful of what were essentially organic batteries was less than appealing. Even if he could somehow force them down, there was no telling what might happen subsequently. The inside of his stomach was not the place to risk a series of secondary shocks.

In the end, it was Pip who provided dinner.

In fairness, she was attacked first. The flock of aerial predators that swarmed around her were smaller than the single soaring, graceful carnivore with the transparent wings that had tried to make a meal of her earlier that day. Given their smaller size, only a drop or two of accurately spat venom was enough to send one after another of the fluttering, fuzz-covered fliers crashing to the ground. When she had effortlessly dispatched half a dozen of the persistent but overmatched hunters, the survivors sensibly broke off the assault and hastened for the cover of the nearest low-lying cloud.

Flinx paused to examine the broken corpses. While their brown, furry wings were as long as his forearm, none of the creatures' bodies was much bigger than his closed fist. Though far smaller and tinted green, their eyebands were not unlike those of the Tlel. Short, powerful jaws were lined with small serrated teeth for slashing and tearing at prey. Instead of talons, their limber feet terminated in clusters of tiny suction cups that were equally adept at grasping tree branches, tree trunks, or unfortunate prey.

As he knelt examining one, Pip dropped down beside him. Folding her pleated wings against her sides, she dislocated her lower jaw and began the slow, steady process of swallowing the smallest of the dead predators. Picking up the one he had been studying by its X-shaped tail, a hungry Flinx contemplated joining her, though he knew he could not do so right away. He knew from experience that by tomorrow morning the caustic poison that had killed the creature would have degraded to the point that it would be safe for him to eat. Pip, of course, was immune to her own venom. Furthermore, self-defined by its teeth and actions as a meat-eater, the dead flier's flesh was unlikely to contain any dangerous plant toxins. Or so he argued to himself.

His insistent, demanding innards made it difficult to wait out the night. The following morning, when he felt sufficient time had passed for the minuscule amount of venom in the creature's system to have degraded sufficiently, he considered tearing off the wings and tail and emulating Pip by swallowing his meal raw. While the idea was acceptable to his advanced, developed mind, his more discriminatory primitive stomach rebelled. Virtually empty it might be, but it was not yet wholly indifferent. While Flinx felt that he could repress his gag reflex, the entire exercise would be useless if he promptly threw back up anything he succeeded in choking down.

What he needed was a fire. How did one make a fire in the absence of tools? Fallen branches lay everywhere, some in places where they had remained relatively dry. Utilizing a bit of ancient lore known to his kind from when it had first stood upright on the mother planet, he proceeded to gather an armful of likely kindling. Selecting the two driest pieces, he set to work rubbing them together.

They broke almost immediately. It was the same with each pairing he tried, irrespective of origin. Tree-like the forests of Gestalt might be, but they were composed of alien growths, not solid Earth-like trees. Rubbing bits of them against each other did indeed generate friction, but only enough to cause every piece to crumble to a powdery substance. Hours of hard work brought forth no flame and no heat: only a pile of what looked like a mixture of sawdust and crumbled sponge.

A lesser individual might have given up. Flinx had been through too much, had endured too many similar desperate circumstances, to abandon hope. Then he remembered the seeds that had given him such a jolt, both literally and figuratively. Retracing his steps, he gathered up as many as he could find, stuffing them into pockets while being careful not to touch any that had been opened.

Returning to where a now stuffed and contented Pip was relaxing, coiled between two folds of a tree, he dumped the nuts on the ground next to the pile of fibrous powder his energetic but so far useless rubbing had produced. While the preponderance of his attire was decidedly nonferrous, the front seal on his boots was fashioned of flexible adhesive metal. Although the morning had dawned cold and he did not have the means to accurately gauge the temperature, the air continued to warm as Gestalt's sun rose steadily higher in the sky. He did not think frostbite would result from a short period of semi-exposure.

Sitting down near Pip, he removed his left boot. Carefully gripping one of the cracked but unscavanged nuts by its neutral outer shell, he brought it toward the boot's open metal seal. How would the nut react to the possible contact?

The consequent flash and crackle that jumped the gap between seed and boot seal brought the first smile to his face in a long time.

Though not strong enough to ignite something as dense as a branch, the spark was more than hot enough to ignite the pile of powder that had resulted from his heretofore futile stick-rubbing. Quickly piling first small and then larger punky branches onto the flames, he soon had a respectable blaze going. Carefully watched over and maintained, it would allow him to cook the small predators Pip had brought down.

Choosing the largest of the deceased carnivores, he shoved the sturdiest branch he could find down its gullet. Gripping the remaining exposed length of the stick in both hands, he held the incipient meal out over the open flames and settled himself down to wait until it was thoroughly cooked. It was hard to be patient. The pungent aroma that arose from the fire as animal fat dripped into the flames and was incinerated was almost overpowering.

Happily, the small carcass did not take long to roast. Torn from the cartilage-like internal support structure, the meat tasted faintly of bad fish. He devoured it nonetheless, wolfing down mouthfuls as if he were dining in the finest restaurant on Earth itself. Fur that had been crisped but not burned off added an attractive crunchiness to the rudimentary meal. Forthrightly omnivorous, Pip was happy to clean up those parts, such as the predator's diminutive organs, that despite his hunger her master simply could not stomach.

When all but the last of the deceased, crumpled aerial predators had been roasted and consumed, he shoved the remaining well-cooked corpse into a pocket to gnaw later and prepared to continue following his chosen path downriver. He was careful to scatter and douse with pink snow the remnants of the cook-fire, making sure not to leave so much as a single glowing coal or warm ember behind. Given the spongy composition of the woods through which he was hiking and the higher oxygen content of Gestalt's atmosphere, it would take no time at all for a forest fire here to rage violently out of control. While such a conflagration might attract distant observers to his present desperate situation, the attention would prove moot if he was incinerated before anyone could spot him.

His one lump of heavily carbonized "trail food" made for a bland supper. Although no stranger to cooked food, Pip would not swallow any but the least burned pieces of meat Flinx stripped from the modest carcass. After that, there was nothing. Two days later, she killed and consumed something small and dazzling that she cornered in the upper floral spread of an unusually narrow growth. It left her weak and listless, barely able to fly. Though Flinx's own body demanded sustenance and his belly was once more growling ferociously, he thought hunger the better part of expediency and declined to try the remaining fragments of glistening meat his smaller companion had eschewed. If the flash flesh made her sick, there was no telling what it might do to his already stressed digestive system.

By afternoon of the next day, he was so famished that he considered retracing his steps to recover that which he had shunned the previous afternoon. He did not do so only because it would have involved trekking uphill. With little strength remaining, he could not afford to waste any on doubling back.

That meant he and Pip would have to find something to eat somewhere downstream.

An hour later they encountered a new species of flier no bigger than his thumb. Observing these small aerial grazers feeding on flat, low-lying deep blue ground cover, he scattered the flock as he fell to his knees to share the bounty they had identified. The fingernail-sized, sickle-shaped seeds the fliers had been eating had virtually no taste, but neither did they outrage his stomach. He picked and downed handfuls in hopes that they were more nutritious than they looked. Most of them, alas, passed through his gut unaffected by his human digestive juices. Eating them had briefly taken away the emptiness inside, but the effort had delivered precious little in the way of sustenance. In a couple of hours, he was hungry again. Pip did better, disdaining the seeds in favor of catching and gulping down a number of the seed-eaters.

Clouds began to veil the sapphire sky during the day and the stars at night. Intermittent bursts of silver moonlight shivered and shimmied until the last of them finally melted into dirty sunshine. The hours, like the days, became indistinguishable. Native fauna howled, peeped, squealed, and rustled in the occasional blue copses whose tempting interiors he forced himself to bypass. Lie down among welcoming alien boughs, he knew, and he might not rise again.

By now, his shuttlecraft should have received instructions from the *Teacher*'s AI to start looking for him. The same ought to be true of the firm from which he had rented the skimmer, anxious for the return of their now overdue property. He needed to be vigilant lest searchers miraculously appear in the vicinity. Unfortunately, lack of nourishment had steadily sapped his alertness along with every other aspect of mental acuity.

Once, he thought he sensed the faint presence of human emotion and tried to stagger in its direction. It was very faint and distant, cutting in and out on the edge of his perceptiveness like a bad radio signal. Either that, or he had begun to hallucinate. That led him to consider if one could hallucinate feelings. While it brought forth no rescue, the mental exercise did help to keep him conscious and aware.

I'm losing it, he had sense enough remaining to realize. He was too tired to be angry at the turn of events. His remaining strength was focused on remaining upright and putting one foot in front of the other while hoping Pip might kill something that was even remotely edible. Tracking the treetops, she evidently succeeded in finding enough to keep her going. None of it fell his way, however, and he had never tried to train her to hunt on his behalf. There had never been any need to do so.

She was at his side in an instant when he stumbled, going down hard. His right knee protested when he tried to rise. Clenching his teeth, swaying slightly from weakness, he managed to straighten and resume the plodding downward tread that had kept him going. Next time he tripped, or the time after that, he knew he might not have the strength to get up again. Everything revolved around time, he mused. Or perhaps it was time that revolved around everything. Learning the truth of his origins. Trying to find something with which to counter that which was coming out of the Great Emptiness. Clarity Held healing from her injuries, waiting for him to return, *expecting* him to return. Understanding himself. Acquiring wisdom. Finding his father. Time, time, time . . .

Time to rest.

Was he still moving downslope? Was the nearby grumbling that of the river that had swallowed his skimmer so long ago, or did the rising rumble exist only in his ears, in his head?

He straightened slightly and strained his eyes against the muted daylight. Ahead he could see only alien flora, rock outcroppings, scatterings of half-melted snow that bled pink. But with his erratic Talent still apparently functioning he thought he perceived something else. Something new.

Emotion. Not human—even in his seriously debilitated condition he was certain of that—but arising from a sentient source. It was off to his right, away from the river that had served as his guide ever since the crash. He tried to bring some coherency to his thoughts. What kind of guide had the river been? Cold and indifferent. He could continue to follow it, but for how much longer?

The faltering feeling came again, not filling his mind so much as teasing it. Was that anxiety he perceived? Or determination? It was often difficult to be sure he was interpreting alien emotions correctly. In his present situation, however, it was not vital that he infer them accurately: it was only important that they *were*.

The river could guide him, but it could not save him. Reaching a decision, he turned to his right and started in the direction of the emotions he was convinced he had detected. He had gone less than half a kilometer when they began to grow noticeably stronger, validating his choice. He had not quite completed the first kilometer in their direction when his shivering legs finally gave out, and he collapsed.

He had been fortunate most of his life. That luck stayed with him at least in some small measure when he fell. Instead of the hard ground to either side, he landed in a patch of soft snow that lay directly in front of him. This time when he tried to get up, he only managed to raise his torso slightly off the ground. When his arms refused to obey him and finally gave out, his resultant slump was utter and complete, as much mental as physical.

It was not so much that he minded dying, he realized as he lay there unmoving. He just did not want to die in a cold place.

Pip tried fluttering in front of him, beating at his face with her wings. When that failed to rouse him, she landed on his back, slithered forward, and used her pointed tongue to flick rapidly and repeatedly at his face. He tried to generate the kind of emotions necessary to reassure her, but in his enfeebled state managed to project only a weak smile. Bit by bit the air around him, the snow and soil beneath, seemed less cold than they had when he had first fallen.

She stayed with him for almost an hour, warming his face with her coils, licking at him repeatedly. Except for the slow rise and fall of his chest, he did not move. Finally she rose, circling above him as she gained height. She hovered there for a while, watching, looking down. Then she turned and glided away to the west, the chromatic blur of her wings diminishing rapidly among the blue growths.

Overhead, a single pale yellow shape settled into the crown of an indigo trunk. Sporting dozens of tapering, centimeter-wide wings, it trained eyes like black ball bearings on the prone, motionless figure far below. Rafts of needles protruding from its four gripping feet flexed expectantly. Within its spade-shaped jaws, small razors dripped acidic saliva. As it sat staring fixedly downward, it was joined by another of its kind. The pair fussed for a moment, each reluctant to make room for the other. They were swiftly joined by a third, then two more. All focused their single-minded attention on the still-breathing but unmoving shape below. They were in no hurry.

They had time.

CHAPTER

8

With long, slender arms the length of his body, Zlezelrenn did not have to bend over to adjust the bottom of his leggings. Prehensile cilia coiled around the rear straps and tugged them tight. While the leggings that covered his lower limbs were striped and swiped in the traditional patterns of his clan, the fabric of which they had been fashioned was wholly artificial. In fact, the material had not even been woven on Silvoun. The colorful synthetic textile had been imported from some far-off world in the sky whose name Zlezelrenn did not know. Its alien origin did not matter to him. While Elders among his sociel decried the loss of ancient crafts, the younger Zlezelrenn and his contemporaries delighted in the many choices introduced fabric had made available. They lasted longer than his ancestors' attire, held their colors better, were cheap and easy to customize, and, unlike treated valask hide, were impervious to water rot. He still championed the weaving of valask-hide apparel by others, however. Traditional textiles were very popular with tourists.

He cradled his puronn lightly against his left arm, the grasping cilia lightly fondling the trigger at the far end. The five other members of the hunting party trailed behind him, their eyebands alert for telltale movement among the rocks and trees, the sensitive special-ized hairs on their flat, disc-shaped skulls attuned to the slightest rise in feral *flii*. An intermittent breeze caused their inscribed transparent vests to flutter around them. The weapons they bore were a far cry from the primitive slingstones and jabsticks employed by their an-cestors. Like his leggings, their weapons were also imported.

Life on Silvoun had changed in significant ways ever since it had agreed to join the vast multispecies galactic authority that called it-self the Commonwealth. His kind had adapted more easily and suc-cessfully than many others to that all-embracing, system-spanning authority. Even on their homeworld, the Tlel were not numerous, and they were by nature nonconfrontational. They represented no threat to the largely benign control exerted by the Commonwealth's two dominant species, the hairless mammalian humans and their partners the insectoid thranx. The Tlel did not even particularly mind that when discussed elsewhere, their homeworld of Silvoun was usually referred to as Gestalt, a name bestowed on it by its well-meaning but initially uninformed human discoverers.

Silvoun, Gestalt, Zlezelrenn—names were unimportant. What mattered in life was boon companions, a sated digestive system, en-tertaining art and inspiring music, spiritual fulfillment, intellectual discourse, respect for one's Elders (if not for their clothing) and for tradition. That was why he and five other members of his sociel were out hunting in weather that, judging by a glance at the sky, was threatening to turn bad. They did not need to hunt. No Tlel needed to hunt for food any longer. The galactic economy that had arrived with the Commonwealth had flooded Silvoun/Gestalt with a steady and sometimes bewildering variety of manufactured goods, foodstuffs included. The larder in his own dwelling was well stocked with pro-cessed provisions, including introduced exotics that had been tested and approved as safe for consumption by his kind. These would be prepared to order by machines designed to accomplish in minutes what had taken his primitive ancestors entire days to render edible. Like many (though not all) of his friends and relations, Zlezelrenn did not mourn for the Old Days. The "Old Days" might epitomize greater adherence to tradition and family life. They also meant disease, starvation, and war.

Hunting, however, was another matter. So ingrained was it in Tlelian life, so much a part of his people's customs, that someone who did not participate in the time-honored endeavor was not considered to be wholly Tlel. No native would have seen any contradiction in the traditional Tlel respect for life and the need to hunt it to sustain tradition. Live and let live was the Tlelian way—except when it was time to kill.

Personally, Zlezelrenn enjoyed the activity. It was bracing to be outdoors, tracking the forest's abundant wildlife utilizing ancient techniques, killing something that you and your friends would then skin, butcher, and eventually consume. It was even better to do so using modern weapons. Some Elders complained that this diluted the respect that ought to be accorded the prey. Zlezelrenn and his friends would have argued that their own possible deaths by goring, trampling, or biting would have left them in positions to deny the prey any respect whatsoever.

They tracked, and camped, and traveled in the Old Way. But when it came to facing down a charging chasinx or kasollt, it was unarguably better to be holding a puronn instead of a slingstone.

A cold gust caused his vision to momentarily darken as it brushed his eyeband. Though his vest was tight around his tapering torso and he had not shaved in a cycle, he found himself wishing he had let his fur grow even longer. It was, after all, the season for it. Then there was the matter of his most recent full-body dye job. Streaking, he decided, did not become him quite as much as the fast-talking village stylist had insisted it would. He vowed that next time he would abjure all bright colors in favor of his usual taupe.

Though he picked up the movement almost as soon as he per-

ceived the first hint of *flii*, he recognized neither. Visually, the creature seemed more dream than reality. Its *flii* pattern was as erratic as
it was alien to his experience. Finding himself awash in uncertainty,
his instinctive reaction was to raise the puronn. Behind him, the unsettled murmuring of his companions indicated that they, too, had
detected the airborne anomaly.

Almost as if it was reading their intentions, the strange flying
creature that had surprised the hunting party promptly ducked behind
the central bulge of a trio of large, linked, cerulean huluds, worming
its way into their festering hoop of cauliflorous blossoms.

Zlezelrenn's companions gathered around him. In a prelude to
shooting, energetic discussion ensued. This was accompanied by
much waving of long arms, fluttering of cilia and chin appendages,
and contentious phraseology.

"I have never seenseen anything like it," declared an astonished
Hluriamm as she checked her gun to make sure it would be ready to
fire on a moment's notice.

Vlashraa extended an arm in the direction of her fellow sociel's
weapon. "Nono, we cannot shoot! It is clearly a spirit creature and
must therefur not be harmed."

Half raising her puronn, Hluriamm stepped forward and took
aim at the cluster of bright flowers where the creature had taken
refuge. "If it is a spirit creature, then ur simple weapons will not be
able tu harm it. If it is not a visitor frum ur ancestors' hypothesized
spirit world, then it is fair game—whatever it is or wherever it comes
frum." She raised the puronn the rest of the way. "Easy enough tu
find out."

Elder among them, Klerjamboo placed a slim forearm on the
barrel of the female's weapon, applying just enough weight to ruin
her aim. "Tuu easy by half, tu slay that which we du not understand."

"Then yu agree with me," Vlashraa said earnestly, "that we should
not attempt tu kill it."

"No, I did not saysay that." Ever courteous, Klerjamboo was

quick to correct the younger female. "I implied that we should try tu understand it." He gestured with his own somewhat smaller and lighter weapon. "*Then* we can kill it."

While the discussion around him grew more animated, a curious Zlezelrenn continued to focus on the place where the unfamiliar apparition had disappeared. As long as it remained concealed within the dense cluster of hulud blossoms, he could not see it. But its strange *flii* was as clear and discernible to him as if the creature were wrapped around his neck.

Could it wrap around his neck? Might it possess other, even more threatening capabilities? Visibly alien, its potential remained as mysterious as its origins. Which led to the most interesting and equally obvious question of all.

What was it doing here, in an isolated river valley of the Anuvu Range? Was it possible it had been lost by its owners and had subsequently flown here all the way from Tlossene, the only nearby place where one could reasonably expect to encounter exotic offworld creatures? If so, why it had chosen to travel all the way to these northern mountains and this valley? Many places much closer to Tlossene would offer more hospitable surroundings to an abandoned offworld animal. Such questions only added up to more questions, none of which would be answered if they simply shot the thing.

As she sensed a surge in its *flii,* Vlashraa began gesturing excitedly. "It's coming out—there it is again!"

Hesitantly, the creature had emerged from the cover of the huluds and was flying toward them. Its wings beat in a fashion Zlezelrenn had never seen before, so fast that they were little more than a gaudy blur. Everyone was looking to Elder Klerjamboo for a hint on how they should proceed. Holding his fire, the Elder scrutinized the slender flier as it halted to hover before them, seeming to sit on the wind. After a moment it turned and zoomed back toward the cluster of trees from which it had just emerged. Reaching these, it pivoted in midair and came back. It repeated this maneuver several times.

"It wants us tu follow it," Zlezelrenn heard himself saying. He wiped cold moisture from his eyeband. It was beginning to snow. They had to make a decision.

Nlowwnee spoke up, his speech as clunky as his aim. "It is said that those whu follow spirit creatures may follow them tu their deathdeath."

Zlezelrenn could barely hide his disdain. "What are yu, some kind of primitive? This is the six thousand and twelve cycle uv the Raised Aborning. The Tlel are become a modern folk, members of galactic civilization. There are no such things as spirit creatures."

As an angry Nlowwnee started forward, Klerjamboo stepped between them. The specialized hair-like receptors on his head parted, half focusing on the intemperate speaker, the other half on the heftier hunter who was ready to make a bracelet of Zlezelrenn's eyeband.

"The observation is unnecessary," the Elder declared. Eyeband bright, Nlowwnee continued to glare at Zlezelrenn. "Spirit creatures emit no *flii*," Klerjamboo continued. "This one does, therefur it cannot be a visitor frum ur ancestors' spirit world. It is a normal being made uv meat and fluid, albeit one notnot frum Silvoun."

Though clearly disappointed at the Elder's analysis, Vlashraa was forced to agree with his logic. "It seems extraordinary tu encounter it here."

"I was thinking the same." Slipping his puronn into the long, narrow holster strapped across his back, Zlezelrenn focused on Klerjamboo. "Du we let it go—or du we follow?"

The Elder consulted the sky. There was little wind, which meant the approaching storm would be slow moving. It would be inconvenient to move about in such weather, but not especially dangerous.

"Not being an expert in offworld biology, Zlezelrenn, I cannot say fur certain which would ultimately prove tu be the wiser course. But I see no harm in doing so fur a little while. We might learn something. And," he added as an aside to the stymied Hluriamm, "if it proves tu be expedient, we can always shoot it later."

To Zlezelrenn, at least, the validity of this decision was soon confirmed. Though it could easily have done so, the alien visitant never flew out of view. It would wing its way ahead of them only to pause in midair or linger on a branch until they caught up again. Then it would resume its course.

"It seems tu know exactly where it is going," Vlashraa pointed out.

Huffing to keep up behind her, Hluriamm was less sanguine. "You ascribe Tlelian motivation tu a creature about which we know nothing. I, fur one, have no intention uv following it interminably. What will yu say if it crosses the Balamm?"

"We will not cross the Balamm," Klerjamboo assured her. "If the creature does so, we will turn back. Crossing the Balamm would put us in the territory of the Tl-racouuy."

Not even Zlezelrenn would go that far to satisfy his curiosity about the outlandish visitor. Like a number of other gr-sociels, the Tl-racouuy were Revisionists who rejected many of the new ways. Conflict between such social groupings was not inevitable, but was best to avoid whenever possible. For himself, he could never be an associate of such a strictly conservative and conformist gr-sociel. Nlowwnee, now, would be a ready candidate except that he was a blood member of the same group as Zlezelrenn and the other members of the hunting party.

Such philosophical and social conflicts had always raged among the Tlel. Instead of bringing the adherents of different gr-sociels together, the advent of the Commonwealth and everything it had brought to Silvounian society had only added another layer to traditional Tlelian squabbling. Though exasperated by this unexpected development, Commonwealth officials were prevented from interfering by regulations governing interspecies contact and by the strictures of their United Church.

The hairs on his head were all inclined forward as Zlezelrenn tracked the airborne alien's *flii*. The shock he experienced when they detected a second flash of otherworldly energy was profound. It was as strong a burst of *flii* as he had ever encountered. He had no idea what could generate such a flare-up. Superficially, it reminded him of the erratic *flii* of those few humans he had personally encountered. Only this was far more powerful.

Without warning, it faded almost to nothingness, then flared again. Though its origin was undeniably organic, it was as if it were being controlled by a switch, like a piece of electrical equipment. From the writhing of facial appendages and twisting of mouths among his companions, it was clear that they were suffering from identical perceptions.

"If this nu being I detect is not a spirit creature," declared Vlashraa, "then it surely must be one whose spirit is tormented by them."

"The second certainly seems tu be in distress." Klerjamboo had lengthened his stride, his bound foot-pads leaving slushy imprints in the leisurely accumulating snow. His younger companions were hard-pressed to keep up with the Elder. "If that is the case, we must help it, even if it is an alien."

"Better tu shoot both," Hluriamm grumbled as she struggled to maintain the pace. No one commented aloud, but Klerjamboo threw her a look that had the effect of forestalling any further comments.

Zlezelrenn sensed the new alien emissions weakening. Having momentarily lost sight of the flying creature, he was afraid they had run past the source when Hluriamm halted sharply and pointed to her left.

"There!"

Though initially reluctant to do so, the beautiful flying thing finally rose and moved away from the body that was lying on the ground. Snow had not yet covered much of the human's face. As Zlezelrenn and his companions gathered around the figure, the flying beast hovered nearby. While watching intently, it made no move to interfere.

Klerjamboo started to reach down for the offworlder's arm. Hesitating, he looked around at the others. "Does anyone here know anything about the physiology uv humans?"

"I have dealt with some settlers." Shifting his position slightly, Zlezelrenn regarded another of the hunters. "So has Vlashraa."

"Only cursorily." She was uncharacteristically reticent. There was nothing tentative in her physical response, however, when she reached down and ran the gripping cilia of her left hand over the human's bulbous face, lightly making contact with its assortment of peculiar bulges and protuberances. "I du know that they are less tolerant uv cold than the Tlel. This one seems tu me tu be badly chilled." She continued to study the angular, motionless form. "Unless attire deceives its shape, I believe it is a male."

"And its *flii* is alternately feeble and overwhelming." Klerjamboo looked upon the figure without fear. Tlel and human had lived together for a number of generations now. Mutual respect had long ago eliminated any apprehension.

"At least that denotes life." Much like his character, Nlowwnee was direct and uncomplicated.

Vlashraa eyed the silently staring Hluriamm. "Do yu still want to shoot it?"

The larger female considered the recumbent body. "Let me think. I am trying tu decide if its skin is thick enough tu be mountable." She was only being half facetious. The other half . . .

The human put an end to any such tawdry speculation by moaning and trying to roll over. The Tlel surrounding him held their ground, though Hluriamm and Nlowwnee flinched slightly.

"We must raise its body temperature." Straightening, Vlashraa studied the surrounding vegetation. "As it is tuu heavy tu be carried in the traditional free manner, we must make a carry-sled."

"A chance tu practice a traditional craft!" Klerjamboo was clearly delighted.

If the carry-sled was fashioned of traditional materials taken from the forest, however, the means used to put it together were decidedly updated. Instead of strip-stem stitching, the use of cutting and sealing tools made short work of binding together the necessary lengths of tree. When all was nearly finished, a somewhat chastened Hluriamm remarked on a deficiency that was immediately apparent.

"There is no cushion of material tu support the neck."

Here Vlashraa's knowledge of the offworlders came into play. "None is needed. See how much thicker and more muscular is the portion uv the body that supports the head? Unlike urs, it can lie out straight fur a long period uv time without snapping."

"Without moving adequately, either, I would imagine." Hluriamm, who could turn her flattened skull a full 180 degrees, could not envision how the creature could possibly see what was behind it without having to turn its whole body.

When they lifted the limp, remarkably flexible form onto the finished carry-sled, the flying creature darted close to monitor their actions. While its lesser *flii* remained more or less constant, that of the human continued to fluctuate like an erratic dynamo. Once, while they were pulling the sled behind them, the silent human emitted a burst that nearly caused them to drop their gangly burden.

The hairs on her head twitching, Hluriamm hastened to employ her cilia to massage and relax the sensitive organs. "Nevernever have I been around a human such as this! One would almost think it was hiding a small generator on its person."

Zlezelrenn looked back at her from his position near the front of the slapped-together carry-sled. "Not this one. I've checked his clothing. It's definitely emanating frum within."

"Maybe he swallowed a generator." It was with decidedly mixed feelings that Hluriamm continued to study their newly adopted responsibility as well as the flying creature that presently lay coiled on the rectangular chest. That portion of the human's torso continued to slowly rise and fall, indicating that air was still circulating within. Though Hluriamm had no idea of the mechanics involved, she had been assured by Zlezelrenn that it proved the human was still breathing and was therefore still alive.

It was not that she wished to be ignorant of the species that now shared a small portion of Silvoun with her people. It was only that in her village, opportunities to interact with and learn more about the strange creatures were infrequent at best. One day, she promised herself, she would have to go to Tlossene.

Meanwhile, a wandering human had come into her community and that of her friends, and she would do her best to learn what she could from him. Especially if, as her more knowledgeable companions Zlezelrenn and Vlashraa were inclined to believe, this human appeared to be something out of the ordinary even for a member of his own kind.

Flinx awoke with a familiar weight on his chest. As soon as she saw her master conscious, and sensed no panic, Pip uncoiled, unfurled her wings, rose into the air, and flew over to settle down in the pool of intermittent sunlight that was pouring through the triangular window. The material of which the transparency was composed appeared to be normal spray glass: nothing exotic or alien.

He had no difficulty sitting up, since the bed rested at a thirty-degree angle. That was how the Tlel slept; if compelled to lie on a completely flat surface, their naturally low center of gravity would put too much pressure on their thin necks and, eventually, on their heads. There was even a pillow of sorts—a soft balloon-shape that had been placed not under his head but under his neck, Tlel-fashion. Whereas whoever had provided it had doubtless done so with the best of intentions, the result was that Flinx sat up with a neck that was more than a little stiff.

He swallowed hard, fighting back his digestive system's initial adverse reaction to his surroundings. While the room in which he found himself was neat, orderly, and well-appointed, it stank like an unfumigated old fish locker. He needed no further sign that he was in a Tlel dwelling and not a human one. Straightening, he surveyed his surroundings. The functions of some of the devices and furniture he saw were self-evident. Others remained a mystery to him. In one corner he was startled to see a garish tri-level twizzat—three iridescent discs that spun around a common center, flashing colors in series. Though nothing more than a cheap child's toy, it was conspicuously out of place in the otherwise altogether Tlelian room. He perked up at the sight of it. Its presence signified that whoever had found him, freezing and unconscious out in the forest, had contact with Commonwealth goods and services. Perhaps the twizzat's owner had even bought it in Tlossene.

A shape ambled in, ambulating via the now familiar side-to-side rocking stride of Gestalt's natives. Flinx recognized female accoutrements. She carried a sealed container. Flinx reached up to his throat to make sure the translator necklace was still dangling in place. Like the rest of him, it was battered but still functioning.

"My name is Vlashraa. My friends and I were out hunting when we found yu and yur creature."

Nodding to indicate that he understood, he gestured in the direction of the single window. "Her name is Pip. Mine is Flinx." He turned back to her. "I lost my identification and everything else in the river when my skimmer went down."

The tone of her reply suggested sympathy. "Yu were very cold-cold when we found yu."

Squinting, he peered out the window. A number of unpretentious single-story structures were visible among clusters of trees similar to those where he had collapsed. "Thank you. How *did* you find me?"

"Yur creature led us tu yu. When we drew near, it was possible tu sense yur *flii*." Her eyeband focused intently on him. "Very strong *fliiflii* yu emit, Flinx."

Interesting. No one had ever commented on his *flii* before. With reason, since the Tlel were the first sentient species he had encountered who possessed the necessary sensory mechanism for detecting it.

She set the container she was carrying down on a low table. Several notches cut into the sides of the stand allowed room for the stout Tlel to more easily access their food, since they ate standing up. When she unsealed the very contemporary container a flurry of attractive aromas filled the room, doing battle with the otherwise noisome atmosphere. None of which the Tlel themselves could detect, he knew.

Taking a step back, she indicated the open container. "This is food yur system should be able tu tolerate. Among ur Elders, Klerjamboo has several times observed humans feeding and marked what they ate. It was he whu suggested and oversaw the preparation uv the dishes that are included here." Like a tilting platter, her head dipped in Flinx's direction. "If there is something in it that does not agree with yu, please tell me. We need no false reticence here."

"Don't worry." As he stepped away from the bed and moved toward the table, a hungry Pip joined him. "I'm not shy."

Since the Tlel used beds and tables but not chairs he was forced to stand as he sorted through the steaming packages stacked inside the container. Choosing the one that smelled the best, even though he knew that odor was no especial indicator of palatability, he peeled it and took a bite of the spongy material inside. Though it had the consistency of packing material, the flavor was pleasantly peppery and his stomach did not reject it out of hand.

"You saved my life," he finally thought to mention as he dug into the nourishing contents of a second package. If not for the tiny eyes located on the end of each steaming tubular shape within, he would have thought it contained poached mung beans. Resolutely ignoring the miniature eyeballs, he bit into the stringy shapes with relish.

Vlashraa studied the process with interest. Unlike Elder Klerjamboo, this was the first time she had observed a human eating. The mechanics of it looked awkward, as if with each bite the offworlder might sprain his narrow jaws.

"Yu say yur skimmer went down. We saw no sign uv it."

"The river swept it away." He spoke while masticating another mouthful of the beady-eyed sprouts.

"What caused yu tu crash?"

Flinx did not hesitate. "Mechanical malfunction. The escort who was with me died. I tried to save her, but she was too badly injured in the crash."

Vlashraa contemplated the human. His words were accompanied by a noticeable spike in his *flii*. Most likely a reflection of the honest emotion he must be feeling—though there was no proof of that.

"Yu are vertical. Would yu like tu go outside?" With its gripping cilia pressed together to form a single tapering point, one long attenuated arm motioned in the direction of the doorway. "Fluadann, who is senior Healer among us, says that fresh air is reputed tu be as restorative fur humans as it is fur Tlel."

"I wouldn't disagree. Yes, I'd like that."

Noting that his clothing had been as neatly cleaned and laid out as if it had been treated and returned by a modern automated sanitizing unit, he dressed slowly and carefully. Though it appeared nothing was broken, he wasn't about to take chances by making any sudden, sharp movements. Also, he was still weak from his arduous sojourn in the forest. Sending out an emotional call, he beckoned Pip to join him. As soon as she was snuggled beneath his jacket, he turned and smiled at the inquisitive Tlel.

"It's not that Pip is shy," he explained. "She gets cold even easier than I do."

More village than city, Vlashraa's town of Tleremot presented an amalgamation of old and new Silvoun he had not encountered previously. Built on a slope, the village offered sweeping views across a wide forest-filled valley all the way to the mountains that rose anew on the opposite side. The river that had claimed his skimmer and his escort could be glimpsed through a gap in the trees. Modern sprayed, prefab, and custom structures, primarily individual homes but with a few commercial buildings also visible, stood arrayed around an open circle that was the Tlelian equivalent of a public square.

A road led through the town and down to the river. Smaller structures were visible on its banks. He saw no sign of dray or other domesticated animals, though he knew that the omnivorous Tlel kept some. When not walking, the adaptive natives made use of small, powered personal transports. The largest of these could hold as many as half a dozen travelers. Though he was disappointed not to see any skimmers or aircraft, that did not mean the village was devoid of such fast means of transport.

In striking contrast with the newer part of the community, older habitations and storerooms had been dug into the side of the hundred-meter-high cliff that formed the back of the village. Over time, natural caves that a much higher, faster prehistoric river had once excavated from the rock had been walled in and enlarged. It was to one of these ancient, traditional dwellings that he had been taken, and it was there that he had been nursed back to consciousness.

As they walked through the community, Vlashraa greeted and was greeted in turn by fellow citizens. Though he could not see all of it at one glance, Flinx estimated Tleremot's population at no more than a couple of hundred. That was not necessarily a drawback. Though small in size, the nature of its buildings, the modern accoutrements he saw in use, as well as elements of Vlashraa's speech, all pointed to regular contact with larger, more advanced communities. His hopes were quickly and easily confirmed.

"You have communication with other towns and—cities?"

"Of course," she told him. "We are serviced by multiple satellite relay. Is there perhaps someone in Tlossene or elsewhere on Silvoun that yu wish tu talk tu? Tu assure them that yu are alive and well, if momentarily stranded?"

Flinx considered contacting the company from which he had rented his skimmer. Better to delay reporting that awkward bit of news, he decided. Not only to avoid having to argue about circumstance and money, but because he was not yet ready to announce his continued existence among the living. Whoever had come hunting for him might also have the expertise and the wherewithal to monitor an unknown variety of communications, including any intended for a certain skimmer rental company. The longer he kept knowledge of his survival quiet, the longer his privacy and safety would be ensured.

"Maybe later," he told the helpful Vlashraa. Refusing to take a backseat to his brain, his stomach chose that moment to speak up forcefully. The Tlel stared at him but otherwise did not react to the peculiar sotto voce growl. Even so, Flinx looked apologetic. "What I'd really like is something more to eat. I appreciate what you've given me already, but I'd be lying if I denied that I'm still hungry."

"There is no need tu apologize. I am pleased fur yu. Hunger is a sign uv good health. We will pay a visit to Healer Fluadann, whu will best know what additional foods uv urs tu recommend fur yu now that yu are walking once more."

"I have some idea," he told her. "I've kept down what I've already eaten, and I also shared some of my escort's food." Bleshmaa had been accommodating that way, he recalled. Though he had thought many times of the ever-helpful escort since losing her to the river, it was only at that moment that he found himself choking up.

Observing the phenomenon in silent amazement, Vlashraa found herself wondering at the seemingly inexplicable shedding of water that had commenced from the corners of the human's eyes.

CHAPTER

9

Nearly an hour passed before Halvorsen finally stopped yelling at the supervisor of the repair facility where he had left his damaged skimmer. The frustrated hunter was nothing if not consistent: every facet of the necessary repair work, from what needed to be done to get the skimmer back in working order to what the repairs were going to cost, had brought forth from its owner an inventive, odious fulmination covering everything from the shop owner's professional ineptitude to doubts regarding the nature of his ancestry. Having dealt with Halvorsen before, the shop owner suffered through it all without comment. Early on he had learned the important lesson that in business it was better to cultivate a spiteful client who paid in full and on time than one who was charmingly and consistently impecunious.

Halvorsen's wrath was muted by the knowledge that the reward he was about to claim would more than cover the repair cost to his vehicle. In fact, if he so wished, he would be able to buy a new one. Having verbally relieved himself on the unfortunate but tolerant shop owner, he turned his attention to filing his claim. Since like all space-minus communications it would have to cross the relevant interstellar gap via Tlossene's projector, he could not very well have his dimensional avatar standing forth declaiming, *The one you wanted killed is dead—I took care of it myself*. While admirably succinct, such a straightforward admission could potentially expose him to awkward inquiries. While modest in size and limited in experience, Gestalt's planetary law enforcement entity was not entirely incompetent.

Consequently, he took the time to make efficient use of code words and intentional misdirection. Those receiving the message would know exactly what was being talking about. Developed and refined through hundreds of years of use, space-minus communication was swift and efficient. Everything being equal, the response to his communiqué should take the form of a series (a series being employed to avoid drawing attention to the overall sum) of substantial transfers that would significantly augment his bank account. Just thinking about it almost allowed him to forget what it was going to cost to repair his damaged skimmer. Almost.

Descending on his quarry with surprise on his side, he'd expected no resistance. That his youthful target had managed to put up much more than a cursory fight spoke highly of his abilities. It went a long way toward explaining why the cryptically yclept Order of Null was willing to pay such a large amount to arrange for his demise. It did not give a reason why the unknown faction wanted him dead. This dearth of detail did not trouble Halvorsen. It was none of his business.

A couple of days, he told himself confidently. Receipt, response, and transfer should take no more than that. How wonderful were the advanced communications that allowed a citizen to be broke one day and drowning in costly purchases the next. With his skimmer temporarily out of action and having nothing else to do, he set about planning in meticulous detail exactly how he was going to lavish a lordly chunk of his ample new funds on what promised to be a binge of estimable depravity.

Watching the young Tlel at play on the cliff edge, Flinx could not help but marvel at how readily the locals had adapted not only to a fad current among young humans, but to one that required special modifications to the necessary equipment. There were only four of them. That was the Tlel way. Other than for traditional exceptions such as a rescue or hunting party, it was best to have no more than four in a group, though he still did not know if the reason for this unswerving, self-imposed limitation was social, psychological, or physical in the sense that it might be somehow related to their ability to perceive *flii*.

Though the side street where he was standing was steep, he had no difficulty keeping his balance as he tilted back his head and stared upward. Built to accommodate the cloddish, blocky feet of the Tlel, the street had been deeply incised with horizontal ripples. The footing thus provided even in damp, slippery weather was as advantageous to a human as it was for the villagers.

Shading his eyes with his right hand he watched as one of the youngsters, unburdened by any complicated apparatus, stepped calmly off the edge of the hundred-meter-high cliff and plunged downward. Immediately, the adolescent's three friends raced toward him on their lifters, riding air as each sought to be the first to partner with the plummeter. They bounced and spun off one another, jockeying for position.

Having spread wide her long arms and thick legs, the seemingly suicidal youngster who had initiated the contest fell surfaceward. She was in no danger, Flinx knew. Continuously monitoring the distance between itself and the ground, the fail-safe lifter strapped to her back would engage in time to slow her descent and set her down safely on the pavement. Assuming, of course, that her plunge was not first interrupted by one of the three other youngsters presently competing to do just that.

Skill at levitating, falling, fighting, and catching combined to award points to the most adroit and successful. Looking on, Flinx had no difficulty understanding the game's attraction. The part of him that was still an adopted orphan boy freely roaming the bustling streets of distant Drallar, on Moth, wanted to don a lifter of his own so he could participate. He knew he could not. More important, more adult objectives demanded his energy and attention. He was not a kid anymore. Not that he had ever really been one, he mused wryly.

Someone else was not as constrained, either by past or present. Sunlight glinted off a small winged shape that darted recklessly in and among the competing lifters as well as the targeted plummeter. Gleefully welcomed into their midst by the soaring, maneuvering Tlel youth, Pip's joyful presence added a new and stimulating element to the game. For a change, the feelings that washed over Flinx as he intermittently connected with his colorful winged companion were entirely free of everything but joy.

I should get a lifter, he kept telling himself. Show them how it's done. He stood and watched, pondering, wishing. Approaching from behind, a more multifaceted set of emotions caused him to turn away from the juvenile aerial contest. More multifaceted and more—mature. Ordinarily open and receptive, he found that at that moment he did not especially welcome them. As brief as they had been heart tugging, memories and thoughts of his carefree youth evaporated as quickly as a snowball on the sun.

His irritation was unfair to Zlezelrenn and Vlashraa, whose feelings were nothing if not kindly disposed in his direction. Having no way of perceiving his melancholy, they could not sympathize. Dragged back to the present by callous reality, Flinx forced himself to greet them politely.

Raising a long arm, Zlezelrenn indicated the contending youngsters. "Going tu join in?"

"No," Flinx told him tersely. "It's just a kids' game. I don't have time for kids' games." His translator could only convey the meaning of his words and not the bitterness behind them. He put his disappointment out of his mind. "This is the last place I'd expect to find youngsters of another species playing gravgrave."

Satisfaction was evident in the sentiments the Tlel projected, if not in the minimal distortions of his alien visage. Natural physiological constraints prevented the Tlel from being physically expressive. "As yu have been told, ur people were and remain quickquick tu import frum the rest uv the Commonwealth whatever is deemed useful. Cultural influences are as readily welcomewelcomed as technology."

"It's not usual." Accompanied by the adult Tlel, Flinx started back down the street. Stabilizing ripples in the pavement notwithstanding, he was careful to watch his step on the steep downhill grade. "Especially at first, less technologically developed species tend to resist such influences."

"We have alwaysalways been highly adaptable." Vlashraa indicated their surroundings: the deep valley cut by its unnavigable river, the dense blue and green forest, and the towering peaks beyond. "Ur world demands it. We have always welcomed anything that makes a hard life easier."

Flinx glanced down at her. "Is that why you agreed almost immediately after first contact to allow individuals of other Commonwealth species, especially my kind, to settle here? Visitation is one thing, but actual settlement is something else again. The matter of granting permanent residency to large numbers of another species is a question that many other sentient races find very—" He sought for the right Tlelian term. "—touchtouchy."

After his escorts exchanged a glance, it was Zlezelrenn who replied. "Stars, river, forest, sky—these things belongbelong tu all. Humans and Tlel—and other intelligences—may be very different physically, but what is necessary tu create happiness among us is not so dissimilar. Silvoun is like a house with many rooms that is owned by small family. Better empty rooms should be used tu make people happy than stay empty."

"Besides," Vlashraa added, "we have always gotten along well-well with yur kind, frum very beginning. Though we not look alike, we likelike many uv same things. Clean air, beautiful mountains, gud food. Human settlement has been gud fur Silvoun and gud fur Tlel. It is much easier tu participate in something vast and nu like interstellar commerce when one is partnered with humans whu are already familiar with its workings. We have made manymany successful and useful enterprises together."

"Still," Flinx argued, "it's not usual for indigenous people to readily sell property to offworlders. Much less to accompany it with citizenship."

The feeding appendages beneath Zlezelrenn's chin rippled in reaction. "The Tlel have ample land fur all."

How long would that attitude last? Flinx wondered. While it was true that for now, at least, Gestalt/Silvoun was hardly overrun by humans, conflict over property rights was an inevitable occurrence on many more developed worlds. He wondered why this should trouble him. Why should he care? In all likelihood he would be long dead before any such conflict arose. Or at the very least an old man on some other world, in another system parsecs distant. Pondering the question, he supposed he cared because he had always cared about such things. Mother Mastiff, on the other hand, would have urged him to rush out and buy land.

Well, he wasn't here because he was tempted by the possibilities inherent in local real estate, he reminded himself firmly. Tomorrow he would see about trying to arrange some form of transportation back to distant Tlossene. It looked like he was going to have to organize his journey to visit the shadowy Anayabi all over again.

Propped up in the semi-vertical sleeping position not only favored by but in fact essential to her kind, Vlashraa was slumbering soundly when she was awakened. By the light he held, she saw that it was

Zlezelrenn who had roused her. A simple voice command activated the illumination in her sleeping quarters. She was startled to see that he was accompanied by several others, Healer Fluadann among them. Stepping off the sleeping platform, she confronted her nocturnal visitors. The flutter in their *flii* told her immediately that something was wrong.

"It is the guest," one of the other callers explained in response to her question as she hurriedly donned leggings and transparent work poncho. "He tosses and turns and cries out in his sleep."

"This not typical uv human sleep." Though not a multispecies practitioner, Fluadann knew enough to know when one of the furless bipeds was acting in an abnormal manner. "The guest is clearclearly in considerable distress."

Vlashraa was almost ready. "Why not just wake him?"

"We would," Zlezelrenn told her, "but the flying creature will not let us near him. Making noise tu wake him might cause more harm than gud." Reaching out, he let several cilia make contact with the side of her head. "Once all whu have knowledge uv humans, and this particular human especially, have assembled, we will try tu decide how best tu proceed."

"Unless of course," Healer Fluadann declared hopefully, "the guest's slumber has eased."

It had not. Poncho closed tight around her body to ward off the cold night wind, Vlashraa joined the others in traipsing through the darkness until they reached the large cliff dwelling where the guest was being housed. She sensed his disturbed *flii* even before she started up the sloping walkway, heard his eerie moans and cries before she entered his sleeping area, and saw him tossing and rolling about on the sleeping platform before her view was blocked by the determined, hovering shape of the flying creature that accompanied him everywhere. Claiming the space between the distraught sleeper and the single triangular doorway that was now crowded by Vlashraa and her friends, it left little doubt as to its purpose. So long as it could stay airborne, no one else would be allowed to approach the figure whose rest was so obviously and vehemently unsettled.

"What are we tu du?" a concerned Zlezelrenn murmured aloud.

"There is nothing we can du," Vlashraa responded. "At least, not until and unless the flying thing allows us tu go tu the unsettled one." Following her words, the figure on the angled bed twisted sharply to his right, simultaneously uttering a long, drawn-out, pained ululation. Well-intentioned but helpless to do anything as long as Pip prevented access to the sleeper, the mindful Tlel could only stand by and watch.

It was closer now, Flinx saw. Vaster and faster, enveloping and obliterating everything in its path. Organic life-forms that hardly had time to cry out before they were annihilated, cold uninhabited rocky worlds and riotous seething gas giants, suns primeval and suns aborning—all gone as if they had never been; wiped out, eradicated, swept from reality like grains of sand from a shore. The dark evil that had extinguished them surged onward. Mindless but mindful; uncaring, sinister, and unstoppable.

His galaxy would be next. Millions of stars would vanish together with their companion worlds and nebulae. The Commonwealth and its tentative, burgeoning civilization, the Empire of the avaricious AAnn, species independent and isolated, all would be erased from existence, eradicated as effectively and efficiently as he would delete a file from quantum storage. Ever unsated, the incalculable malevolence would sweep on to the next galaxy, leaving in its immeasurable wake only emptiness where intelligence had once dared to peep outward and contemplate itself.

Clarity and Mother Mastiff, Bran Tse-Mallory and Truzenzuzex: everyone who had ever meant anything to him would be gone, gone, gone. In the end of ends it would not matter because he would be gone, too. Nothing could halt the oncoming void. Nothing except perhaps an alien weapons platform deficient in memory and lost in time. Nothing except that, and by a quirk of fate as indifferent and uncaring as the Great Evil itself, one minuscule organic blip. The blip had a name attached to it: Philip Lynx. One who ought not to be alive was expected to try to save billions who should be, who deserved to be.

He was not entirely alone. There was the trio of inscrutable sentiences that frequently participated in his uneasy dreams and helped to sustain his sleeping sanity: the hard, cold thinking of an ancient artificial intelligence that was intimately related to the weapons platform for which he was supposed to be searching, a feral green life-force that he now felt had something to do with the place called Midworld, and a warm-blooded intelligence that remained unidentified but was definitely nonhuman. Having recently been saved once again by his friends the brilliant but child-like Ulru-Ujurrians, he was now almost certain this last could not be them. One component of the supportive dream triad he knew, one he emfoled and empathized with, and the third remained an enigma. Hardly a reliable army with which to try to oppose peril on a cosmic scale.

And he the key. The trigger, he had been told. The trigger to what? *I am not a gun!* he howled at himself and at the eavesdropping cosmos. Nor part of one, he added more calmly in his restless sleep.

Catalyst, the uncompromising artificiality countered.

Medium, insisted the persistent emerald city.

Sad trigger, declared the sympathetic but steadfast passion.

No! *No more . . . !* he screamed.

And sat up.

He expected Pip to be eyeing him, watching over him, as she always did when he slept. He did not expect to see the half a dozen or so slightly reflective eyebands of solemn Tlel arrayed nearby. There was no need to blink away sleep. As was frequently the case following such episodes, he woke up already wide awake. The back of his head and neck felt as if a pair of tiny but muscular invisible figures were taking turns using a large sledgehammer to pound steel rods into his skull.

"How long have you been watching me?" he muttered, simultaneously embarrassed and pleased by the attention. Though the odor of so many Tlel packed into the space just inside the doorway bordered on the overpowering, he determined to ignore it.

"Long enough." Healer Fluadann stepped forward. Her master awake, Pip retired to the top of the sleeping platform and settled herself there, as exhausted by her discomfited master's Morphean anguish as he was. "We speculate on what could inspire such terribleterrible night-dreamings."

"We wonder if we can help," Zlezelrenn put in without waiting for the Healer to finish.

Flinx rubbed hard at his eyes with the heels of his hands. "There's nothing you can do," he replied disconsolately. "There's nothing anyone can do. It's my burden. My suffering. I just have to live with it—until I die."

While he heard Vlashraa's response, it was the authenticity of her feelings that caused emotion of a different kind to well up within him. Their heads might be shaped like platters, their hands might terminate in a snarl of glistening filaments, and their body odor might be stomach churning, but these were good *people* who genuinely wanted to *help*.

"There must be something we can du," she whispered earnestly.

Others have tried, he was about to say. About to, because he remembered that he did need help, albeit of a kind that had nothing to do with his dreams and nightmares. Perhaps, if they were as concerned as their straightforward feelings seemed to indicate, they might even be able to provide more help than he dared hope for.

"There . . . is something that might ease my distress. I hesitate to mention it because it's a lot to ask. Even if you'd still like to help after hearing the details, you might not have the wherewithal to do so."

Emotions among the assembled Tlel grew confused. Zlezelrenn

spoke for them all as well as for the community. "We cannot demur until we are asked."

Flinx nodded perceptively. Behind him, from the top of the inclined sleeping platform, Pip surveyed with interest the small room that was now flooded with emotion. Open, guileless emotion, Flinx was convinced. For a little while at least, in this good company, he felt confident he could let down his guard a tiny bit. He plunged onward.

"I've come to talk to someone who might or might not be my father. It's very important to me that I try to meet with this person or I wouldn't have come all this way." In the dim light, multiple impenetrable eyebands shone back at him. But the emotions that stirred behind them were as clear and easy to follow as the veins on the back of his hand. "Your village is very close to where this person lives. I can wait until I can get transportation back to Tlossene, hire a new skimmer and escort, and start out again. But if you really want to do something to help me, and we don't have to go on foot, it would be a lot faster and easier to go to this place from Tleremot." He did not add that in that way, whoever had tried to kill him would miss out on the chance to try again in Tlossene.

The assembled Tlel murmured among themselves. Finally, Vlashraa turned back to him. "Yu du not know if this individual is yur male parent or not?"

Flinx shook his head. "No. I've been looking for that person for a very long time. I was raised by a single nonparent."

Further discussion ensued before she spoke again. "Where is the place tu which yu wish tu go?"

"I know the coordinates that were entered into my skimmer's navigation system. I'm fairly certain I could also find it on a map."

"Maps we have," Healer Fluadann confirmed.

The youngest of Flinx's nocturnal visitors was sent running, to return soon after with a small projection unit in hand. The three-dimensional display it generated showed not only river valleys and mountain ridges but also forests and talus and caves, not to mention the current weather, continuously updated. Observing that Tleremot was the only community in the immediate vicinity of the river, Flinx realized how truly lucky he was to have been found by Zlezelrenn and Vlashraa's hunting party.

Drawing upon his excellent memory, he identified a small valley at the confluence of two tributaries. "That's where I need to go." According- ing to the map and in accord with his best guess as to where his craft had gone down, it was not far from the village—as the hlusumakai flies. Or the skimmer. Getting there by any other means was certain to take longer than a couple of days. How much longer would depend on what mode of transportation was available to the villagers.

Vlashraa gestured at the location Flinx had indicated. "There is some difficult terrain between. It would require a number of days tu reach the place yu have specified." She looked over at him. "There are also possible dangers."

"On the positive side, there will also be opportunities fur hunt- ing," Zlezelrenn pointed out encouragingly. "There is nothing along the obvious route that gaitgos cannot negotiate."

"Gaitgos?" Flinx inquired. No one answered him. The Tlel were too busy chattering among themselves.

"This is a venture fur volunteering." Healer Fluadann studied the human. "Having treated youths whu have lost parents, I believe I un- derstand better than most the importance of this tu yu. I will go."

Zlezelrenn and Vlashraa added their assent almost before Flu- adann had finished speaking. By the time word had spread through the rest of Tleremot, the proposed expedition was oversubscribed with volunteers.

The Tlel might have skinny arms and funny-shaped heads, an overcome Flinx reflected somberly, but there was no disputing the size of their hearts.

A gaitgo's function was immediately apparent even to an outsider such as himself. Each of the motorized walking devices would accommodate a single Tlel comfortably. Behind the padded, slanted seat there was storage for supplies. Though open to the weather; the extremely lightweight frame formed a protective cage around the driver. Designed for travel in Gestalt's rugged backcountry, the individualized transports boasted eight legs. Or maybe, Flinx thought as he studied the line of waiting vehicles, eight arms. Since the mechanical limbs were attached to both the bottom and the top of the transports, he was not sure how to label them.

Vlashraa explained the design. "Yu have seen enough uv ur mountains tu know that it is as important tu be able tu climb and descend as it is tu travel in a straight line. The gaitgo has the ability tu du both. It can even travel sideways across a vertical wall. That is not the problem we face right now." She studied the tall, lanky human. "The problem lies in finding one tu fit yu."

In the end, it was decided not to try to supply their guest with a transport of his own. That suited Flinx just as well. Time that would have been spent instructing him in the use of Tlelian controls and instrumentation was time better spent crossing open country. His dignity would not suffer from having to make the journey as freight. As for Pip, as soon as they settled into the modified open cargo bay in the back of Zlezelrenn's gaitgo, she rose and found herself a perch atop one of the protective composite honeycomb beams that came together above the Tlel's head. The multiplicity of openings in the material offered dozens of gaps into which she could insert her coils. If her presence riding directly above him in any way unsettled Zlezelrenn, he did not comment on it.

There were a dozen gaitgos in the expedition. All were the same size, all individually piloted. Comparable scaled-up devices could be used for transporting cargo and multiple passengers, but for those purposes imported skimmers were more practical. Able to ascend precipices, crawl through narrow tunnels, ford rivers, and even climb trees, the one-Tlel gaitgos were the favored means of mechanized local transportation among the inhabitants of Gestalt's innumerable smaller communities. And unlike skimmers, they were manufactured right on Gestalt, in its other major city of Tlearandra.

All those villagers who were not engaged in essential work turned out to see the travelers off. Yet again Flinx was struck by their kindly nature and general geniality. He could not have been rescued by representatives of a more affable species. At ease around humans and secure in their relationship with them, the Tlel were in no wise subservient. As equals, they truly wanted to help.

And, as Zlezelrenn had pointed out previously, the expedition offered those participating a fresh opportunity to engage in traditional ritual hunting.

While it may have felt perfectly natural to his Tlel driver, it took Flinx awhile to get used to the gaitgo's rocking forward motion. Considerably more unsteady than a skimmer, the vehicle's movement was defined and made possible by the smooth operation of no fewer than four and sometimes as many as all eight of its mechanical limbs. Once most of him (with the notable exception of his cramped backside) became accustomed to the jerky, uneven motion, he was able to marvel at the device's abilities. He found himself wondering if it had been designed by the Tlel themselves and made a mental note to put the question to his new friends at the first opportunity.

By the end of the first day he was convinced that, should it have been necessary, Zlezelrenn and his fellow villagers would have been able to find the valley of the two tributaries even without the aid of a map. Several times he was certain the expedition had made a wrong turn or had begun to retrace its course. Each time he was assured by his hosts that they had not deviated from the predetermined itinerary, and that sometimes the shortest and quickest route to the next waypoint was not a straight line.

In addition to the awkward walking motion, the gaitgo's climbing ability took some getting used to. It was one thing to be striding along up a gentle slope, quite another to find himself dangling out over emptiness as Zlezelrenn sent the multilegged mechanical clambering up a sheer rock wall. Not once, however, did one of the unique grasping legs lose its grip.

Strange, Flinx thought, how one could wholly without fear traverse immense distances when traveling between star systems through space-plus, yet suffer panic and disorientation when suspended only a few dozen meters above solid ground. It was all relative. Or a matter of relativity. One just had to have confidence in the relevant machinery. In that respect the gaitgo was no *Teacher*. It wasn't even a rented skimmer. But after a day of watching it clamber over and around seemingly impossible obstacles without losing so much as a composite digit, he finally found himself starting to trust the vehicle as much as its operator.

One time the gaitgos in the lead touched off a small landslide. It was at once frightening and enlightening to see the several machines caught up in the slide skitter downhill among the tumbling rocks without a single one toppling over or losing its gyroscopically enhanced balance. Eight computer-coordinated legs provided the kind of stability that would have eluded a tracked or wheeled vehicle. Once the rockfall had rumbled to a stop, Vlashraa led those who had successfully ridden out the slide back upslope to rejoin their companions.

When it began to snow lightly, a touch on a control caused the protective arching framework to unfurl a lightweight, transparent rain shield that kept both driver and cargo clean and dry. Streams were easily forded and deep, narrow canyons effortlessly negotiated.

"Tu more days," Zlezelrenn called back to where Flinx had folded himself into the gaitgo's modified cargo compartment. "Then we will arrive at the valley yu seek."

"I won't be there long." Flinx shouted to make himself heard over the steady, metronomic thudding of multiple artificial feet. "It should only take a short while to find out if this person is the individual I've been looking for."

"Take yur time." Everything was running smoothly, and Zlezelrenn was very much at ease. "We are all uv us enjoying the change frum daily routine." From the emotions that emanated from each of the gaitgo drivers, Flinx knew that Zlezelrenn was telling the truth.

It was the following day when a different and less enjoyable change in routine interrupted the morning meal. The disturbance also served to remind Flinx that while his new friends and companions might be wholly civilized, the world that they had so magnanimously agreed to share with humans was not.

He had just finished eating and was watching the Tlel pack the last of their supplies and equipment onto their vehicles when activity ceased. Whatever realization was dawning over his companions, it occurred progressively instead of all at once. First Sladehshuu, their lead driver, stopped what he had been doing. From busily adjusting the seals on his gaitgo's storage locker, his cilia stopped moving. His attention shifted not to another member of the party, not even to the surrounding dark blue forest, but to the mountainside that loomed off to the left. Then he was shouting as he hopped—given their low center of gravity, the Tlel could not leap—and pulled himself into the driver's cage of his vehicle.

"Ressaugg, ressaugg!" he yelled. The word was new to Flinx, did not translate, and sounded as much choked as spoken.

The cry was rapidly taken up by the others. Zlezelrenn was at Flinx's side in seconds, urging him to mount their gaitgo. With his escort not lingering to answer questions, Flinx had no choice but to throw himself into the open cargo bin that had been adapted to accommodate him. An increasingly agitated Pip swooped back and forth overhead, rising skyward in ascending spirals until she had climbed above the treetops.

Gaitgos were starting up all around Zlezelrenn. Supplies and personal gear not yet packed were abandoned where they lay. Casting aside any pretense at organization, drivers slammed their machines into sprint mode and began to race away in all directions. No attempt was made to coordinate the wild flight. Unlike every previous morning, the Tlel did not line up themselves and their machines in single file. Witness to the near panic, Flinx had the distinct impression that for the first time since he had known them, the best and brightest of Tleremot's normally mutually supportive inhabitants had degenerated into a self-centered mob. There was no avoiding the impression that, whatever the cause of the confusion, at that moment it was every Tlel for itself.

Though he had no way of realizing it at the time, the apparent randomness of the scattering and flight was not indicative of panic. It was a proactive reaction, the defensive opposite of fish schooling.

Concentrating on his driving, Zlezelrenn ignored his passenger's increasingly anxious queries. Seeking the source of the disorder, Flinx looked around repeatedly. He found what he was looking for moments later, and not by picking up on any broadcast emotions.

How had he overlooked something so massive when every Tlel in the group had detected its presence? True, it was projecting nothing in the way of strong feeling, but its size alone should have revealed it to him more or less at the same time his friends became aware of it. As he stared at the onrushing monster, the explanation presented itself to him.

Something that big, he realized, must generate a proportionate quantity of *flii*. Every Tlel in the traveling party would have picked up the monster's particularized electrical field at approximately the same time. It was an identifying characteristic Flinx could not have detected even if the creature was right on top of him.

Which, if Zlezelrenn's gaitgo could not muster more speed, was liable to be exactly the case.

CHAPTER

10

"It is a ressaugg!"

Flinx could barely hear Zlezelrenn's shouted words. Not because the smooth-running, engine-dampened gaitgo was making too much noise, nor because its composite feet were making loud scraping sounds each time they slammed down onto the rocky ground, but because the monster his Tlel friend and driver had finally identified was smashing down entire trees and splintering them beneath its weight as it barreled toward them. The deafening electric *crack* of wood being violently splintered combined with the rumble that accompanied the creature's attack to drown out all but the most penetrating cries.

Superficially it resembled the round, furry rollers that had come bounding toward and past him on the tarmac of Tlossene's shuttleport as they had frantically sought escape from the kasollt that had been pursuing them. Sheer size was the most obvious difference between those panic-stricken herbivores and the creature that now threatened the fleeing Tlel. The largest of the rollers had been thirty or forty centimeters in diameter.

The gigantic mass of dense pale pink and white fur that was bearing down on him now was bigger than his shuttlecraft.

Like the harmless rollers, the ressaugg was also propelled by four limbs. Unlike them, these did not terminate in flat, fleshy pads. Instead, each tapered to a single five-meter-long curving claw. As the creature rolled downhill, the fully extended arms rotated madly. So, naturally, did the four scythe-like claws. The spinning blades sliced through tree trunks as if they were made of gelatin. Clearly, they would effortlessly and instantly dispatch anything softer they happened to come in contact with. Prey, for example. Himself, for example.

Almost lost against the booming hulk of onrushing inimical whiteness, a tiny pink-and-blue shape was whizzing back and forth just in front of it and out of its reach. Realizing her master was in danger, Pip responded as she always did: by confronting the threat. That was all she could do. Somewhere within that tumbling mass of fur there were likely to be eyes, or an enormous eyeband akin to those of the Tlel. It didn't matter. Whatever organ or organs the creature utilized to perceive the world around it was completely hidden within the rolling thunder. Even if she attacked randomly with her poison, the corrosive effects of her toxin could not halt so mammoth a monster in its tracks. Much less the avalanche that accompanied it.

Not only did the ressaugg half bury itself in a snowbank to mask its presence, but when it had started downslope on the attack it had brought all that snow along with it, Flinx realized. Though he had spent time on many dangerous worlds and had emerged unscathed from a number of hostile environments, this was the first time he had encountered a predator that utilized snow as a weapon. If prey was not cut to pieces by the monster's extended, rotating talons or crushed beneath its massive weight, there was a good chance it would find itself buried beneath the snowfall the ressaugg deliberately brought crashing down around it. At the bottom of the slope atop which it had positioned itself the patient carnivore could then collect itself, gather its quadruple limbs around its enormous body, and leisurely set about the task of picking up the pieces of its sliced or smothered quarry. The ressaugg's method of hunting was exceptionally energy-efficient: it did not even have to walk, much less run, after its intended prey.

Flying ahead of the oncoming predator like dozens of small, stinging, winged scouts, snow at the forefront of the avalanche struck Flinx's face as he looked out over the back of the gaitgo. He could no longer see Pip. He could see nothing but hungry, flying pinkness. The expansive *flii* of the rolling, tumbling ressaugg remained invisible to him.

Then the wall of snow slowed, along with the beast it shrouded. The roar of the avalanche faded together with its force. Pink snow settled into drifts against the splintered shells of smashed trees. Looming above it all and now clearly visible against dark rock and blue sky, the ressaugg retracted its scythe-tipped arms and began burrowing into the new snowfield. A worried Flinx strained to see even as Zlezelrenn's gaitgo continued to put distance between its two passengers and the spherical monster shoveling snow behind them. Had any of his newfound friends been too slow in initiating their escape? How many Tlel lay buried beneath the combined weight of snow and ressaugg?

None, as it turned out. Individually and in pairs, gaitgos and their drivers reassembled on the far side of a small but fast-moving tributary of the main river. Stimulated by the near escape, the collective pong they emitted was heady, almost overpowering. It did not affect them, of course. Among the group there was in fact only one who had to struggle not to gag on the stench. As visitor and guest, Flinx would have been too polite to mention it. He would have been wasting his time if he had, since his olfactory-deprived companions would not have had the slightest idea what he was talking about.

A final head count confirmed that everyone had survived the assault. Having now lived through it, Flinx did not need to ask anymore for an explanation of the seeming panic that had enveloped the party when the attacking ressaugg had first been detected. The predator's method of assault was clearly designed to take down as much prey as possible as quickly as possible. Since its mass and lack of bona fide legs rendered it incapable of swift pursuit, it had to situate itself to bring down not just a single animal but an entire herd at one swoop. By scattering as they had when the attack had first been detected, the Tlel had deprived the ressaugg of an obvious target.

As the re-formed expedition resumed its course, Flinx found himself frequently glancing up at overhanging ledges and heavy snowbanks that he'd previously ignored. What else might lurk among Gestalt's mountainous heights, waiting to roll, plummet, or perhaps drop down on unsuspecting passersby?

"A great many harmful creatures make their lairs and nests in such places," Zlezelrenn elaborated in response to Flinx's inquiry. "Usually they leave signs that can be recognized, so that they may be avoided." Raising a long, slender arm, he used his cilia to point to the lead gaitgo. "That Sladehshuu did not detect the ressaugg before it attacked shows how effective was its camouflage."

Flinx considered. Once again tucked comfortably beneath his jacket, Pip had finally relaxed. He wondered if the minidrag was experiencing frustration at her continuing inability to counter the threats this world posed.

"I'd think more than one of you, not just Sladehshuu, would have sensed its *flii* before it started toward us."

Zlezelrenn looked back at him, the sun glistening off his eyeband. "Did yu not know, Flinx, that many predators possess the necessary biological mechanisms tu suppress their *flii*?"

Of course they would, he told himself reprovingly. Now that it had been pointed out to him, it was obvious that such an ability was vital. Otherwise *flii*-sensitive prey would always be able to detect the presence of those stalking them. A predator unable to mask its *flii* was less dangerous to prey able to sense it than a cat with a bell around its neck was to a mouse. He should have realized that before he asked a Tlel what must have sounded like a stupid question whose answer was blatantly obvious.

"You said *a great many harmful creatures,*" he submitted. "I take it there are worse dangers in these mountains than the ressaugg?"

"Yes," Zlezelrenn told him. "Much more dangerous. And probably not like what yu think."

Flinx eyed the immense bulk of the rocky spire that dominated the terrain to the immediate left of the advancing column. "How do you mean?"

"Why waste warmth forming the words? We have just escaped a ressaugg." Though he could not be sure, Flinx thought his friend sounded slightly testy. "Those whu speak uv trouble often find it. Better tu focus on the way ahead, and tu think instead uv gud weather and safe traveling."

It was an approach Flinx could understand, even if his everactive imagination prevented him from dropping the subject as easily as Zlezelrenn. While a part of him wanted more of his curiosity concerning the nature of hazardous Gestaltian wildlife satisfied, the rest concurred with his host. With luck, he would remain ignorant for the remainder of the journey as to the precise makeup of the threat to which Zlezelrenn had alluded. They had already been lucky in their surprise encounter with the ressaugg, however.

As one who had counted on the Bank of Luck to bail him out of numerous difficult situations in the past, Flinx knew well that his account was seriously overdrawn.

While unlike his sensitive Tlel companions he could not detect the *flii* of a flea, his own singular Talent continued to function, interrupted only by the occasional pains that flashed through his head. As always, the frequency and intensity of these were utterly unpredictable. Sometimes he would go for days or weeks without so much as a twinge. Then there would come a morning when he felt as if his head were going to explode every hour on the hour. He dreaded his repetitive dreams because the worst cerebral attacks always seemed to follow close upon each occurrence. An ordinary day might pass, or two, or several, without any discomfort. But every time his somnolent visualizations interrupted his sleep, he knew that without fail a fiery, stabbing headache would not be far behind.

Having recovered fully from the most recent of the trance-like dreams, his mind was clear when he picked up the first faint stirrings of unsettled stress. They had the feel of emotions distant but closing, of the faraway coming inexorably nearer. Straining for clarification, he perceived hostility underlain with tension merged with apprehension. Considered as an emotional whole, not an altogether comforting mix.

He would have informed his companions, who continued onward entirely ignorant of the stress-laden feelings that were inclining in their direction. Doing so, however, would have meant revealing his ability. Justifying a warning by saying that he "just had a feeling" would carry no more weight with the Tlel than it did with any other intelligent species, including his own kind.

But as the line of gaitgos ambled through a section of particularly dense forest and growths from green to turquoise to near indigo in color closed in claustrophobically around them, he grew more and more uneasy. The enmity he sensed was thickening in his mind like a fog, threatening to drown out his perception of his amiable companions. That the hostility he was identifying arose from Tlel minds and not those of primitive carnivores rendered it no less troubling.

He finally decided that he could no longer keep his concerns to himself. If one of his friends questioned his "feelings" or means of perception, he would extemporize some kind of explanation or excuse. Debating how best to proceed, he leaned forward to address himself to Zlezelrenn.

He never got the chance.

Where his singular ability was concerned, continued silence

would keep his secret safe. However, it would do him no good if he ended up dead. That seemed a very real possibility as the forest around them erupted with gunfire. Though not nearly as advanced as the gaitgos, the weapons that were being brought to bear on the line of travelers were more than adequate to accomplish their intended task. Rock-hard projectiles whizzed around his head as Zlezelrenn took immediate evasive action. Small projectiles of forced metal capable of killing simply by unlocking the kinetic energy they possessed slammed into the forest on all sides. Trees exploded noisily.

Zlezelrenn was yelling at him to stay down. Flinx needed no incentive. Though ignorant of the motivation and identity of the attackers, he still found himself wishing for his pistol. Regretfully, along with the rest of his equipment it lay somewhere at the bottom of the river that had swallowed the skimmer.

Still and as always, he was not entirely defenseless. There was his functioning Talent—and Pip. As sensitive as her master to threatening emotions, she had slithered out of his jacket and taken to the air before the first shot had been fired. Now she patrolled overhead, singling out potential targets, flying cover for Flinx, marshaling her venom. Instinctively aware that it was limited in quantity, she would not dive to his defense until her master was more openly threatened.

It was the appropriate, sensible reaction, he knew as he hunkered down in the back of the dodging gaitgo, but her efforts would arrive too late if he caught a stray shell from an assailant who was not intentionally aiming in his direction. That was the trouble with being caught in a random assault by many attackers who were not specifically hunting him. Flinx had been able to deal swiftly and effectively with whoever had attacked his skimmer because there had been only one assassin and that individual's attention had been concentrated solely on him. In contrast, as just another gaitgo rider he was only one potential target among many for the unknown number of unidentified assailants.

Zlezelrenn's words of the previous day returned to both enlighten and disturb. There were far more serious dangers in the mountains than avalanche-exploiting ressauggs, his friend had told him. *Probably not like what yu think,* the gaitgo driver had stated knowingly. Realizing from the storm of confrontational emotions he was currently perceiving the nature of what Zlezelrenn had meant, Flinx now knew why the citizens of Tleremot traveled with what at first glance seemed to be a surfeit of arms. Yes, weapons were needed to fend off impressive predators like ressauggs and kasollts.

But more significantly, and in yet another blow to his already badly battered sense of optimism, they were evidently also needed to defend in conflicts with others of their own kind.

As he was brooding over this disheartening state of affairs and the revelation that the cheerful Tlel were, like all too many supposedly sentient species, not above slaughtering their own kind when circumstances required, Zlezelrenn ran the gaitgo in behind a thick stand of particularly large growths.

"Stay here!" he admonished a dispirited Flinx. A touch on a control caused the protective cage that surrounded him and his guest to pop open like a blossoming flower. Climbing out, the Tlel first removed his brightly colored leggings and then the largely transparent poncho that covered him from neck to knee. Unclothed, he pulled a slender but lethal-looking weapon from its brackets on the side of the vehicle and began to weave his way forward toward the heart of the conflict that was now raging among the trees. As he moved away, his fur changed color. White and mottled brown shaded to white and mottled blue-green. Flinx looked on in surprise. He had not known that the Tlel were capable of chameleonic transformations.

It was certainly effective. Though the woods echoed with gunfire, from his place of concealment behind the trees he could not make out a single combatant. Not with his eyes, anyway. His Talent allowed him to perceive individuals as clearly as if with a field scope. It would have enabled him to greatly assist his friends—except that he was without a weapon. Pip continued to swoop back and forth above him, restraining herself from engaging hostile assailants who did not directly threaten her companion. Yet.

He considered trying to project on the attackers. While it was an aspect of his Talent that he had grown more adept at applying, most recently to overcome the hired killer who had shot down his skimmer, the presence of so many attackers was likely to render it much less effective. On a crowded battlefield where he could only sense rampant hostility, it was difficult to separate friend from foe. Straining, he found that he was able to recognize Zlezelrenn's emotional signature, and Vlashraa's, and to a lesser extent those of villagers such as Fluadann and Hluriamm with whom he had also had previous contact. Unable to identify and isolate the other members of the expedition, he ran the risk of projecting on them if he tried to incapacitate their attackers.

He *could* attempt to generate a really serious, wide-ranging projection that would immobilize the entire field of conflict, friend and enemy alike. If successful in the effort, he could then pick through the dazed and revitalize only his friends, one at a time. There was no guarantee that this would work, however. The disabling projection might not be all-inclusive. Or, striving to revive his companions, he might inadvertently restore one or more of the attackers. Mentally projecting a disabling or distracting emotion was not the same as blanketing a combat zone in a soporific gas. His ability to focus his Talent had improved considerably, but it was still nowhere near as precise as an actual weapon.

He felt he had to do something, but without a gun of his own, let alone his own familiar pistol, he could not decide how to proceed. If he left the shelter of the trees and wandered out into the line of fire, Pip would immediately descend to take out any Tlel aiming specifically at him. That would work—so long as he was singled out by only one enemy combatant at a time. Eventually she would run out of venom. She would have to retire and wait for her body to produce more, an inescapable biological interval that would leave him without any personal protection beyond what he could conjure from his all-too-often unresponsive and erratic mind.

As was so often the case in the course of combat, circumstances eventually overwhelmed logic and reason and he was forced to defend himself.

Perhaps the duo who attacked him thought his human appearance was some sort of clever subterfuge on the part of their enemies. Plainly, they were not put off by the fact that he was non-Tlel. It was apparently enough that he was occupying a Tleremot gaitgo. Reasonable or not, that was sufficient to brand him an ally by association. Had some of his fellow humans participated in battles like these among the natives? Flinx wondered. The notion was too depressing to contemplate.

In any case, he didn't have time.

Altering the color of their fur to take full advantage of the position of the sun, the group of assailants who came up behind him was camouflaged nearly perfectly. There was a good chance the well-conceived flanking movement could have fallen upon the rear of the villagers' position without being detected until it was too late. Only one thing stood, or in this particular instance sat, between them and their intended targets—the tall, lanky, bundled-up visitor who would greatly have preferred not to get involved. Convinced they were well concealed, two of the stalkers broke off from the main body of silent infiltrators and came toward him. Even looking straight in their direction, they were difficult to make out against the rocks and snow.

Their homicidal emotions, however, burned like torches.

Flinx was not the only one to detect them. Pip perceived them also. Folding her wings against her sides, she dropped from the sky like an arrow, a blue-and-pink blur. Flinx's stalkers never saw her.

The nearer of the two caught the full force of her venom square in the center of his eyeband. Letting out a high-pitched squeal, he dropped his weapon and fell backward onto the ground, kicking wildly with uncovered legs while frantic cilia fluttered futilely at his rapidly liquefying vision. Taken aback, his female companion hesitated, then tried to aim the pistol she was carrying at the darting, dodging, impossibly agile alien shape. She lowered her gaze just in time to get a faceful of the replacement strut that Flinx brought down across the top of her flattened skull. The disc-shaped head collapsed, folding inward like a pie plate chopped in the middle. Blood flew, splattering Flinx. Simultaneously stunned and disgusted, he stumbled backward. But he kept his grip on the now bloody strut.

Their position revealed and the surprise they had been counting on lost, the remainder of the flanking attackers rushed the villagers. Alerted by Flinx's self-defense, not to mention the rapidly fading screams of the Tlel whom Pip had brought down, the travelers from Tleremot were ready. Flinx was spared the need to kill again as his friends began to gain the upper hand.

They did so by means of an advanced piece of technology that had been developed in concert with human and possibly thranx expertise. When its properties were explained to him, Flinx realized that the device had all the hallmarks of skillful thranx engineering. How it had come to be designed, sold, and deployed on bucolic Gestalt was one tale he preferred not to hear told.

There was no mistaking its efficacy. Wholly contrary to his profession, Healer Fluadann wielded the apparatus while being defended by armed villagers standing on either side of him. Observing its effectiveness, Flinx wondered why the device had not been brought into use at the start of the skirmish. Only later did he learn that it took some time to activate properly—because no one dared risk its accidental activation.

The weapon emitted a broad but intense electrical field strong enough to overwhelm any Tlel caught in its beam. An analogous human weapon would have been a sonic projector powerful enough to burst eardrums. That the attackers were overwhelmed was evidenced by the speed with which they fled. Not all made a successful escape. Those who caught the full force of the device went mad on the spot, the part of them that was able to sense *flii* shattered by a storm of discharge emitted by the weapon. Blood dribbled from mouths whose owners had lost control of the relevant musculature. Blood gushed from ears that led to hemorrhaging brains.

There was entirely too much blood, a dismayed Flinx observed.

The civilized, gentle, rustic citizens of villatic Tleremot did not enhance their stature in his eyes as they moved across the now quiescent battlefield, breaking the fragile necks of the wounded and scavenging their personal effects. Only when these grisly tasks had been concluded did they retire to redon their discarded leggings and ponchos. No matter where one traveled, he was forced to remind himself yet again, the veneer of civilization was very thin. Would it be so terrible if that sliver of sentience slipped into oblivion, obliterated forever by whatever was coming out of the Great Emptiness?

Then Vlashraa was at his side, and the emotion that poured forth from her reminded him yet again why consciousness and intelligence in this part of the galaxy were worth preserving.

"Yu are all right?" Her concern was sincere. She tilted back her head so that her eyeband was able to meet his binocular gaze. "The miserable GrTl-Keepers are not recognized. They are not frum this area, and came only tu foist their heresies on NaTl-Seekers such as urselves." She eyed him intently. "Had they succeeded in proceeding undiscovered and unchallenged, they would have raided Tleremot. We owe yu much fur yur help, Flinx."

"Always pleased when I can repay a debt," he replied mechanically. He surveyed the section of forest where the bulk of the fighting had taken place. The snow was now spotted with death. "I'd nurtured hopes for—I didn't know that the Tlel fought among themselves. I wasn't prepared for such ferocity. Internecine warfare is rare within the Commonwealth, although not unknown historically." He smiled tightly. "My own species offers ample proof of that. But except for small-scale, usually highly personalized conflicts, we no longer war among ourselves. We and the thranx are too busy dealing with, for example, the AAnn. And—other threats." His tone reflected bewilderment as much as honest curiosity.

"Why *do* you fight?" He gestured in the direction of the recent field of battle. "You said these who attacked you came from outside the area. Is there some kind of dispute over land, maybe? Or is it an ancient rivalry of some kind that social maturation has failed to dispel?"

"Land?" Vlashraa looked at him askance. "Why would we fight one another over land? Yu have already been told that the world belongs tu all, and specifically tu those whu make use uv it. What an absurd notion, that intelligent beings should slay one another over dirt!"

Different species, Flinx mused, different motivations. "If not land, then what?"

"It is not ancient, as yu suggest," she told him. "But the dispute isis old, and intense. It originated before yur kind came to Silvoun—though it must be acknowledged that participation in the Commonwealth has sharpened the divide between the two groups."

Flinx made no effort to hide his confusion. Experiencing a sudden chill, he shivered sharply. The perspiration he had generated in the course of the fight was evaporating, leaving only cold behind.

"Two groups? What two groups?" For the second time, he pointed to the battleground. "Is it just between the people of Tleremot and these folk? Or is it more extensive and others are involved? You said it's an old quarrel."

She let out a soft whistle. "Regional affiliations have always been important tu the Tlel. Zlezelrenn, Klerjamboo, Hluriamm, myself, and everyone else on this journey is proud tu hail frum a village as progressive as Tleremot. If they were here, ur neighbors and friends would express similarly."

Reflecting the uncertainty he felt, Flinx drew his brows together. "So this is a disagreement between towns? Something political?"

"Not political," she corrected him. "Regional and civic affiliations are determined by birth. One does not get tu choose them and one cannot change them. Yu are a citizen uv where yu were born and that cannot be changed. What yu cancan change, and modify, and alter, are yur individual beliefs."

As her words sank in, Flinx found himself more troubled than ever. Knowing from his pre-arrival research that the Tlel were a prosaic, largely nonreligious society, then what a somber Vlashraa was telling him suggested that . . .

"You're fighting over *philosophy*?"

Gesturing with the cilia at the end of her right arm, she indicated in the affirmative. "Among the Tlel, how one thinks is far more important than where one happens tu have been birthed. Frum an early age, we form and are bound tu one another by sociels. Fur example, Zlezelrenn and Hluriamm are both part uv mine. Healer Fluadann and Elder Klerjamboo are not. A base sociel consists uv four individuals. Similar sociels promulgate similar philosophies. In this way are like-thinking groups expanded and developed. Among the Tlel there are at present tu great competing sociels.

"Foremost are the NaTl-Seekers, uv which the sociels of Tleremot are but one small component. NaTl-Seekers believe in showing respect for the established order while simultaneously far-seeking. That is why we are happy being a part uv the Commonwealth. We keep ur traditions while adopting that which is nu and useful."

Flinx nodded. "And the others?" A hand waved in the direction of the silent battlefield. "Those?"

"Adherents uv the GrTl-Keepers. They believe that by engaging fully in the Commonwealth we risk losing ur heritage, that we will become something that is no longer tru tu the Tlel self."

"I see. Maybe that's why they didn't hesitate to attack me. As a human, I present the face of the Commonwealth they consider invasive."

"Not at all." Her correction was as swift as it was unexpected. "There are humans whu support the GrTl-Keepers. Some settlers are allied with them, others with the NaTl-Seekers." Her gaze was fixed on him. "Yu were attacked not because yu are human, but because they assumed since yu were traveling with us that yu are a NaTl-Seeker."

"I'm just a visitor," he protested. "I don't favor either argument. I'm not an ally of either side."

She pointed to a body lying nearby, its fur stained red. "The GrTl-Keepers did not know that." She started to turn away, then paused. "We du not hate the GrTl-Keepers. We just find them and their philosophy deathly passive. They're misguided, not evil. But they would withdraw frum the Commonwealth if they could. Undu all the progress that has been made, renounce all the marvels that have been brought tu Silvoun, forsake all the scientific and techno-logical advances membership in the Commonwealth has brought us. The GrTl-Keepers du not want tu go backward so much as they wish tu freeze time."

"So you fight." On his shoulder, Pip regarded the Tlel thought-fully. "And employ whatever marvels and wonders and advances you can lay your hands on to murder one another. I have to say that when I first arrived here, Vlashraa, I was inclined to think better of your kind."

She stared at him. Her expression, such as it was, meant nothing at all to him—but her emotions were roiling.

"I am sorry if we disappoint yu, Flinx. I have studied something uv other sentient species, including yur own. At least we fight over ideas, and not fur dirt, or meaningless property."

He sighed tiredly. "It's just that I was hoping, that I'm always hoping, to find something better."

She indicated understanding. "Yu would make a gud NaTl-Seeker."

A sudden thought made him ask, "What does the Common-wealth representative on Gestalt think of your internecine warfare?"

She had turned away from him. Now she looked back. "Though

both greater sociels vie fur Commonwealth favor, the representative refuses tu take the side uv the NaTl-Seekers over the GrTl-Keepers. As a supporter uv the more progressive sociel, this is something I and my friends cannot understand."

It's called politics, Flinx thought as he turned and headed back in the direction of Zlezelrenn's gaitgo. While his view of the Tlel had changed, and not for the better, his opinion of at least one unnamed and as yet unencountered Commonwealth functionary had risen considerably. The local bureaucrat sounded like someone who, if contacted, could undoubtedly help him in his ongoing search.

Unfortunately, as had all too often been the case throughout his life, those best positioned to aid him were the very people he had to take care to avoid.

CHAPTER

11

Halvorsen restrained himself. Another talent he had developed over the years. While suffering impatience waiting to receive payment from a client was perfectly understandable, he knew from experience that it would do no good to rush such people. He'd worked hard to build a reputation not only as an independent contractor who could be relied upon to perform a job in an efficient and unobtrusive manner, but also as one who would not tiresomely dun a patron for payment. Usually there was no need to do so. Those who failed to pay up invariably found that in the absence of the payment of timely and agreed-upon compensation, Halvorsen's reputation would sooner or later be followed by Halvorsen himself, with predictably dire results for the tardy.

Of course, on those rare occasions when a client was situated offworld, implied threats carried correspondingly less weight. Only once had he been forced to travel to another system in order to collect on an overdue payment. The mayhem he had delivered on that occasion remained as a clear warning to any others who might entertain thoughts of trying to stiff the contractor from Gestalt.

Anticipating no problems with his most recent contract, he was therefore surprised to find waiting for him when he returned home that evening a terse coded communication from the individual representing the so-called Order of Null. Conveyed via space-minus to the core receiver at Tlossene and thence through the planetary Shell to his home subox, it arrived in lieu of the anticipated fiscal deposit. If not to boiling, the unexpected substitution at least raised his emotions to simmer.

Easy, he told himself. Sometimes critical information, such as a single key for unlocking and facilitating a monetary transfer, could arrive encrypted in such communiqués. But no matter how many times he ran the message through his personalized, advanced decoding system, no such propitious revelation proved forthcoming. If funds were being sent to him, the means for accessing them was not provided in the newly received message.

Fuming in his seat, his temper held preternaturally in check, he settled down to read the words that had been sent to him in lieu of money.

The half-meter-high, fully dimensionalized avatar that appeared above his scuffed, well-worn desk was that of an attractive middle-aged woman. Her attitude, however, was as cold as the domesticated photons of which she was spun. She wasn't hostile, Halvorsen decided as he listened to her. Just distant. At least she did not equivocate.

"The information provided together with the imaging included in your last communication have been thoroughly examined and analyzed," the lambent avatar declaimed, "and have been found wanting." The fingers of Halvorsen's gnarled right hand slowly clenched into a fist, tight enough so that the knuckles began to turn white. He stared at the hovering, orating image, listening intently.

"It is clear from the evidence that you have succeeded in seriously damaging a nondescript transport skimmer somewhere in the wilds of the world known as Gestalt. Beyond that, nothing conclusive is established. The nature of any passengers on board the assaulted craft in question cannot be ascertained even from an enhancement of the image-by-image breakdown of the recording you supplied. Your assertion that the individual of mutual interest was aboard this particular vehicle and perished with it cannot be proven. Your word, while it has been found to carry weight in certain circles, is insufficient to justify disbursement of the amount of credit under discussion."

Halvorsen very badly wanted to place his hands around the neck of the woman who was dismissing him in such cool, dispassionate terms. His grasping fingers would only pass through the avatar, of course, and would have no effect on the actual speaker, who had stood for the recording on a world distant in truspace and time. That was the trouble with dealing with clients over interstellar distances: swindlers and their ilk were immune from something as straightforward as a kick to the kidneys. He could only sit and listen and take it—a posture he found worse than infuriating.

The avatar was not finished. "You will doubtless argue," she continued, "that given the damage inflicted by you on the craft in question and the rugged, uncivilized terrain where it presumably went down, no one could have survived the inevitable crash. You further state that for reasons unknown to you but suspected by us, the individual of mutual interest who rented the transport caused its integrated tracker to be removed prior to his departure from the nearest town. This more than anything else, more than the rental documentation and visuals you have provided, leads us to believe that the individual of interest to us all was indeed on board the skimmer you attacked."

Hearing this grudging assessment somewhat muted Halvorsen's distress. At least they weren't dismissing his claim utterly. Leaning forward in his seat, he waited for the avatar to conclude.

"While we are not willing to transfer the specified funds on the basis of the limited information you have thus far provided," the female projection went on, "we have agreed to initiate the necessary preliminaries. On receiving satisfactory proof of the demise of the individual in question, monetary disbursement in full will transpire without delay." Shifting her position, she momentarily must have stepped out of range of the recorder. As a result, the subsequent message was somewhat disconcertingly delivered by only half a woman.

"You must understand," the semi-figure declared earnestly, "that we hold this individual to be capable of certain exceptional feats of the mind. The one opportunity we had to kill him ourselves, we failed. The experience that resulted from that encounter was most enlightening, however. It is this enlightenment, of which you are unaware, that leads us to exercise caution in light of your claim to have accomplished the requisite task. This person is not one to expire easily."

What kind of proof will satisfy you? Halvorsen found himself muttering silently. The question was anticipated.

Shifting her stance again, the woman was once more visible in full figure. "No transfer of credit will be initiated by us without incontrovertible physical proof of the death of the subject under discussion. In addition to unmanipulated visual confirmation, a DNA analysis from an established autolab is required. Until such documentation is provided, I and my colleagues must reject your request for payment. This is a more serious matter than you can imagine, Mr. Halvorsen. Substantiation must be incontestable. We look forward with great interest to your next communication."

The avatar vanished as the message ended, leaving Halvorsen's desk once more empty and bare above the concealed projector. He sat staring at it in silence for several moments. *Capable of certain exceptional feats of the mind,* the woman had said. What did that mean? What did it imply? Thinking back to the confrontation, he remembered the still-baffling mental collapse he had suffered. It had been severe enough to cause his skimmer to automatically break off the clash and return home. How to explain what had happened? How to explain the inexplicable? By a *feat of the mind*? Or perhaps something equally subtle but far more reasonable had been involved. Maybe he had been hit with some kind of undetected gas projectile that had affected his skimmer's internal environment.

He was in no mood to waste time trying to diagnose incomprehensible absurdities. Attempting to make any sense out of the female avatar's outlandish warning was making his head hurt. Any effort at analytical thought found itself drowned by his escalating anger. Rising from the chair, he cursed, turned, picked up the piece of furniture, and heaved it against the far partition. It bounced once off the floor before slamming into the barrier. Molded of liquid composites, the chair did not break. It did, however, leave a sizable dent in the less robust wall.

How did they expect him to come up with that kind of information? he fumed as he donned outdoor gear and stalked down the stairs. Hadn't he shown them the damage that had been done to the quarry's skimmer? Were they blind? Didn't they look at the recording that had accompanied his message? If the target hadn't been killed outright, he surely would have died in the inevitable crash. And if he hadn't perished immediately, the icy and inhospitable mountains of northern Gestalt would surely have finished him by now.

As a matter of course, the ever-cautious Halvorsen had monitored every transport report and transmission subsequent to his limping return to Tlossene. Plentiful cargo and numerous passengers had come in and gone out of the city since then, but neither a communication nor a manifest had contained mention of anyone matching his quarry's description. It was unlikely a gypsy transporter would have misdescribed a young redheaded offworlder nearly two meters tall.

No, the intended victim was "intended" no more. He was dead, finished, properly deceased, somewhere up in the northland. How did his clients expect him to provide further proof of that? He did not know where the fatally wounded skimmer had gone down. It might have stuttered along for a considerable distance, in any direction, before finally coming down among the trees. Absent its intentionally removed tracker, there was no way to find it. Even if he somehow managed to do so, any bodies not carbonized in the consequent wreckage would by now have been dismembered and consumed by wandering, foraging fauna. The ever-hungry and grimly efficient scavengers of Gestalt would leave not even bones, ingesting them down to the last knuckle in order to obtain their marrow and calcium.

Safe on their far-distant, civilized world, these naïve Nullites wanted proof he could not supply. How was he supposed to obtain DNA from a nonexistent corpse—let alone images of a dead body sufficiently clear to provide indisputable visual evidence? Downstairs, he waited impatiently for the temperature to equalize in the building's semi-lock exit. Storming out into a light snowfall, he headed straight for Tlick's Tlounge. The occasional Tlel he encountered paid no attention to the stocky, purposeful human in their midst, but those humans who saw him coming and noticed his expression made it a point to cross the street, temporarily change direction, and avoid eye contact at all costs.

Tlick's Tlounge had no class. Certainly far less than those establishments that catered to the city's elite, its healthy middle class, or visiting travelers. It did, however, make available honest rations of often illegal stimulants without judgment or comment. It also welcomed nonhumans including Tlel, a fact that on more than one occasion had almost induced him to switch to another dive. Instead, he continued to direct his patronage to Tlick's because its prices and portions were peerless. As was ever the case with Halvorsen, money invariably trumped principles.

Feats of mind indeed. They were stringing him, these cold, colorless Null folk. Using every trick and elusion they could think of to avoid paying him his rightful due. Satisfying their request had caused his skimmer to suffer serious, expensive damage. How was he going to pay for that now, when the credit transfer he had expected and had been counting on was being unjustly withheld? Carrying out the contract had nearly cost him his life. Didn't that count for something? Did they really believe he was so stupid and incompetent that he would put his life on the line and nearly get himself killed hunting down the wrong man, or failing to do a proper job of it?

PATRIMONY

It was an unfair universe indeed, and Halvorsen hated it with a passion few could equal.

The interior of Tlick's Tlounge was dark and warm, two qualities much prized by Tlossene's human inhabitants. Though a great deal of what institutions such as Tlick's provided was available for enjoying within one's own dwelling, since the beginning of human civilization people had congregated in places where they could also indulge in the company of their own kind. This gregariousness was shared by many other sentients. While some sought out establishments that catered solely to their own kind, others were generalists who chose to patronize a specific business on the basis of ambience, price, and offerings rather than species exclusivity.

So it was that Halvorsen found himself having to compete with non-Gestaltians for a place in the crowded circular main room. Ingrained xenophobia combined with recent infuriating circumstances to raise his blood pressure. Most of those nonhumans present he merely disliked. Hatred was a stronger emotion he reserved for the native Tlel. There were no thranx among the crowd. Thranx he liked. Thranx and humans. Bugs and apes. All the rest, he thought, could head for the giant black hole at the center of the galaxy and take the fatal final protophysical plunge. He wouldn't miss a one of them.

How could the eponymous Tlick allow natives inside? Bad enough one had to encounter them on the street, but at least outside one could avoid the bulk of their stench. In an enclosed, heated establishment such as Tlick's their stink was inescapable.

The bar that was his intended destination might well have been recognizable to a human visitor from several thousand years ago, but sight of the automatons working behind it would have sent them fleeing in fear. His order arrived in chilled glass that had been formed in the shape of a pyramid. As red-orange lights danced within its transparent substance, he sucked liquid through a pressure-activated siphon and stared moodily at the crowd.

He didn't really hear the music that was being played or the soundscapes that accompanied it. Music, he felt, merely filled up synapses more profitably occupied dealing with problems. The noise added to his anger and did nothing to lighten his mood.

He drained the pyramid and had it refilled, drained it again. The potent blend of alcohol, locally manufactured deinhibitors, and imported stimulants soon had him feeling better. Much better. When the automaton that was filling his orders suggested he take a break and accompany it with a shot of moderator, he waved it off. So what if the crazies who had refused to pay up wanted more proof? He would find it or, failing that, he would find a way to fake it. If he, Norin Halvorsen, couldn't get the money due him out of a bunch of fish-faced, stiff-spined, otherworldly cranks, then he might as well pack it all in and start a small specialty store. Norin Halvorsen, shopkeeper.

Not likely, he growled softly to himself. Dead first.

What bothered him was that someone else was already dead first, and he was not receiving credit for it. The gangly youth he had pursued was properly demised. Halvorsen was sure of it. It was only a matter of returning to the scene of the confrontation and collecting the necessary corroboration. A smidgen of DNA, that was all that was needed. Surely the scavengers had left that much. After paying for his pleasure, he started for the pulsating portal that marked the distant doorway.

The performance floor was lit by effervescent luminants whose shapes morphed from those of naked men, to naked women, to unclothed creatures whose assorted pulsating extremities and orifices repulsed rather than interested him. Making a face, he pushed and shoved his way through a drifting chartreuse chanteuse. Her disembodied head continued to croon at him in some obscure Terran tongue that was equally melodic and incomprehensible long after he had walked on past. Disappointed, the light fixture recongealed rapidly behind him.

Distracted by the luminant, which if he had lingered would have tried to sell him something, he failed to see the pair of Tlel who were in the process of crossing his path. As he stumbled into them, one straightened and thrust its eyeband in his direction.

"Forgiveness is made, since yu are so clearly inhibited by ingestments." It added something deeply laryngeal in its own language.

"Go forgive yurself!" Halvorsen growled warningly as he sought to go around the couple. He added something colorful in unaccented Tlelian.

The pair looked genuinely shocked. If they had simply bagged their outrage and continued on their way, the exchange would have ended there. But being duly stunned by Halvorsen's response and sufficiently concerned that they somehow might have offended, they persisted. Both scuttled sideways to block his path.

It was surprising that the fury of emotions Halvorsen was generating was not enough to whisk them aside. "Get out of my way."

"There was no call fur that language, no call at all," the male declared straightforwardly. "We cannot demand, but can only request, an appropriate apology."

"Apology?" Very slowly, Halvorsen turned to fully confront the native. Its odor filled his olfactory sense to overflowing and threatened to leave him dizzy. "I'll give yu an . . ." Before he could finish, the Tlel did something. It was the wrong thing.

He put his hand on Halvorsen.

Or rather, dozens of soft, gripping cilia fastened themselves to the human's thick upper right arm. It was a gesture intended to simultaneously reassure and restrain, an indigenous means of physically punctuating the request for an apology. Another time, another place, Halvorsen might well have interpreted it appropriately. Doubtless he still would have responded with harsh language. Given his current mental condition and emotional state, it was not surprising that in this particular instance he reacted physically.

By Halvorsen's standards it wasn't much of a shove. But in his moderately impaired state, it was more forceful than he might otherwise have intended it to be. Furthermore his right hand, the one that pushed, instinctively assumed a fighting position: fingers drawn back, heel of the hand thrust forward. More by misfortune than intent, it struck the politely protesting Tlel at its most vulnerable point.

The thin neck snapped like a twig. Instantly the male's eyeband darkened. The flattened head flopped loosely to one side. Though Halvorsen had lived on Gestalt for some time, the female was making sounds he had never heard before. It struck him that he had just killed. Not, as was commonly the case, for something honorable such as money, but out of foolish anger. However briefly, he had lost control. Knowing that upset him far more than the actual killing.

It was an accident, pure and simple. He could claim, rightly, that the native had put its cilia on him first. He could claim, wrongly, that it had done so roughly and with hostile intent. He had only been defending himself. Looking around wildly, he fought to clear his mind. They were alone on the luminant-infested corner of floor. There did not appear to be any other witnesses.

So he killed the female.

The prim and proper Tlel-loving authorities might accept a plea of self-defense and they might not. What they were certain to do was fatally delay his attempt to collect on the debt due him from the Order of Null. He could not afford that. In addition to the repair work being done on his skimmer there were other arrears outstanding. He was not the only disagreeable self-employed entrepreneur on Gestalt. Before long, others to whom he was in hock would come looking for him. He had been counting on the Null payment to take care of that. He had been counting on the Null money to take care of a great many things.

No, he had no time to waste, especially on explaining his actions as they concerned the now deceased pair of Tlel. Hastily he cleaned the scene, wiping away or removing anything that might be traced back to him. Surely any investigation would not last long. They were only natives, after all. Stinky, smelly, gag-inducing natives. Two fewer of them made for a cleaner world.

By the time he stepped out of the transport pod halfway across the city, he felt much better about the annoying inconvenience to which he had been subjected. The authorities would conduct an investigation. Finding nothing, they would hypothesize. Only the clan to which the deceased belonged were likely to press for an extended inquest. By that time Halvorsen would be long gone from the city. He would do nothing to conceal his departure, of course. Nothing would be more certain to draw attention to himself than to try slipping out of Tlossene or offworld while a murder investigation was under way.

He could, however, reasonably be excused for making another trip to the northlands. A slow, unhurried journey. Relaxing, even. Nothing out of the ordinary for someone such as himself. He was not fleeing, exactly. Not hiding out, quite. Simply finishing a job he had begun earlier.

If he did not finish it, to the satisfaction of his clients, then the entire effort would turn out to have been for nothing. The tracking, the hunting down, the chase, the fight, and his subsequent survival— all for nothing. An unforgivable waste of time. Halvorsen had done many things in his life, but wasting time could not be counted among them. He would return with all the proof the cheery scions of Null demanded.

As he cautiously and methodically worked his way back to his residence, he did his best to stay inconspicuous. Snow that was falling more heavily helped to mask his movements. Meanwhile, in the absence of credit, he had his anger to drive him onward. He made something of a game of it, trying to decide whom he hated more: his quarry, who had been inconsiderate enough to fight back and to die somewhere chill and distant, or the otherworldly mooncalves who by refusing to pay him had set him on his present path.

He did not wrestle overmuch with the distinctions that existed between them. There was plenty of time and energy with which to hate them both, he reassured himself.

CHAPTER

12

It was possible that none of them saw the danger because of the storm. Had the expedition been intended as a hunting party, they would have found or fashioned shelter and squatted down inside to wait until the weather improved. Flinx certainly would have been amenable. Though he was in a hurry, as always, to get where he wanted to go, his present need was not so desperate that he could not have stood a delay of a day or so. He would have been content to hole up in a cave or beneath some trees until the snow stopped. Instead it was Vlashraa and the others who insisted on continuing forward with the gaitgos. He was glad they were the ones who made the decision to keep going.

He was not sure he could have dealt with the result had the consequent calamity been his fault.

They were passing through a narrow, scree-framed canyon. Riding on the back of Zlezelrenn's gaitgo and freed from the need to concentrate on the route ahead, Flinx was able to study the imposing rock walls at leisure. Despite the steepness of their slopes, they looked solid and stable enough. Clumps of thick, gnarled growths in shades ranging from cobalt to cyan clung tenaciously to ledges and other places where sufficient soil had accumulated. Periodically, he paused to wipe blowing snow from his face and eyes. Among his possessions lost in the river with the drowned skimmer were a pair of photosensitive protective goggles. How he wished for them now.

Might as well wish for a synsteak with flash-frozen dirla curls and steamed green vegetables, he told himself. Surfing the bitter cold, the blowing snow only bothered his eyes. The rest of his face was now too numb to feel much. In contrast, from the neck down he was reasonably warm, thanks to the output of the integrated thermothreads that formed part of the weave. Also, the walls of the storage compartment served to shield his lower body from the wind. In contrast with her master, Pip was not suffering from the weather. Inside his clothing and smooth against his bare skin, multiple minidrag coils lay unwound against his waist and chest. Not for the first time, Flinx envied his companion her exceptional flexibility. At least one of them was comfortable, he mused.

Somewhere in the general vicinity of his waist, need clashed with determination. It was not that hunger was gnawing at him so much as the knowledge that his body needed fuel to fight the cold. The sooner they made camp, the sooner he would be able to warm the inside of his body.

That wouldn't be for a while yet. Despite the snow, the line of mechanical walkers and their Tlel drivers were making good progress. Probably pushing themselves to get through the pass, he told himself. Once clear of the canyon walls, it would be much easier to find a campsite out of the wind.

Then he heard the rumble.

It started slowly. A steady whisper that rose swiftly to an ominous growl. Zlezelrenn heard it, too. His flattened head turned sharply to the left and tilted back, the glistening eyeband focusing on something heard more than seen. Recalling the previous attack on the column, Flinx's breath came a little faster as he fought to peer through the falling snow. This time there was no sign of a plunging, ravenous ressaugg. No exotic alpine predator threatened the line of travelers. No raiding party of maniacal GrTl-Keepers had been lying in wait to ambush their philosophical opposites. Only Nature, in her purest Gestaltian guise, had chosen to attack. He did not detect any hostile emotions behind the gathering avalanche because there were none to detect. There were only steep slopes, wind, damp, and too, too much accumulated snow on the heights directly above the column of gaitgos.

Grinding hoots of alarm rose from the line of travelers. There was no chance to escape the swelling cascade by reversing direction: the pass was too narrow and the opposite slope too steep to be negotiated in time. Flinx was slammed roughly backward and nearly out of the modified cargo compartment as a desperate Zlezelrenn demanded full speed from the vehicle's compact engine. Nothing Flinx had undergone since they had left Tleremot compared to the violent mechanical leg action and severe jolting he experienced now as Zlezelrenn and the others desperately tried to outrun the avalanche. Far from being able to ask questions or offer suggestions, it was all Flinx could do to hang on and keep from being thrown out. Pip was sufficiently startled to spread her wings and take to the chilly air, keeping pace directly above the pounding gaitgo.

Pushed ahead of the cascading snow, freezing-cold air ripped at the exposed skin of his face. He ought to have turned away from it. He did not. What froze him in place was not the ambient temperature but the sight that was roaring toward them. It looked like half a mountain was racing at incredible velocity straight toward the machine on which he was riding. The immense wall of pink snow bore down on the frantic expedition like a bloodstained flare. There was no place to run, no place to jump. No place to hide. Above him, the minidrag suddenly rose higher, ascending into the flurry of falling flakes and out of sight.

"Pip!" he shouted, trying to make himself heard above approaching thunder that shook the ground. Incongruously, he suddenly found himself thinking of Midworld—hot, steamy, and tropical, where a mountain of snow wouldn't last an hour. The thought was a refuge of wishful thinking.

It was his last one before the full force of the avalanche hit.

It felt as if a trio of that distant green world's helpful, lumbering, bearcat-like furcots slammed into him simultaneously. As the wind was knocked out of him he felt himself being ripped out of the cargo compartment, over the side of the gaitgo, and away from the fast-moving vehicle. Stunned by the unrelenting ferocity of the snow, he could only clutch and scrabble futilely at the cold pink mass that enveloped him. It was not unlike being caught and spun by a big ocean wave, except that he could breathe a little.

He had no idea how long he tumbled or how many times he was rolled. It might have been seconds or it could have been minutes. Eventually, thankfully, the avalanche slowed, then stopped, its energy spent. He and the snow came to a halt simultaneously. The deafening roar that had a moment earlier been all-pervasive vanished. It was absolutely, totally, utterly silent—as still and quiet as the vacuum of space outside the *Teacher*.

Little by little, his respiration steadied. He swallowed a couple of times. Then he called out: first Zlezelrenn's name, then Vlashraa's. There was no answer, no response. Taking in measured breaths he started to rise, only to find that he could not.

He was buried.

Slowly, breathe slowly, he told himself. Panic and fast breathing will only use up more rapidly whatever air has been trapped with you. He had never suffered from claustrophobia. That was fortunate, because the gap between his face and a solid wall of snow was only a few centimeters wide. In the complete absence of light, he had to estimate the distance using his fingers.

He had come to rest on his side. Trying to turn onto his back, he found that he could not. He was encased in a frozen loose-fitting strait-jacket, and the weight pressing down on him was oppressive. His lost service belt held several devices that he could have used to cut through or melt away the icy prison that now surrounded him. More wishful thinking. Entirely too much of that going on, he decided decisively.

Grim-visaged, he started digging. Lying on his side, he clawed with his hands at the imprisoning wall on his immediate right. Though heavy, the snowfall had not yet solidified around him. It was critical to get out before it became too compacted to work.

He did not slow or pause even though the cold began to penetrate his gloves. Occasionally, he would get rid of a tiny bit of the snow by swallowing it. Not only did this procedure open up another handful of space, but the cold meltwater helped to refresh him as well. Hot chocolate or Parian syrup would have been more welcome, he thought. What body heat leaked out through his clothing melted a little of the snow beneath him, providing slightly more room in which to work and enough space for him to slightly move his legs. As he dug with his hands, he kicked and shoved with his feet, compacting the snow under his boots.

You weren't going to waste any more calories on wishful thoughts, he admonished himself. Not even on imagining drinks that were hot, warm, thick . . .

Stop it, he told himself.

As soon as he had managed to excavate a small cavity in front of his face, neck, and chest, he altered his angle of attack and began digging upward. He knew he was tunneling in the right direction only because he could perceive a small emotional presence some-where overhead. The anxious and vital directional beacon that was Pip alternately strengthened and faded in his mind. He could envision her diving restlessly back and forth above the settled snow, able to sense the presence of her longtime companion but unable to see him. It would be better for him if she settled down on the surface directly above him and remained in one place, but he had no way of telling her to do so, and he was not about to waste any energy on pointless shouting.

He did not know how long he scraped and clawed at the imprisoning snow. Much longer than it had taken it to entomb him, anyway. Though he made good progress at first, the lack of food together with the increasing buildup of carbon dioxide inside the cavity he had excavated combined inexorably to slow him down. He was nearly vertical within the avalanche now. Thankfully, the snow overhead was now packed solid enough that it did not collapse on top of or around him. Suffocation was a bad way to die. But though he reached as high as he could to dig and pulled away more and more of the frigid roof over his head, each handful he drew downward and shoved toward his feet exposed only more of the same.

What if he was buried too deep? What if there were meters of the heavy, smothering wet stuff above his head instead of centimeters? First to go would be the ability to dig; then he would lose consciousness. If his Tlel friends were looking for him, could they even find him? The avalanche had swept him not only out of Zlezelrenn's gaitgo but also an unknown distance down and possibly across the canyon. How far did their ability to perceive another individual's *flii* extend? If they *were* searching for him, they might not even be looking in the right area.

It was getting difficult to breathe. Hard as he fought to regulate his respiration, his lungs kept shouting for more air. Soon they were demanding it, then screaming for it. Survival quickly became a race between how fast his hands could pull away the snow over his head and how long his lungs would continue to function before collapsing: a battle between desperation and suffocation.

The former was not enough to overcome the latter. Utterly exhausted, he lay trapped within a drift of unknown depth, the remaining air around him polluted by his own exhalations. Through sheer force of will he thrust his right arm upward yet one more time, made it scoop another handful of pure cold. But he didn't have the strength to pull it down and shove it beneath his feet. As the snow clasped in his cupping fingers began to melt slightly, the small rivulets tickled his fingers beneath the glove, tickled and teased and . . .

That wasn't water, he told himself. Whatever was caressing his fingers was solid and dry.

The realization was enough to summon forth his last reserves of strength. Shoving his hand down, he dumped the snow and reached up again. Once more something that was neither snow nor water ran back and forth over his questing fingers. Forcing back his head, compacting snow behind it, he looked upward. Something twisting and worm-like kept flicking in and out of a hole no bigger than his thumb.

Pip's tongue.

It took another agonizing half an hour for him to fully extricate himself from the massive snowbank. The first thing he did was allow the half-frozen Pip to snuggle down inside his jacket and inner shirt. She was shockingly cold, but he did not for a moment consider denying her the body heat her serpentine form was stealing. Lying on his back on the beautiful, lethal pink snow, he realized that the fast-moving storm was ending, trailing away to the south. He also realized something else.

He was still surrounded by the same all-encompassing silence. Deathly silence.

It was clear now why there had been no attempt to rescue him. No one had tried to dig him out because there was no one left to do so. He and Pip were the only ones alive. All the others, every one of his new Tlel friends, lay entombed in the increasingly hard-packed snow. Zlezelrenn, Vlashraa, Healer Fluadann, Hluriamm—all dead, all gone, flicked away like ants and buried by the avalanche. Because they had tried to help him.

Don't go there, he told himself firmly. Nature killed them. The avalanche. They could have perished the same way in Tleremot, or while out on a hunting expedition. It's not your fault. *It's not your fault.*

Those four words became a mantra. In spite of his exhaustion he rose and began searching. With the storm fading, any hint of color should stand out starkly amid the pale pink of the fresh snow. A shred of clothing, a suggestion of composite, a loose fitting—a limb—he ought to be able to spot it. What he chose not to acknowledge was the complete absence of emotion. Maybe, he told himself uneasily, he perceived nothing at the moment because his erratic Talent, shocked by his own ordeal, was not working. It was more encouraging to believe that than to concede that there was nothing left to perceive.

The longer he searched without finding anyone alive or sensing any other emotions, the more convinced he became that his own survival was due not to any special determination or unique ability but rather to a fortuitous bit of anatomical evolution. His gloves shielded and protected strong digits built of solid bone that were attached to equally robust arms. Working together, hands and arms were capable of steady digging. With their thin arms tipped by flexible but internally unsupported cilia, the Tlel would not be nearly as efficient at the primitive procedure. It was the ape in him that had been able to move snow and dig himself out. Differently built, differently evolved, the Tlel had been unable to emulate his disciplined tunneling.

In spite of this realization, a surge of hope rose within him when he spotted portions of a gaitgo's protective cage work sticking out of the snow. Stumbling over to it, he began shoveling recklessly with his hands, throwing snow in all directions. He had excavated halfway down to the vehicle's inclined seat when he realized that the driver had been pulled out of the torn and broken enclosure and swept downslope. Though he continued to dig in and around the machine until he had both it and a substantial area around it cleared of snow, he found no sign of its former occupant.

There was nothing more he could do. Properly searching the huge area that had been swept clean and buried by the avalanche would require either dozens of searchers or specialized rescue equipment capable of locating the bodies buried within the pink mass. He had access to neither. Even if he found someone, enough time had passed to reduce to near zero the chances of finding any of his friends alive.

He sat longer than he should have contemplating the shattered remnants of the gaitgo. Only when Pip shifted against him inside his shirt did he finally bestir himself. Having begun the journey in search of answers, he now needed to keep moving in hopes of finding something more prosaic—food and shelter.

The first revealed itself to him after a little work. The gaitgo's storage compartment had stayed intact and was still packed with the supplies that had been intended to sustain its driver. There were bottles of a thick, almost gummy, but palatable protein-rich liquid; neat squares of various dried foods; some packaged nutrients he did not recognize but crammed into a makeshift backpack anyway; and assorted nutritional supplements. Enough to keep him alive for a number of days—if they didn't turn his digestive system inside out. Some Tlel foods he could tolerate; others would be rejected by his body. While he disliked the idea of subjecting his stomach and organs south to satiation by trial and error, he had little choice.

Some of the tools he found in another compartment were simple and straightforward enough that he recognized their function immediately. There were others whose purpose he would divine by experimenting with them. Most welcome of all was the portable cooker that was included with the food. While provisions imported from offworld were usually self-heating or self-cooling, according to the nature of the item, the Tlelian victuals were not. Though at this point more than willing to sample raw any and all of the salvaged rations, he had another equally important use for the cooker. He spent the next fifteen minutes in a state of pure bliss, using the device to lightly heat first his face, then his hands, and lastly anything else he could warm without having to expose too much of it to the icy air.

Later, while Pip lay in a happy, tight, thawed coil atop the cooling cooker, Flinx sampled some of the Tlelian provisions. With the exception of something purple and puffy that momentarily made his insides feel the way it looked, everything went down easily enough. More important, all of it stayed down. Finally warmed within and without, he rose from the site of the ruined gaitgo with a renewed sense of purpose and a fresh resolve to press on. Having little choice in the way of destination he had no real option but to continue northward, his present position lying far closer to his intended target than to now distant Tleremot. It seemed that one way or another he was destined to find what he had come for or die trying.

It would hardly be the first time he had found himself in such a situation, he observed sardonically.

As he started for the near end of the canyon he entertained thoughts of someone arriving to rescue him. The *Teacher*'s shuttle, perhaps, or even his remarkable, inscrutable friends from Ulru-Ujurr. As he slogged onward through the deep snow, neither ship nor aliens magically materialized to extricate him from his present desperate situation.

It soon became evident, however, that he was no longer alone.

The feelings that began to tease the edge of his Talent were simple, basic, primitive. Barely perceptible. The kind of elementary emotions generated by something very low on the scale of sentience. Devoid of refinement or the distinctive overtones associated with higher cognizance, they were easy to interpret. Anticipation. Excitement.

Hunger.

Though he saw the first of them before he stumbled out of the pass, it was quickly evident that their habitat was not restricted to that deadly, snow-packed canyon. They followed him out and beyond as he began to make his way downslope and away from the worst of the accumulated pink drifts. Whenever he stopped to rest, they paused with him, maintaining their distance. Now that the sun was out, he had to squint to make out his new companions against the painfully reflective brightness. He could identify them, but he could not count them. There were too many.

Perhaps dozens, he decided. Maybe more than a hundred. They were unlike anything he had yet encountered on Gestalt. No avalanche-embracing ressauggs, no ominous vacuum-equipped predators these.

The largest of them stood no more than half a meter high on its two thick legs. Varying in mass from ten kilos down to one and completely covered in short, dense fur, they sported a surprising range of colors: everything from pale cerise to dark mauve. The broad panoply of hues would allow some of them to blend in perfectly with the snow, others with the varied vegetation, still others with the bare rock on which a number of them were presently standing. They contemplated him out of eyebands the thickness of his little finger. Parted jaws revealing rows of short, sharp, needle-like teeth were set in flattened skulls that reminded him of upside-down dinner plates. While different in several respects, the similarity to the skulls of his native friends could not be denied. Several members of the sprawling pack sported colorful, flexible crests. When not lying flat against the backs of their heads, these semaphored like so many miniature flags.

Though they stared at him with undisguised intent, he was not the sole focus of their attention. Some dug and kicked at the ground with their clawed feet, searching for anything edible. Others fussed and squabbled among themselves. They emitted a surprisingly wide range of sounds: from soft, almost imperceptible squeaks to an intermittent coughing that sounded like a metal file being slapped back and forth across a log. There was something about them . . .

In spite of the obvious danger they posed, he found himself smiling when he realized what had tickled his imagination. More than anything, the pack brought to mind a bevy of miniature, many-toothed, blank-faced Tlel. The superficial resemblance extended beyond the similar shape of the skulls. Though it seemed unlikely there could be any kind of close relationship between the short-statured scavengers and the much larger, infinitely more intelligent masters of Gestalt, the physical resemblance could not be denied. Convergent evolution, Flinx found himself wondering, or simply coincidence? He did not think Hluriamm, in particular, would have found the comparison flattering.

Thinking of his recently deceased companions caused the smile to fade from his face. The pack of voracious little bipeds tracking his progress did not want to help him: they wanted to gnaw his bones. Peering out from beneath her master's jacket, Pip studied them with undisguised animosity. He kept her restrained. Short of the creatures making a direct assault, it would be wasteful to have her harass the pack. If she was going to expend more venom on his behalf, they needed to wait until any such defensive exertions became unavoidable.

Would they attack? There was no misconstruing the ravenous desire their dozens of feral little minds were projecting. He had no weapons except his own hands, feet, mind, and Pip. The radiant cooker he had salvaged from the ruined gaitgo could not be turned up enough to expel harmful heat. Indeed, if he tried to modify it to do so, its integrated safety features would cause it to shut down completely. His ability to defend himself by projecting conflicting emotions on potential assailants depended on those assailants having developed a certain level of emotional complexity. Based on what he could perceive, the scavengers determinedly trailing him rated very low on that scale, even more so than other carnivores he had confronted on other worlds. Projecting onto even highly evolved animals as opposed to representatives of sentient species was always a hit-and-miss proposition. On the other hand, there were plenty of exposed rocks lying around.

Rocks. A citizen of the most technologically and scientifically advanced civilization in the history of his kind, and it was looking more and more like he was going to have to defend himself by throwing rocks.

Notwithstanding their ongoing attentions, it was possible he might not be reduced to such desperate measures. They might decide he was simply too big or too alien to take on. Or perhaps their preferences precluded predation and they would not attack, preferring to wait until he collapsed from exhaustion or lack of nourishment before trying to feed. If he needed further stimulus to keep him going, the pack's persistent presence provided it.

For now, anyway, he chose not to dwell on what might happen when night descended and fatigue forced sleep upon him. In the event any of the two-legged carnivores came close enough to take an exploratory bite out of him, Pip would drive it off and the ensuing commotion would wake him. But her venom would last only so long. She could fight off and dispatch one or two dozen of the persistent little monsters, but not more. Certainly not hundreds of them, if others were trailing the main pack or hiding among the boulders and trees.

In that event his defense was straightforward: don't sleep.

He didn't, not all that night nor into the following morning. The whistling, skittering, restless pack settled down nearby for the night and was with him when the sun rose the next day. They stood or squatted in a respectful arc behind him, looking on as he warily cooked breakfast.

"See, you eyeless little bastards!" he yelled challengingly as he waved his heated food in their direction. "I've got plenty to eat and pink snow to drink. I'm not going to die here. Why don't you go and dig up some nice smelly carcass somewhere else and leave me alone?"

Glancing up from where she was swallowing the bite-sized crumbs of food he had broken off for her, Pip eyed him gravely. In the absence of other voice-capable respondents, her master was not much given to talking out loud. It worried her. Her concern did not keep her from eating, however.

After finishing the last of the insipid but filling meal, Flinx badly wanted to relax with the cooker running and just bask in the limited heat it generated. That would be, he realized tiredly, a waste of time and fuel, neither of which he had to spare. Forcing himself to rise, he packed up the cooker and resumed the arduous downhill trek.

As if his situation was not bad enough, dark clouds began to spill over the eastern horizon, portending the onset of another storm close on the heels of its recent lethal predecessor. Fortune, which had been so kind to him on so many previous occasions on so many other worlds, seemed to have deserted him.

Too cold for Fortune here, he told himself as he shouldered his makeshift pack and strode grimly on. Too cold for me, too.

Thankfully, the new weather front brought no snow with it. Unfortunately, it hit with a solid wall of wind, hail, and sleet. He kept going, pushing himself onward, afraid that if he stopped to seek shelter and rest he might fall asleep only to be awakened as he was being torn to bits by his eager and unwelcome Gestaltian entourage. The pack was still with him, he saw through the freezing rain. Plodding along methodically in his wake, waiting for him to drop. The faint vestiges of comic ambience he had initially attached to them had long since fallen away. He no longer saw them as amusing downsized versions of the Tlel. In his mind's eye their faces and feet had faded from view, leaving behind only the gleam of claw-equipped paws and razor teeth.

Pain flared in his right ankle. Looking down he saw that one of the creatures, bolder than the rest, had darted forward to try to take a bite out of his leg. Though sharp, its numerous teeth were too short to penetrate his winter attire. The pain had come from its nipping jaws pinching his flesh. The skin had not been penetrated. Sensing the attack, Pip struggled to escape his jacket.

Her assistance was not needed. Using his other foot, he pushed the determined scavenger off his leg. Bringing his boot down hard a second time snapped the vulnerable neck. Breathing deeply while angrily wiping moisture from his face, he looked up through the driving sleet. Having witnessed the short, deadly encounter, no other member of the pack showed any inclination to sacrifice itself in an attempt to exact revenge on behalf of a deceased comrade.

There were definitely more of them now, Flinx decided. Whether drawn to the pursuit by smell, or movement, or sound he could not tell. Hundreds of them, certainly: not dozens. At what point would some critical mass, some unestimatable number be reached when they felt there were enough of them to safely rush him? Turning and lowering his face into a blast of pitiless sleet, he resumed walking.

He could not tell the number of times he thought seriously of giving up. Food was sufficient to stave off, but not entirely mitigate, the effects of exhaustion. No matter how much he ate, however, the activity could not compensate for his ongoing lack of sleep. In some ways, eating only made it worse. It would be so much easier just to lie down in the soft, inviting snow, close his eyes, and finally embrace the rest that forever seemed to elude him. For him, for Philip Lynx, rest was all too often little more than an unattainable goal, a destination devoutly to be wished for but never to be reached.

Why was he bothering? Why did he continue to push himself, to voluntarily submit to the repetitive torment of responsibility? Civilization could look after itself without him, the menace posed by the Great Evil notwithstanding. What was worth such continued suffering? Even the Tlel, whom he had initially thought endlessly cheerful, helpful, and at peace with the cold world around them, engaged in murderous internecine conflict. GrTl-Keepers and NaTl-Seekers slaughtered one another—over sociophilosophical differences, of all things. Yet another in a too-long list of examples of sentience wasted on those whose social maturity had failed to keep pace with their achievements in technology.

The sleet had let up but the wind was still blowing hard. When one boot slid sideways on a rock buried in the snow, he stumbled and dropped to one knee. Reading his resignation, an alarmed Pip struggled to free herself from his jacket. As soon as he went down a pair of scavengers, eyebands glistening in expectation, sprinted forward and started gnawing hungrily at his boots. Sensing the end, the rest of the swollen pack crept steadily forward, holding back only to see if these two most aggressive of their number met the same fate as the solitary individual who had attacked earlier.

Flinx's head had started pounding. It looked as if his unremitting headaches would not even let him die in peace. He started to rise from the one knee, failed in the effort, and fell forward. Behind him a harsh, collective alien ululation rose from the pack as it surged forward in its hundreds. Trapped within her master's jacket, a pinioned Pip fought frantically to free herself.

Flinx felt a sudden surge of heat. It came not from the crush of dozens of energized scavengers finally swarming over him, nor from an inadvertently activated cooker, but from a new source. It lanced one, two, four of the closely clustered carnivores, searing flesh and fur. He was barely conscious enough to recognize the coarse stink of smoldering tissue.

The heat had passed over him. It was followed by a second burst. This was enough to send the rest of the pack fleeing in panic, scrambling and scrabbling over one another in their frantic haste to find cover among trees, rocks, and snow.

A shape appeared in front of him: a large, irregular, looming shadow. Standing straight and tall, leveling an unusual weapon in both gloved hands, it defied the wind as audaciously as it had the threat posed by the now scattered pack. His conscious fading, Flinx heard a voice. It was as forthright and snide as that of a retired professor.

"Anyone stupid enough to be out in this country in this weather by themselves deserves to be left here. On the chance that it wasn't planned, and against my better judgment, I suppose I'm obligated to save your life."

CHAPTER

13

Taking pity on him, a fickle Fate (if not Fortune) decreed that his head should cease throbbing—for a while, at least. When Flinx finally awoke, the debilitating pain had disappeared. So, too, had the wind, the sleet, the cold, and—it was immediately apparent—the pack of scavengers that had been on the verge of scouring the meat from his bones. Two other particulars struck him simultaneously. First, the familiar weight of a tightly wound serpentine coil asleep on his bare chest, indicating that Pip had survived with him. Second, the realization that he was, for the first time in a great many days, actually warm.

Continuously adjusting itself to his stabilizing body temperature, the physiosensitive blanket beneath which he was presently reclining backed off another fraction of a degree. His entire body was numb—but for a change it was just from fatigue, not from cold. Blinking once, he turned slightly to his left on the padded couch to examine his unexpected but welcome new environs. His muscles protested even this modest exertion.

The room was larger than it needed to be. Taking the shape of a gently curving dome reflecting unmistakable Tlelian influences, the ceiling was high enough to accommodate the tallest visitor. Lined with irregularly shaped gray and green tiles, its means of support was cunningly concealed. Some of the tiles had been randomly silvered so that they shimmered like mother-of-pearl. Indirect light from hidden sources enlivened these with sparkle. Sealed portals off to left and right doubtless led to other rooms.

Directly across from where he was lying, a crackling blaze filled a traditional triangular Tlel stone fireplace. Though its function was likely more decorative than necessary, he welcomed the supplementary heat. Everything else in the room shouted contemporary technology. The presence of the wood fire was more a testament to the owner's aesthetic tastes than to any need.

Replication artwork of a high order decorating the walls indicated that he was in the presence of someone who possessed a measurable degree of cultural sophistication as well as good taste. In addition to copies of famous works drawn from the history of human creativity there were also a few striking Tlel originals. A pair of large, comfortable chairs were angled toward the fireplace, extending an invitation to contemplate the wood fire blaze that, in its primitive fashion, constituted a work of art in itself.

As he let his attention skim over his surroundings, Flinx recalled the circumstances that had brought him to this place. Most recently, he remembered little beyond being picked up off the snow, carried a short distance, and unceremoniously dumped onto some form of transportation. This had been followed by an indeterminate period of unexpectedly smooth riding. The steady, gentle vibration had combined with his advanced state of fatigue to put him almost instantly to sleep. How long he had reposed in that state of blissful insensibility he did not know. Now fully awake and aware once more, he was immediately cognizant of more than just his physical surroundings.

First and foremost, he sensed the presence of another sentient. Reaching out, Flinx probed for emotions. He touched on them without difficulty or opposition. At present they were diverse and nonspecific. What was more important was that they were indisputably human.

Try as he might, he could not keep his heart from racing as a figure appeared in the right-hand doorway and entered the room. He was just as Rosso Eustabe had described him: tall, though not as tall as Flinx, with dark eyes to match his close-cropped black hair. Well-built beneath his pale yellow, loose-fitting, one-piece winter garb. Skin almost the same shade of olive as Flinx's own, though it was impossible to tell if the color was natural or the result of cosmetic enhancement. A neatly trimmed white spade beard ran from beneath his nose to end in a point below his chin. Eustabe hadn't mentioned a beard. Possibly an oversight on his informant's part, or perhaps a recent addition.

It would be more than just slightly ironic, Flinx reflected as he stared, if the man who had rescued him turned out to be his own father.

Walking over to the fire, the man used a small manipulator to adjust the position of several blazing logs. Fire-weakened wood crumbled in on itself, allowing a shower of sparks to escape up the flue. Primitive sight, primitive sound. Turning, the man noticed Flinx gazing back at him. Without hesitation the older man reached down, picked a pistol up off a table that was blocked from Flinx's view by one of the chairs, and calmly aimed its business end at the lanky figure occupying the couch.

Looking to her master for direction as she sensed a surge in emotion, Pip barely lifted her head. If Flinx's feelings were not roiled, there was no reason for her to be alarmed. Closing her eyes, she resumed her nap.

Her perception was not mistaken. Flinx saw no cause for alarm. If the man wanted to shoot him, he could easily have done so when Flinx lay semi-conscious at his feet somewhere out in the snow. Nor did his host's emotions betray any hint of overt hostility or aggression. There was wariness, yes, but that was perfectly understandable. He knew nothing of the lean and unblinking visitor lying on the couch. Had their situations been reversed, Flinx would have been equally cautious, though he would not have been so quick to bring a gun into the equation.

Of course, he had Pip.

Though the man's voice was genial enough when he finally spoke, his tone was clipped, and the gun constituted a rather severe form of punctuation. "What are you gaping at? Who are you, what are you doing out here alone, and what do you want?"

"I wasn't alone." Flinx chose to answer the easiest part of the question first. "I was with friends. Tlel friends. I was traveling with them."

Behind the man, the blaze in the fireplace popped noisily. The muzzle of the pistol did not waver. "I didn't see any Tlel."

Flinx swallowed. "Avalanche got them all. In the canyon. My friends, their gaitgos, nearly all the supplies, everything. They were— good people."

His host grunted softly. "The Tlel are like any other sentient species. Some good, some bad. I'll grant that on balance they seem happier than most. Which is something, when you consider how in- hospitable is a good chunk of their home planet. Well as they've adapted, Commonwealth membership has still been a godsend to them. Right from first contact they were smart enough to recognize the potential benefits, accept them, and run with them." He gestured meaningfully with the pistol. "Decent little civilization they've built up here."

"I've seen that they're very welcoming of settlers, which is un- usual," Flinx commented.

"Yes. Most intelligent species dislike the idea of having other sentients living permanently among them. Not the Tlel. In that, they're a lot like the thranx."

While the small talk was stimulating, there was one thing Flinx felt he could not put off any longer. "Thank you for saving my life."

"Somebody needed to. *You* were doing a pretty piss-poor job of it." The older man nodded to himself. "Though if you were traveling with Tlel it explains how you made it as far as the pass. I'm sorry about your friends. Lucky for you I was out checking traps."

"Traps?" Flinx blinked. Pip opened her eyes.

"The Tlel aren't the only sentients on this world who take hunting seriously. Call me atavistic, but there's something soul-satisfying about bending Nature to one's purpose."

Flinx wondered what lay behind those black eyes besides cool self-control. "Bending—or twisting?"

His host frowned. "There's a difference?" When Flinx did not respond, the man continued. "Anyway, once I put a dozen or so kerveks out of their squabbling misery the rest scattered quickly enough. I dumped you on the crawler and brought you back here." With his free hand he indicated the dozing minidrag. "Your pet there gave me a bit of a start when it peeked out from under your shirt. Since it ignored me, I ignored it, and we got along fine for the remainder of the trip back."

Reaching down, Flinx stroked his pet's iridescent spine. Folded against her sides, her wings quivered slightly. "Her name's Pip. She sensed you meant me no harm."

"I suppose she must have." Flinx's host did not realize that his young guest was being literal. "How are you feeling? You can't stay here, of course. I place quite a high value on my privacy."

"Sorry to have intruded." Where another might have been offended, Flinx kept his tone carefully neutral. "I feel okay. Better than I expected to after half freezing to death." Reaching up, he rubbed the back of his neck.

"Better than you have any right to. I pumped two ampoules of Refreshain into your gut. That should keep your system going until this evening, by which time the transport I've arranged for you is due to arrive and take you away. Since I don't know where you came from or where you'd prefer to go, I took the liberty of designating Tlossene as a destination. From there you can arrange transportation to any point on the planet." His expression did not vary. "You can pay? If not, the government has an emergency fund that can be tapped for evacuating stranded backcountry travelers." Reaching down, he picked up a tumbler from the same concealed table as the gun and swallowed some of the metallic container's contents.

"You've only answered a third of my question."

Pulling aside the blanket, Flinx sat up and swung his legs off the side of the couch. As he met the other man's gaze Flinx tried to fathom what, if anything, was going on behind those ebon pupils. All his life he'd tried to imagine the possibilities of the moment that now loomed immediately before him: the ramifications, the import, the potential emotional resonance. Strangely disconnected, he felt as if he should be feeling something else, something more. Hope, joy, anger, relief, sadness, fear, desperation. Love.

Instead, he felt nothing beyond an abiding hope. That was, he decided, eminently reasonable and rational. The individual standing before him might be nothing more than just another émigré artist; timidly introverted at best, violently antisocial at worst. While Flinx realized that his emotions might jump the gun to make certain assumptions, the rational part of his mind would not. Could not. The time for resolving the two was—now.

"My name is . . ." Astonishing himself, he hesitated briefly. ". . . Flinx."

Brows drew together as the other man frowned at him. "*Flinx*? Just one name? That's unusual."

Flinx nodded. "You ought to know—Anayabi."

As expected, this revelation sparked the first stir of deeper emotion within his host. "I thought there must be something awkward involved to motivate someone like yourself to travel out this way. Can we now assume that at least a part of your journey involved coming to see me?"

"Not a part," Flinx corrected him. "All of it."

The hand holding the gun steadied. "How do you know my name, where I live? What do you want with me, Mr. Flinx?"

"Not *Mr.* Just Flinx. If anyone should be calling someone mister, it's me."

His host was growing visibly impatient. "You're not making sense. I don't much care for people who are deliberately mysterious."

"I'm not trying to be mysterious." Flinx took a deep breath. "I'm looking for my father. Without going into a lot of detail right away, I have reason to believe you—might be him."

Anayabi was one of those rare individuals who always seem to be ready for anything—but it was obvious he was not ready for that. His expression betrayed his surprise and confusion as clearly as did his emotions. After a long, incredulous pause, he finally managed to articulate a reply.

"You lay out in the cold too long. You can only hope the damage isn't permanent."

"If it is," Flinx replied slowly, "maybe you can find a way to fix me. To *improve* me."

Still the other man refused to bite. Or maybe, Flinx mused, the bait he had extended had no attraction for his host. Having come this far at the sacrifice of time, money, and a sorrowfully large number of now deceased friends, he was not about to give up meekly.

"My real name is Philip Lynx. I am an unmindwiped, unreconstructed, surviving experiment of the outlawed, edicted eugenics association that called itself the Meliorare Society. One of at least two known such survivors. My mother was a Terran lynx named Ruud Anasage. My father—my father is known to me only as the sperm donor. I've been looking for him, trying to discover his identity, for a very long time. Research leads me to believe that you could possibly be him. Research, and the dying testimony of citizen Shyvil Theodakris of Visaria. Whose real name, whose Meliorare name, was Theon al-bar Cocarol."

Visually, Anayabi's expression did not change. Verbally, he responded straightaway with, "All of that means nothing to me."

Emotionally—emotionally, he convulsed. It was as potent a conflicted upwelling of sentiments as Flinx had ever perceived. Beyond subterfuge now, he challenged the other man's denial head-on.

"You're lying." Having slithered down to his lap, Pip was now wide awake and alert, her attention focused exclusively on the man holding the pistol.

Anayabi let out a snort of disgust. "I save your life, and ten minutes after regaining consciousness you're calling me a liar." He made a show of checking a chronometer. "The sooner that transport gets here and you're gone, the better I'll like it. And you can be sure I'll think twice about picking up the next fool I find stumbling around in this country."

Having confessed, however concisely, his personal history, Flinx saw no reason to hold back now. His whole life had been pointed toward, had been leading up to, this confrontation.

"I know that you're lying because I can read your emotions. That's my Talent. Experiment Twelve-A's Talent. I'm an Adept."

A moment in time passed during which a great deal was said even though nothing was spoken. After, Anayabi did not so much crack as subside. When his lips finally parted again, the voice that emerged was altered from what had gone before. It was still firm, still resolute, but at the same time subdued. The same held true for his emotions. Voice and feelings and posture pooled to put Flinx in mind of a prize-fighter who had taken one too many punches, was barely able to stand within the fighting cube, and could do nothing more except wait for the final blow to land.

"Theon Cocarol." Anayabi was slowly shaking his head. "Hadn't thought of him in—years. Many years." From staring into the distance, he now looked up and across at his guest, seeing him in an entirely new light. "Dead, you say?"

Flinx nodded. There was nothing to be gained and possibly much to be lost by going into detail concerning the means and manner of the other surviving Meliorare's recent passing. "He told me that he knew where my father was. *Gestalt,* he said. That was all the information on the matter I managed to get out of him before he died. So I came here, did my best to initiate a search based on some preconstructed paradigms, and interviewed a lot of potential candidates. Too many, in retrospect." He sat a little straighter on the couch. "Then you came to my notice."

He expected the inquisitive Anayabi to inquire how that singular revelation eventuated. Instead his host eyed him with fresh curiosity. "You really are who you claim to be, aren't you?" Flinx nodded, just once. "Then you're not a peaceforcer or other government or Church agent, here to arrest me? You really are just on some kind of insane quest to try to find your paternal parent?"

Flinx replied softly, "Insanity has nothing to do with it. If you could read my emotions the way I can read yours, you wouldn't be asking that question or couching it in such terms."

Sitting down in and swinging around on one of the large chairs, Anayabi rested the pistol on his right thigh. For a long time he just sat staring at the tall young man seated across the room from him. Occasionally, he would shake his head and an odd expression would momentarily transform his features. Emotional resonance aside, Flinx was unable to tell if this was a grin or a grimace. Anayabi's corresponding feelings likewise remained ambiguous.

"Maybe I can't read your emotions, Twelve-A, but I can see your solemnity and I can sense your desperation. It's all true, then. You knew Theon. You are familiar with a certain significant amount of your personal history. You know about the Society. And you're sharp enough and smart enough to have found me." He shook his head more strongly. "I didn't think anyone would ever find me here, in the northlands of an unimportant incorporated world like Gestalt."

"I wouldn't have either," Flinx told him, "if not for Cocarol."

The placidness went out of Anayabi's voice, to be replaced by the steel Flinx had encountered earlier. His host's voice dropped to a growl. "Theon always was one to favor the grand gesture. The old bastard could have done me a favor by keeping his dying mouth shut."

"Maybe he wanted you to see that one of your experiments had survived the Commonwealth crackdown."

"Maybe, maybe . . . ," Anayabi muttered. "So you're an empath—you can read emotions. I can't recall what the specific objectives were for the Twelve line. It was all so long ago . . ."

"Not so very long." Flinx's voice was taut, barely controlled. "Only twenty-seven years."

"Twenty-seven years," Anayabi echoed more calmly. "An empathic Adept. What do you know." His emotions shifted in a way Flinx did not like. "There should be more. Or at least something else. Tell me, of what else are you capable?"

"Nothing, insofar as I know," Flinx lied. He lied without hesitation and without thinking. It was easy. He'd been doing it ever since he was old enough to realize that he was different. "Answer my question. *I have to know. Are* you my father, Anayabi of the Meliorares?"

The man who years ago had fled to out-of-the-way Gestalt in order to avoid the relentless hounding of Commonwealth justice sat pondering silently. When he finally deigned to reply, his words were accompanied by a slight nod.

"Yes, Philip Lynx. Twelve-A. I am your father."

Flinx's heart missed a beat, his thoughts going momentarily and uncharacteristically blank. Before he could respond, Anayabi continued.

"One of them, that is. In a manner of speaking. After a fashion of science."

From unguarded elation, Flinx was plunged into a vortex of bewilderment. "I—what are you trying to say?"

Anayabi then did perhaps the worst possible thing he could have done at that moment and under those emotionally charged circumstances.

He laughed.

Flinx thought his head was going to explode. Combining a suddenly escalating headache with the clashing emotions that were raging inside him threatened to send him spinning back into unconsciousness. With as great an effort of will as he had ever exerted, he somehow forced himself to remain composed and in control.

"Please." A universe of multiple meaning underscored that one word. "Explain yourself."

"Oh, very well." Anayabi was at ease now. Finally convinced he was not about to be arrested and sent off for mindwiping, he had reverted to his natural authoritarian self. "You might as well know the truth about yourself. Everyone deserves to know the truth about themselves, I suppose. Even experiments that ought not to have survived this long." Virtually merry, his improving mind-set contrasted starkly with Flinx's deepening somberness.

"What else did dear departed Theon tell you about your origins, Twelve-A?"

Despondent and confused, Flinx struggled to recall. "Very little. He—wasn't talking much at the time. No, wait—I do remember something else. He said—he said that I was *not the product of a natural union.* I already knew that, of course, since I'd previously learned that my mother was impregnated via artificial means."

"Artificial means." Anayabi chuckled, shaking his head. "Description without being descriptive. I'm afraid that all these years you've spent searching for your 'father,' you've been wandering aimlessly on a bit of a wild-goose chase, Philip Lynx."

Something horrible was growing in the pit of Flinx's stomach. The gathering discomfort threatened to match the throbbing that felt like it was going to blow the top off his skull. On his lap, a suddenly apprehensive Pip twisted around to look up at him. She could not read the expression on his face, but she could perceive his emotions as clearly and sharply as she could detect dead meat at twenty meters.

"Maybe," Flinx said abruptly, "we should stop for a little while."

"Stop?" Anayabi eyed him in mock astonishment. "Why would

you want to stop now, when you're so close to obtaining the truth that you say you've spent such a long time seeking?" Still holding on to the pistol that was resting on his thigh, he leaned toward his newly uncertain, uneasy guest.

"When I say that I am 'one' of your fathers, what I am really saying to you is that you *have* no father. You never did. Not in the traditional patrilineal sense."

Flinx was barely breathing. Head pounding, he desperately wished for the medicine kit that was part of the service belt he always wore. Kit and belt, hope and past, and maybe a great deal more lay drowned together somewhere in a Gestaltian river far to the south.

"Even, even if the name was lost," he stammered, "the identity of the man who donated the germane sperm should be traceable through—"

Clutching the pistol, Anayabi stood up abruptly. "You're not *listening* to me, Twelve-A. *Pay attention.* That's a good little experiment." He smiled as a desolated Flinx stared starkly back at him. The older man's widening smile was far from what anyone would have considered jovial. There was, truth be told, just a faint hint of a smirk about it. It was one more indication, however minor and seemingly insignificant, that the outlawing of the Meliorare Society had not been done in an arbitrary manner but for good and sound and well-researched reasons.

"There was no sperm donor, Twelve-A. Your DNA was mixed in the proverbial vat. Your chromosomes were predesigned in shell and sybfile. You were not conceived: you were sculpted. A strand of protein here, a fragment of nucleic acid there." His voice grew slightly distant, remembering fondly. "We picked and chose and cut and spliced. The most difficult gengineering work ever attempted; the finest ever achieved. You were pasted together, Twelve-A. Like all the others. Some of it worked. Some—did not." His attention returned fully to the present. "You weren't *born,* Philip Lynx. You were *made.*"

Somehow Flinx choked out a response, instead of on it. "To what purpose? To what end?"

Anayabi gestured meaningfully with his free hand. "Isn't it obvious? You yourself already used the term *improve*. Humankind has come a long way since our first ancestors figured out it was more efficacious to throw rocks at their enemies instead of hiding behind them. Time passed, civilization—of a sort—grew. Thousands of years passed. Hundreds of years ago we finally took our first steps out of the nursery and off the mother world. Since then we have accomplished many things, some great, others less admirable. We, along with the thranx, have made the Commonwealth. Yet we still all too often fight and argue among ourselves, act irrationally, neglect our true potential."

No longer the reclusive retiree, Anayabi was now every millimeter the true believer, Flinx saw. The face and voice of the gently inquisitive hermit had been replaced by that of the dedicated fanatic.

"Humankind has always been impatient." Having fully warmed to his polemic, the older man continued. "Those of us who worked as Meliorares were merely a little more impatient than the rest. Tired of waiting for our species to achieve its full potential, we determined to do our best to bring it about. In so doing we dedicated ourselves not just to reach for the next rung of the evolutionary ladder, but to skip as many rungs as possible. We strove to push human gengineering to the next level."

"Without the consent of the gengineered." Flinx's voice was flat.

Unperturbed, Anayabi shrugged diffidently. "It is difficult to consult with an embryo. Yes, there were some failures along the way. It is ever so with science. With each line we strove to focus on a new ability, a new dimension of human consciousness."

"I've scanned the Society's history. Some of your 'failures' died prematurely. Some of them died horribly. Some were not that lucky."

"It was not intentional," Anayabi assured him. "Steps forward are invariably accompanied by steps back. We did everything we could to minimize the discomfort of those lines that did not develop as intended."

"Verily your kindness knew no bounds," Flinx replied acidly.

The other man's expression darkened. "Great leaps in practical, as opposed to theoretical, science are rarely made without sacrifice."

"A noble proposition on the part of those who never have to make the sacrifices." Discouraged, disenchanted, and disheartened beyond measure, Flinx had had just about enough of this smug survivor. "At least I had a mother."

Anayabi eyed the tall young man pityingly. "Twelve-A, Twelve-A—you listen but you do not hear. If you are no more perceptive than this, then despite your claimed Talent you are beyond doubt only one more in an unfortunately long line of failed experiments. I have told you, you were produced. From head to toe, you are a *manufacture*. The lynx-caste ex-courtesan Anasage whom you persist in referring to as your 'mother' was only one of many hired to carry finished product to term. Biological carriers are more reliable than synthetic wombs. Not to mention cheaper." Leaning forward once more, he all but hissed his next words.

"*Listen to me,* Twelve-A. Philip Lynx. There was no sperm donor. There was no egg donor. You are a broth, a brew, an infusement and distillation of thousands of different strands of DNA carefully selected by brilliant if misunderstood men and women, vetted by software and machine, melded together in the simulacrum of a fertilized human egg that was then implanted in a suitable vessel and allowed to mature to term."

Escalating headache ignored, everything else forgotten, a trembling Flinx swallowed hard one more time. His throat was as dry as the time he had been marooned on the deserts of Pyrassis, as dry as when he had gone gem hunting on Moth with an old man by the name of Knigta Yakus.

"Then," he finally managed to whisper, "I'm not human?"

The older man's humorless laugh filled the room. Behind him

the wood fire, forgotten and unattended, was beginning to subside. "Oh, you're human enough, Twelve-A. If anything, you're more human than human. That was our intent, remember. To enhance, not to change. To revise and update, not begin anew. We did not wish to break with the human genetic code. Merely, as with any reliable machine, to give it a tune-up. Working without precedent and in the absence of a suitable manual, we were forced to fall back on trial and error."

He's not looking at me, Flinx realized. He's studying me.

"Stop it," he snapped icily. "Stop it right now."

"Stop what?" Anayabi's emotions belied his innocence. "You have no idea how rewarding your unexpected appearance is for an old man. I am gratified merely to see you alive, Twelve-A. Alive and—"

Flinx could not keep himself from finishing the other man's sentence. "Not warped? Not misshapen? Not some poor, miserable, crawling thing that needs to be put out of its misery?" Now it was his turn, as he stroked and soothed and restrained the increasingly restless Pip, to lean forward. "There are all kinds of distortions, old man."

Though he tried to sustain his anger, he could no more do so than he could continue to deny to himself the truth of the relentless Anayabi's statements. He was too stunned to marshal an appropriate response. What more could he say, what else could he do? The sense of loss, the emotional hollow that had materialized inside him, was overwhelming and threatened to drown him with its import.

After all these years, after more than a decade of desperate, hopeful searching, not only had he not found his father—he had lost a mother.

I am nothing, he thought.

No, that wasn't quite true. He was certainly something. Some *thing*. A human thing, Anayabi had insisted. Had insisted with a hint of an emotional as well as visual smirk. What kind of human-thing not even the last of the Meliorares was able to say. Anayabi's next words indicated that he very much wanted to know, however.

"When the representatives of the sanctimonious United Church combined with ignorant Commonwealth authorities to smash and scatter the Society, a number of incomplete experiments were dispersed throughout the Arm. Preoccupied with saving ourselves from mindwipe, those of us who survived the initial storm and its subsequent outrages quickly lost touch with our test subjects. In nearly every instance we never learned which of these were successes or failures. Tell me, Twelve-A—which are you? Without access to long-destroyed records, I cannot correlate generalized hopes with specific manipulations. Besides reading emotions what else, if anything, can you *do*?"

So earnest was the query, so genuine the request, that for a moment Flinx almost answered honestly. He caught himself in time. The last thing this cavalier toymaker deserved was any kind of insight into the life and nature of one of his unhappy, unwilling subjects. A new kind of calm settled over Flinx.

"Nothing," he replied evenly. "Other than perceiving the emotions of others, I can't do anything. Except, apparently, track down sinister dead ends like yourself."

"Nothing at all? I have already decided from talking with you that your intelligence level is nothing remarkable." Anayabi delivered this observation as coolly as if the subject of the slight were not sitting directly across from him. "No unusual abilities, no great physical strength, no exceptional enhancement of the other senses?"

"No," Flinx told him categorically. "Nothing. Except for being cursed by the need to track down the truth about my origins, I'm— ordinary."

"I see. *Ordinary.* An *ordinary* empathetic telepath." Anayabi nodded at some private thought. "I am afraid, Twelve-A, that in the lexicon of the Society *ordinary,* when measured against the expectations of the Society and even if combined with what is after all not such a useful ability—a talent for reading emotions—must be placed in the same category as failure. Besides which, you now know not only where I live but also who I am." The muzzle of the pistol started to rise slightly. "This has been fascinating and enlightening. Meeting you, reminiscing—but on balance and despite the brief burst of pleasure it has given me, it would appear that I should have left you in the snow."

Preternaturally sensitive to such things, Pip perceived the stark shift in the other man's emotional balance an instant before Flinx did. Unfurling her wings, slitted eyes focused unblinkingly on the other man, she rose from her master's lap.

Possibly she was getting old. Despite his long association with her, Flinx had no idea how old she was and therefore had no idea how long she had to live. For self-evident reasons, records on lethally venomous Alaspinian minidrags were notoriously incomplete. Possibly Anayabi was just lucky. The reason was immaterial.

His pistol blew a hole in her left wing. He could not possibly have focused so quickly on and aimed so accurately at the pink-and-blue blur. One lucky shot in a lifetime of close association with Flinx finally brought her down. Spiraling awkwardly downward, she crashed to the floor and lay there, writhing and coiling in pain. A stunned Flinx found he could only stare.

"It was going to attack me," a defensive Anayabi stated with confidence. "I have this feeling it will try to do so again. As always, first things first . . ." Training the pistol on the helpless flying snake, he took careful aim.

"No!" Rising from the couch, Flinx unhesitatingly threw himself between the weapon and the animal with whom he had shared an unbreakable empathetic bond since childhood. It was not the first time in such a dire situation that he had acted without thinking.

It was not the first time in such a dire situation that something powerful and inexplicable overwhelmed him and consciousness fled.

CHAPTER

14

When light and awareness began to return in equal measure, Flinx found that he was not entirely mystified at what had happened. Because the same thing had happened to him several times before. Most recently on Visaria when an alien assassin had tried to kill him, and again on a previous occasion when the offending party had been comprised of human executioners. While he had confessed to Anayabi his abilities as an empathetic telepath, he had neglected to mention the singular and still-unknown attribute that had sporadically stepped in to defend him whenever he was on the verge of being killed. His impulsive and instinctive attempt to protect Pip had placed him in that position yet again, and had once more caused the mysterious mechanism to engage.

He wondered if Anayabi had survived long enough to be enlightened.

Pip was injured, but alive. She lay coiled on the floor, licking her perforated wing. Picking her up carefully, Flinx cradled her in his left arm while stroking her gently with his other hand and whispering soothing words. While comforting her, he studied the damage that had been done to the room. Though he had a good idea what had happened, he still had no clearer idea how he managed to wreak such havoc. As it had on all previous such occasions, the unidentified, innate mechanism that involuntarily engaged to protect his life had concurrently rendered him unconscious.

A perfectly round hole some two meters in diameter had appeared in the rear wall, about a meter above the floor and halfway between the still-smoldering fireplace and another doorway. Approaching the gap, he saw that another chamber lay beyond the one in which he was standing. Conspicuous in the next room's far wall was a second hole. It was a perfect match to the one through which he was staring. Beyond it, another room and still another corresponding hole. Seen through this third consecutive circular gap, rocky landscape was visible. The faint rush of distant wind could be heard over the crackle of the fireplace. If his shadowy defensive ability had punched a hole in the weather, that was not visible.

Neither was Anayabi. There was no sign of the ex-Meliorare. That is, there was not if one discounted the revealing discolorations that stained the edges of the first hole. These sprayed outward from the still-crumbling periphery in a faint ray-like pattern, like a mottled sunburst. Some of the stains were pale white; others, a very faint red in hue. The explosive medium was comprised of bone and blood that had been powdered and vaporized.

Unaccountably, Flinx felt sick to his stomach. Having in his relatively short life already encountered far too much untidy death, he was no stranger to the ghastly fascia of gore. He had unavoidably been responsible for a portion of it himself. Then why should this one particular incident affect him so?

After all, Anayabi was not his biological father. In detailing Flinx's origins, the Meliorare gengineer had callously admitted as much. He was no more Flinx's father than Theon al-bar Cocarol had been. Their "relationship" to him had been that of manufacturers to a

product, of scientists to an experiment. So what if they were the closest things Flinx would ever know to a paternal parent?

How many men, he mused mordantly, got to kill their father
twice over?

The two Meliorares were not all that his visit to Visaria and now
Gestalt had dispatched. Following Anayabi's harsh and uncompromising explication, something else inside Flinx had died. Whereas
previously he had only felt terribly, dreadfully alienated, there was
now a vast emptiness within him, as if he had gone all hollow inside.
You were made, the late, unlamented Anayabi had told him. *You are a
manufacture.*

A manufacture. A human manufacture. Wasn't that a contradiction in terms? But then, he told himself, what was *Homo sapiens*
stripped of pretension and self-importance if not an organic machine? In the end, was it the process of manufacture that was important, or the product? Certainly the Meliorares had subscribed to the
latter belief. If he believed similarly, was he the same as they? Was
there in the final analysis anything to differentiate him from his cold,
calculating progenitors?

Ethics, perhaps. Morals. A sense of purpose. The last, he knew,
was in imminent danger of slipping away. Concern for others, certainly. He was sure that still held true because he spent the next hour
searching the house for medical supplies with which to treat Pip's injured wing. Careful scrutiny with the handheld scanner he found indicated that the damage was confined mostly to membrane. Given
time and care, it should heal good as new. Pip would soar again.
Would he?

A check of a chronometer showed that several hours remained
until evening. That was when the transportation Anayabi had earlier
unwittingly engaged to take his then as-yet-unidentified house guest
back to Tlossene was due to arrive. Flinx would go out to meet the
transporter as soon as it appeared. It would be more circumspect to

do that than to allow potentially querulous visitors a look at the building's violently altered interior.

While he was treating Pip, yet another unwelcome thought presented itself. Were the Meliorares the only ones who knew the truth of his origins? Could there be others who had been monitoring his progress, his life, his activities, all along? Had the Eint Truzenzuzex and Bran Tse-Mallory really just casually made his acquaintance in Drallar one day all those many years ago? For a moment, feverish suspicion and acute paranoia threatened to overwhelm all other thoughts.

Then his reflections turned to Mother Mastiff. There had been no guile in that gruff old woman, he was certain. If any of the deeply held sentiment she felt toward him was made up, he would long since have perceived its speciousness.

Take one step at a time, she had often told him, wagging a finger warningly in his face as she did so. *Even if it's a small step.*

Very well. That was what he would do. Care for Pip, make his way back to Tlossene, board his shuttle, and rejoin the *Teacher.* Once more back in familiar, secure surroundings, he could then decide how to proceed. With the task Tse-Mallory and Tru had placed on him. With his life. If he decided the first was worth completing. If he decided the second was worth pursuing.

Lost within himself and just plain lost, he also lost track of the time. It seemed that mere minutes had passed since he had finished treating Pip when he heard the sound of the approaching transport. Setting and sealing her wounded wing as best he could, he wrapped her loosely in the same blanket that had warmed him earlier and carried her outside.

While he waited in the open alcove that fronted the residence, isolated flakes of pink snow swirled around him, perishing against the warmth of his face or lingering longer on his clothes. What thoughts he succeeding in mustering were focused elsewhere, on matters and people and worlds far from Gestalt. He had to decide whether to return to deal with them and if so, what questions to ask, what challenges to put forward. He had to decide not only how much he was willing to extend himself to help others survive, but also himself. It was going to be harder than ever to implement such tasks. Coming to Gestalt in hopes of expanding his own reality, he had been left instead with an empty shell.

The approaching skimmer did not bother to circle. Its confident pilot brought it down straight and true onto the small landing pad that fronted a large, nearby storage structure. Blinking away blowing snow, Flinx started jogging toward it, holding a squirming Pip as close to his chest as he could without risking further damage to her wounded wing. As he drew near, he automatically reached out with his Talent to perform a cursory scan of the craft's interior. There was only the one male pilot, whose emotions were controlled, internally focused, and nonhostile.

As soon as the side portal opened he hurried on board, not wanting to delay, not wanting to give the pilot time to inquire as to the whereabouts of the person who had hired him. Once engaged in conversation, Flinx was sure he could talk his way around that absence. Like anyone operating in Gestalt's wild and undisciplined backcountry, the skimmer's pilot would be interested first and foremost in receiving payment for his services. As long as this was forthcoming, he was not likely to question the source of his recompense.

"Find yourself a seat, citizen," a gruff, slightly irritated voice called back to Flinx from the vicinity of the forward console. "I'll have you in Tlossene fast as weather permits." As Flinx had hoped, the busy pilot did not even bother to inquire about Anayabi.

Once above treetop level, the skimmer pivoted cleanly and accelerated. Peering out a transparent portion of the canopy, Flinx watched as the dead Meliorare's dwelling receded into the distance. The damage that had been inflicted by his mystifying, enigmatic defensive capability had never been visible from the craft.

"Don't go wandering around unless you have to," the pilot told him. "We might hit some chop, and I won't be responsible if you go banging off the walls. Your passage has been prepaid, but I guess you already know that."

Flinx had not, and was grateful to hear that was the case. It would allow him to settle back and enjoy the journey without having to worry about monetary negotiations.

Setting the skimmer on auto, the pilot swung his seat around to face the single passenger. "So tell me, how are things up in this part of the northlands? There's talk that several NaTl-Seeker villages are going to combine their efforts to—"

His chatter halted abruptly. Preoccupied with Pip, Flinx had been paying only half a mind to the conversation. The other half now detected a pointed, unexpected spike in the pilot's emotional state. Frowning, Flinx focused his perception. Indifference was replaced in the pilot first by uncertainty, then by excitement, and lastly by a briskly burgeoning antagonism. Without revealing that he was aware of any of these emotional developments, Flinx carefully set Pip and her blanket to one side. It wasn't easy, because the flying snake was doing everything possible to free herself from the encumbrance of the blanket. Try as she might, however, she could not possibly rise on only one good wing.

By the time Flinx had placed Pip out of the way, the pilot had drawn his handgun and taken aim at his passenger. Flinx eyed him evenly.

"Have I done something wrong?"

"Hmm." The pilot's tone turned quietly mocking. "Let's see. You almost destroyed my skimmer, forcing me to rely on this nondescript and thoroughly inadequate loaner until the very expensive repairs to mine can be completed. You did something to me that I still can't fig-ure out. If it feels like you're trying to do it again, I won't hesitate: I'll shoot you before whatever it is can take effect. And you had the indecency not to die conclusively. That oversight can be fixed more cheaply than my skimmer."

The account was detailed enough to tell Flinx whom he was

dealing with. The more he perused the pilot's emotions, the more the memory of his previous encounter with them strengthened, like a blurry picture slowly coming into focus.

"You're the one who shot down the skimmer I hired to come up here," he growled accusingly. "You're the one responsible for Bleshmaa's death."

A blend of amusement and contempt filled Halvorsen's face as well as his emotions. "You had a Tlel with you? Of course—an escort. Customary. Well, if it's dead, then the planet's a slightly cleaner place. It may be theirs by birthright, but frankly Gestalt is too good for the fetid little flat-heads." The muzzle of the pistol did not shift. This man, Flinx saw as well as sensed, would not be easily distracted. He would have to proceed with great care.

He did not wonder why he had failed to detect the hunter's true nature during the skimmer's approach and touchdown, or immediately upon boarding. Unaware that the solo passenger he had contracted to pick up was the very one he had previously tried to kill, Halvorsen's emotions had been devoid of aggression. Ironically, had he known that Flinx was his intended passenger, he would have been unable to mask his emotions and Flinx's Talent would have provided advance warning. Halvorsen's ignorance had proven his greatest advantage.

"I've had to keep busy lately and not hang around places like Tlossene," the man behind the gun was saying. "My automatic monitoring software picked up a request for transport for one passenger. Take him from here back to the city. Since I was toiling up this way anyhow—looking for your body, as a matter of fact—I jumped on the offer. Chance to take a quick break and pick up some easy money. Just goes to show how being first in line can be good for business in ways you never expect."

"Why were you still looking for me?" Flinx felt reasonably certain he already knew the answer, but anything that kept the man talking instead of shooting provided that much more time to consider how best to proceed.

"Certain people are willing to pay handsomely for your demise. Here on Gestalt my reputation would be enough to satisfy a client. They're not from here, though, and they want incontestable physical proof that your life-force has been terminated. So I had to go to all the trouble and time and expense of trying to recover your remains." When Halvorsen smiled, it made the deceased Anayabi's crooked grin look positively jolly by comparison. "And here they are. The requisite remains-to-be." The muzzle of the weapon lifted slightly, to focus squarely on Flinx's forehead.

"This is even better. This skimmer's internal recorder will not only show you dead, it will show me killing you, and will also include the record of this conversation. *That* ought to satisfy the smarmy tight-assed prigs."

Why not just let him shoot and get it over with? a part of Flinx argued despondently. It would put an end to a life that had now become far emptier than it had ever been before. Terminate the anguish, end the despair—the worrying, the desolation, the responsibility. At least someone would benefit from his demise, even if it was only one miserable low-life slayer. Turning to take a final fond look at Pip, he heard himself mumbling, "Go ahead. I won't stop you."

Having previously found himself in similar situations on other equally mortal occasions, Halvorsen had been subjected to a wide-ranging assortment of Last Words. Usually they involved desperate pleading, or sometimes a flurry of furious, frantic curses. Despite his considerable experience, these were new to him. Curiosity made him hesitate.

"Stop me? You can't stop me."

Something flared within Flinx. It wasn't particularly profound, but it was just enough to counteract, at least for the moment, for that particular moment, the utter feeling of futility that had temporarily overcome him.

"You shouldn't kill me."

Halvorsen blinked. It was clear to him now that the offworld Order of Null had contracted for the death of not only a dangerous man, but a crazy one. Still, he had always prided himself on his thoroughness. Having been surprised with an easy triumph, he was not one to overlook even the slightest chance that a greater one might possibly be lurking in the wings.

"Why not? If you're going to offer me more money, forget it. I don't know you, I don't know anything about any resources you might be able to tap, and I don't work that way. When I accept a contract, I stay with it until I can fulfill it. Sorry." Both his smile and tone were tight. "However, there are exceptions to every policy and I'm always willing to be convinced otherwise. You have sixty seconds."

An unblinking Flinx met the hunter's gaze. "Something located behind an astronomical phenomenon known as the Great Emptiness is accelerating toward Commonwealth space. Where it passes, nothing remains. It eats galaxies. There is some tiny, infinitesimal chance that I might be the key to doing something about it. The only key." He took a long, resigned breath. "I may be some kind of trigger."

Halvorsen's thin grin became a smirk. "You don't look like any kind of triggerman to me."

"Not triggerman," Flinx corrected him. "Trigger."

The hunter seated across from him laughed. "Trigger-chigger. You're nothing but a tall, skinny offworlder who looks even younger than he is, and a deluded one at that. I've got to hand it to you, though: in all my years running down and terminating people whom other people wanted dead, that's the wackiest deathbed plea I've ever heard. You're no *trigger*, Philip Lynx—whatever you're babbling about. You're remains. You're dead meat. You're a meal ticket."

"I only wish it was that basic." A resigned, disconsolate Flinx was muttering as much to himself as to the edgy assassin. "I know I can't convince you by talking. I wouldn't be able to convince anyone just with words. So I'll show you." He closed his eyes. Wrapped tightly in the blanket, Pip looked up at him in alarm.

Remembering the inexplicable, overwhelming emotions that had overcome him in the course of their previous confrontation, Halvorsen did not wait any longer to see what might happen. The record of the confrontation that was now safely on the skimmer's recorder was more than sufficient for his purposes. He started to fire, his finger convulsing on the trigger of his hand weapon.

Fire at what? He gaped openmouthed, jaw slack. His target had vanished. So had the skimmer. So, for that matter, had Gestalt. He was flying outward, traveling at incredible, impossible speed. Stars and nebulae and stellar phenomena for which he had no name and no experience flared and erupted around him. He was aware he was not alone. There was another presence with him, carrying him along. He could not see anything, but he could sense it. It was his quarry, unperturbed and in control.

I'm going to kill you now, he screamed, only to suffer another shock. Though he screamed, his voice made no sound. And how was he supposed to kill his victim when he could not even see him? Searching his stellar surroundings, he saw no other living thing. Glancing down, he found that he could not even see himself.

There was something ahead of him, coming nearer. Or he was approaching it. Whatever the explanation, the proper physical designation, it was clear the distance between him and it was shrinking. More than a darkness against the intergalactic vastness, it was a complete absence of light and life that redefined everything he thought he knew about emptiness. He started to make what he believed were kicking motions, flailing also with his arms, as if he could swim away from what was approaching. A sense of terrible disquiet began to waft over and through him, a palpable psychic poison. He knew only that he had to slow down, to stop, to reverse direction, to get away from . . .

Evil. A foulness on a scale unimaginable, of a kind beyond comprehension. He started screaming again, his voice low at first, then rising to a pitch his own throat had never before achieved, a shriek so high he would not have believed it possible for his lungs and larynx and lips to vomit it forth. He screamed and screamed, and heard nothing. The darkness was near. Soon it was proximate. Then it touched him.

Flinx had touched it, and survived. Inside the skimmer, a now completely mad Halvorsen clawed and scrabbled at the internal walls until he had torn the nails from his fingers. He slammed his head against the unyielding plexalloy dome until blood streamed from above his eyes. These had bulged outward until they were now halfway out of their sockets. Questing bloody fingers finally found their way to a portal control.

Halvorsen's horrible screams did not cease until he hit the ground. By the time they did, the skimmer had traveled onward and out of hearing range, slicing smoothly through the falling flakes of pink snow.

Slowly, Flinx opened his eyes. When such episodes engaged his mind, there was always the fear that the part of him that had ventured outward would not come back. That it would remain out where his dreams and projections took him, condemned forever to drift in the vicinity of the galactic horror that was racing toward the Commonwealth, or be swallowed by it and destroyed. Small but strong emotions made him turn and look down. Pip was staring up at him.

If only you were sentient, he thought. If only we could connect on more than just the emotional level. What advice would you give me? What different perspectives on my condition could you vouchsafe? What suggestions on how to continue this miserable existence could you offer?

She could not do any of those things, of course. What she could do was comfort him, simply by her presence. Simply by being.

His head was throbbing. The effort of showing Halvorsen what no one deserved to be shown had triggered yet another of Flinx's interminable headaches. What if for once he chose not to fight the affliction? What if he just allowed it to continue to build, to swell, to expand inside his skull? Would his head explode? Or would he finally and simply go mad, like the hunter?

The pounding intensified. It approached the limits of tolerability. Eyes squinched tight, teeth clenched, Flinx sat in the passenger seat as the skimmer cruised on through the darkening night. Having slithered to his side, Pip looked on helplessly. Through their most intimate connection she could feel his pain without exactly sharing it. But she could not do anything to stop it.

Slumping in the chair, Flinx slid to the floor, unconscious.

They were all there. All three parts of the triangle he had come to know from previous events. Clearer and sharper and easier to perceive than ever before. He knew them well by now. The incredibly ancient yet still functioning alien device, interaction with which had been what had first allowed him to see. The rich, unbelievably fecund greenness, cogitating on a scale and in a fashion no creature of flesh and blood ought to have been able to comprehend, yet he did. Last of all was the all-enveloping warmth, smothering and reassuring and more intimately familiar than either of the other two.

Resignation is no escape, insisted the Krang mind. *This is a fact well known. I know it. I exist it every moment.*

For every tree there is a seed, declared the planetwide forest that was the consciousness of Midworld. *For every seed there is something that sparks life. Water. Sunlight. Something. A trigger. A Flinx.*

We will be there, proclaimed the third component of the triangle. *We will be with you always, as we have always been even when your kind could not see that clearly.*

You cannot die. So insisted the artificial intelligence of the ancient Tar-Aiym weapon.

You will not be allowed to die. Thus spake the green sentience that girdled and encompassed the entire globe known as Midworld.

You will know death as do all living things—but not yet. Therefore concluded the collective consciousness that dwelled on a world called Cachalot.

When he awoke, Flinx found himself lying on the skimmer's deck. His head was still intact and securely attached to his neck. Extricating herself from the blanket, Pip had worked her way over to lie half on, half off his chest. Thanks to the advanced medications he had found in Anayabi's abode, the injured wing he had treated already showed signs of knitting. He sat up, rubbing at the back of his head, then screwing his knuckles into his eyes. Visual purple flashed before his pupils, his own private aurora. Around him the skimmer hummed softly, doing its job, taking itself home on autopilot, back to Tlossene. Little could be seen through the plexalloy canopy. It was now night outside and dark, but not as devoid of light and substance as the darkness he was projected to confront.

An alien machine thought he should do so. A green world-mind insisted that he do so. A combined consciousness that was intimately related to him devoutly wished for him to do so. It all fit the pattern of his life.

Even his death, it seemed, was not to be his own.

Machine, green, serene, he mused. Clarity.

Clarity. A galaxy of potential there, if not a literal one. He sighed. It didn't matter. The triangle of his thoughts would not let him die. The tri-barreled weapon of unknown possibilities would not abjure its trigger. He would live. He would go on not so much because it was his desire to do so but because it was desired by others. His death was not his own and neither, it appeared, was his life. Like it or not, he was an immutable part of something bigger than himself, much bigger. He could not revoke, would not be allowed to revoke, that which minds vaster and more profound than his own had declared irrevocable.

He would continue to search for the gigantic Tar-Aiym weapons platform that disguised itself as a brown dwarf. He would not give up. Never-giving-up, no matter how hopeless things seemed, was something humans did. Only machines analyzed available evidence and, when all appeared hopeless, quietly conceded everything including their own existence. If he went on, if he did not give up, that was at least one indication of humanness he could cling to. No matter how much he had begun to doubt it.

Rising from the deck, he moved forward and settled into the pilot's seat that had been so recently and hysterically vacated. Ahead lay a few hours' travel time. Then Tlossene, his shuttle, and waiting patiently in orbit, the *Teacher*. Waiting for him to tell it what to do, where to go next, which planetfall it needed to plot.

No wonder he always got along so well with the ship-mind. It takes one artificial intelligence, he reflected with bitter irreverence, to know another.

About the Author

ALAN DEAN FOSTER has written more than a hundred books in a variety of genres, including hard science fiction, fantasy, horror, detective, western, historical, and contemporary fiction. He is the author of the *New York Times* bestseller *Star Wars: The Approaching Storm* and the popular Pip & Flinx novels, as well as novelizations of several films including *Transformers*, *Star Wars*, the first three *Alien* films, and *Alien Nation*. His novel *Cyber Way* won the Southwest Book Award for Fiction in 1990, the first science fiction work ever to do so. Foster and his wife, JoAnn Oxley, live in Prescott, Arizona, in a house built of brick that was salvaged from an early-twentieth-century miners' brothel. He is currently at work on several new novels and media projects. For more about the author, go to www.alandeanfoster.com.

About The Type

This book was set in Times Roman, designed by Stanley Morrisons specifically for *The Times* of London. The typeface was introduced in the newspaper in 1932. Times Roman had its greatest success in the United States as a book and commercial typeface, rather than one used in newspapers.